Changed Purpose

Paula Jean Henry

WESTBOW
PRESS®
A DIVISION OF THOMAS NELSON
& ZONDERVAN

Copyright © 2018 Paula Jean Henry.

All rights reserved. No part of this book may be used or reproduced by any means, graphic, electronic, or mechanical, including photocopying, recording, taping or by any information storage retrieval system without the written permission of the author except in the case of brief quotations embodied in critical articles and reviews.

This is a work of fiction. All of the characters, names, incidents, organizations, and dialogue in this novel are either the products of the author's imagination or are used fictitiously.

Scripture taken from the King James Version of the Bible.

WestBow Press books may be ordered through booksellers or by contacting:

WestBow Press
A Division of Thomas Nelson & Zondervan
1663 Liberty Drive
Bloomington, IN 47403
www.westbowpress.com
1 (866) 928-1240

Because of the dynamic nature of the Internet, any web addresses or links contained in this book may have changed since publication and may no longer be valid. The views expressed in this work are solely those of the author and do not necessarily reflect the views of the publisher, and the publisher hereby disclaims any responsibility for them.

Any people depicted in stock imagery provided by Getty Images are models, and such images are being used for illustrative purposes only.
Certain stock imagery © Getty Images.

ISBN: 978-1-9736-4556-6 (sc)
ISBN: 978-1-9736-4555-9 (hc)
ISBN: 978-1-9736-4557-3 (e)

Library of Congress Control Number: 2018913497

Print information available on the last page.

WestBow Press rev. date: 11/30/2018

Dedicated to my Lord and Savior, Jesus Christ,

And to the cherished memory of my
precious daughter, Courtney Ann

From the Author

Have you ever wondered what would have happened if the South had won the American Civil War? I did. After touring the Stone Mountain Park historical attractions with my family in 1999, a spark of this story entered my mind and heart. As I stood before the life-size statue of Robert E. Lee on his horse, Traveller, I wondered what would have happened if the South had won the Civil War. The seed of my idea grew, and with much effort, countless prayers, and many revisions, it became this completed novel, *Changed Purpose*.

If you had a choice, how would you have wanted the American Civil War to end? There are as many opinions about this subject as there are people.

No one can reasonably impose the viewpoints of current standards on what has already passed in our nation's history. All we can do is learn what we can from past experiences and purpose to improve our future as a nation. With God's help we can and shall be successful for the good of our beloved USA and its citizens. Our Pledge of Allegiance states, "One nation, under God, indivisible, with liberty and justice for all." Amen.

Were those in the South right in their pursuit of liberty and autonomy? Were those in the North right for preventing the South from seceding? How can a conclusive, definitive answer be achieved when the basis of the argument comes from clashing opinions?

I am an American patriot. I love my country. People from all over the world want to come here. There is no other country like ours on the planet, and I am thankful to God that I am an American.

Changed Purpose is a time-travel novel, not a true story. Everything that appears to be a convincing fact is really an attempt to capture your attention within its pages. Although a few facts are true, I'm not historically accurate much of the time in this novel.

Some imagination of your own will be needed to flow with the characters and the storyline. I actually had to flow with the characters as they jumped out of my fingertips when I typed. I'm as surprised as you will be by some of their behaviors and words. They took on a life of their own as I typed. It was an incredible, unexplainable experience as the author.

I'm not a historian, but I do enjoy history. I'm stirred when I realize what life was like for people in earlier days. It makes me wonder about the future. How will life be for people who live long after we pass on into our eternity? I have learned that living as God designed is always our best choice, yet right from the Garden of Eden, Adam and Eve's selfishness and disobedience changed our course.

There is no way to avoid our nation's history of slavery. Both the North and the South had slaves, because as original thirteen colonies of England, slavery was legal. After our War of Independence from England in 1776, the USA abolished slavery with the Thirteenth Amendment in 1865. If I had my way, slavery would have never existed in the past, present, or future. I tried to be respectful and kind while imagining a better life by freeing the slaves within their circumstances in this story.

This novel is also a love story. It seeks to portray the love between God, our Creator, and His creation as well as the joys and struggles we face as humans. Hidden within its pages are love notes from God to everyone who reads it. Please see if you can recognize His love notes to you.

References to certain historical institutions, agencies, public offices, public personages, and some dates are mentioned. The characters involved, even in the public domain, are imaginary in this work in the way they behave, think, and speak. Any resemblance to actual persons, living or dead, or actual events and how they happened is purely coincidental. The opinions expressed are from the characters and shouldn't be confused with the author's, nor do they necessarily reflect the views of the author. King James Bible quotes and references are accurate and in the public domain.

Regardless of whether we agree with the main character, Sarah, no one really knows what would have happened if the South had won the American Civil War. Please allow your mind and creativity to flow as you read. I invite you to go on an exciting time-travel journey with

Sarah and discover one alternate history, in Sarah's opinion, that could have been possible if the South had won the American Civil War.

Thank you for taking time to read *Changed Purpose*. I hope you enjoy it and share it with others.

Blessings to you,
Paula Jean Henry

Acknowledgments

My entire existence, life experiences, people in my life, and talents have all come from Jehovah God, my Father; His Son, Jesus Christ; and the Holy Spirit. I pray to honor God in all I do yet know I fall short daily.

Many thanks to my loving, kind, devoted, encouraging husband, Kenley Redditt, who continually reminds me that God told me to write and that I have much to share, many people to reach, and a sacred witness to impart. Kenley suggested a few keywords and ideas for me to develop in the battle scene.

My heart rejoices in my beautiful four children: Courtney, Jacob, Jessica, and Joshua. Many aspects of each of them inspire me in so many ways. I remain forever thankful to be their mother.

I'm also so grateful for my mother, who taught correct grammar to me and insisted that I write and speak correctly and properly. As a teenager, though, I accused my mother of being "too much Emily Post!"

To my precious grandchildren—Andrew, Landon, Khloe (and my future grandchildren)—who give me hope and vision just because they exist. They are the promise of the future and the continuation of our family line. I pray that somehow my writings will lead them to a dedicated walk with Jesus and inspire them to write as well.

Sweet girlfriends in my life have greatly helped me along my path just because they love and encourage me. I acknowledge each with my love and thanks: Tess Q (recently deceased and daily missed), Beverly C, Lisa U, Betty F, Michele T, Kay P, Sylvia T, Carolyn L, Genalee B, Jan C, Rachel B, Frances G, MJ W, Debbie Mc, Emily & Robin B, Joyce B, Jade Lily B, Carol S, Elaine Y, Ellie D, Joy V; and my new friends, Tracy H, Carla, Amy, Nancy R, Danielle P, and Miss Jane … and many more. I am so blessed! You are eternally in my heart, and I am so thankful for our friendships.

I am honored to be part of the Georgia Mountain Writers' Club. Founder and dear friend Ellie Dobson (recently deceased) and all the women and men in the club have encouraged and inspired me over the years.

I even acknowledge the difficult people in my life (you know who you are). Because of the pain and suffering I felt over each of you, I drew closer to God, found comfort in Him, and became stronger as I dealt with each issue you created in my life. I now understand what God meant when He said to be thankful for trials. Each has helped me to grow personally and to become the woman I am today. I now understand that Jesus defines me, values me, and loves me just for being me. You may have meant to do me ill, but instead, you have helped me to be a better person. I forgive all of you difficult people in my life—past, present, and future—and even wish you well.

Blessings to all,
Paula Jean Henry

Chapter 1

The melody from the bagpipes faded into the air. Sarah sat for a moment, her eyes closed. The music not only reminded her of her parents' and Lexi's funerals but also ignited her passion for American Civil War history. The Great Highland bagpipes had inspired many Confederate and Union soldiers, long past their last possible resources, to fight on with their convictions until the very end. Who had been right?

"So many senseless deaths! So many courageous lives wasted! Oh, why can't time travel be possible?" exclaimed Sarah in frustration.

She slowly got up from her rocking chair, turned off the TV and DVD player, and placed the remote on the table. Her fuzzy slippers made a scuffing sound across the wooden floors as she went to the kitchen to eat a piece of toast with almond butter and banana slices. As she munched and drank another cup of coffee, Sarah sat at the kitchen table for a long time in thought.

She remembered the enormous process in preparing her master's degree thesis. She had learned many details about the American Civil War. Her thesis topic questioned who had been on the right side of the American Civil War. Her research had opened her eyes and heart to new opinions. She had set out to applaud Mr. Lincoln for not allowing the South to secede. However, the facts she'd uncovered surprisingly changed her point of view.

The Southerners had been motivated to fight valiantly in defense of their own soil. They had been fighting for their states, their heritage, and their homeland. They hadn't been aggressively trying to take over Northern territory. They'd just wanted to protect their own and govern themselves.

Sarah liked that attitude. She'd also learned that even with cotton and their spirit of liberty on their side, Southern leaders had made the mistake of underestimating the North's economic advantage and their larger forces.

Speaking to herself passionately, Sarah said aloud, "If the

Confederates could have had their states' rights and seceded, so many valuable lives would have been saved on both sides. The South would have surely abolished slavery on Christian moral ground because they valued freedom so highly for themselves." Sarah sighed and went on thinking aloud. "Freedom comes with responsibility. No doubt the South would have instituted new ways to manage their plantations with all men and women free and vital to society. All Northern states finally did abolish slavery after a time, but they had their free choice to do so. Being able to choose freely usually brings out the best in people."

Sarah sighed a deep cleansing breath. *Wasting life in any war is so horrible, and so is taking away God-given freedoms from people.* She also believed that the two separate nations could have lived in peace and in agreement to be protective of each other and to have fair trade. *But we will never know.* Sarah wasn't aware of how she flipped her bathrobe sash back and forth as she thought.

She got up and retrieved her thesis from the filing cabinet. The old metal drawers scraped as they slid. Sarah saw once again what her professor had written on her cover page. "Interesting viewpoint for a northerner. Caveat: Your courage to embrace the southern principles stands alone … like they did." But the paper had received a 98 percent. She had to hand it to her professor to be opposed to her point of view but to grant her an excellent grade. *It was one small victory for the South.* Sarah smiled at her thought and put her thesis back in the cabinet. She closed the drawer with a click of the metal lock, as if concluding the matter of her opinion.

Sarah took the last bite of her breakfast, cleared her place, and went to look out the living room window. Her scuffing slippers announced the rhythm of her footfalls. Most days she was up before dawn. Lately, she had developed an unwanted habit of insomnia and felt tired most of the time. She pulled back the white lace curtain and stared out into the rainy spring morning of Philadelphia.

The deluge made rippling patterns in the pooling street puddles. Shivering, Sarah clutched the collar of her warm bathrobe closed at her neck. Just looking at the freezing rain made her think of how miserable it must be to be cold and wet. The scene blurred before her as she thought about the men of her Scottish heritage and ancestors who'd tragically died in the Civil War. Her heart was struck with deep sadness from viewing the documentary depicting the countless dead and broken bodies, including those of the Highland Regiment and their bagpipers. When Sarah saw Civil War history movies, she became a living part of the event in her mind. She felt like she was there. It was always like that for her.

Knowing what I know, I could have helped if I had been there. If the South had won early in the war, so many lives would have been saved and not been wasted.

"Why hasn't someone invented a time machine yet?" Sarah audibly demanded of the world outside her window.

She felt discontented with her life, with Philadelphia, with the weather, and even with the very century in which she lived. She still profoundly grieved the death of her best friend, Lexi, just last Thanksgiving. As if that hadn't been enough to handle, just days later, her beloved parents died as well. Life without them was difficult at best. A thousand times she wondered whether she could have done something differently to prevent their deaths.

Knowing her life would never be the same, she'd buried herself in her passionate studies of the Civil War to distract herself from the ever-present grief. However, the pursuit only intensified her feelings.

Sarah picked up her copy of a book about General Stonewall Jackson and stared at his photograph on the red cover. She had recently finished this in-depth account of the brave general and felt as if she knew him and respected him. Lovingly touching his portrait on the cover, she whispered, "I'm so sorry that you died by mistake. How tragic that was! I wish I could have saved you."

With a deep sigh, Sarah prayed, *Oh Lord, why did you have me live now? Why couldn't I have lived during the War between the States? I wish I could have done something for those extraordinary, beloved men of valor who fought for states' rights. It is an honorable thing to fight for human rights and freedom. I remember the American Revolutionary War history too, Lord. Our courageous forefathers stood up for what they believed was their right to govern themselves and broke away from the rule of England,*

and they won. I am confused, Lord. Why couldn't the Confederates have won for the same reason as our forefathers at our country's beginning? I wonder what would have happened if the North hadn't resisted.

Sarah thought she had her life all figured out—a master's degree in history, a great job at the museum, a supportive church family, and her plan for Mr. Right to appear, sweep her off her feet, and then start a family. Death had altered her course severely. She had no one close to share anything with now. Even her position at the museum in her field of Civil War history no longer fulfilled her. She prayed, *Dear Lord, what should I do now?*

With increasing force, an army of pouring raindrops beat against the roof and windows. However, Sarah knew colorful flowering buds would no doubt be on the heels of these predictable spring rains. *Life changes.* With that thought in mind, Sarah inhaled a slow, cleansing breath and exhaled just as slowly. She needed to think ahead to the next season of her life. Much like how the warmth of spring brings new freshness following the winter, Sarah felt that her life had to get better.

After minutes of intense thought and prayer, Sarah turned with sudden new clarity and purpose. She quickly picked up her cell phone to call her brother, Colin. He was usually home on Saturday mornings once he completed his hospital rounds. However, it was her sister-in-law who answered after six rings. Tess shouted a harried "Hello," trying to speak over a wailing child.

"Hi, Tess. It's Sarah."

"Oh! Sarah, how good to hear your voice! Sorry for the noise level," Tess replied. Sarah formed an image in her mind of Tess cradling the phone against her neck and shoulder as she juggled her protesting toddler.

"What's wrong with Scottie?" Sarah asked.

"Well, he's just about over my shouting at him for attempting to put the screwdriver into the plug outlet a few minutes ago. Thank the Lord I saw him in time."

"Oh no! That could have been terrible. Well, what I'm calling about might surprise you. I have just decided to move south near you, so I—"

"Yippee!" shouted Tess, interrupting Sarah. "It's about time, young lady!" Tess released her squirming and now-quiet two-year-old son.

Sarah smiled, feeling joy in her new resolve. "I knew you'd say that, Tess. And I agree. It *is* about time. I would like to fly down as soon as possible and look around your area for places to live and work. I'll give my two weeks' notice here at the museum, then work on my plan and direction."

"That will be great, Sarah! *No!* Scottie!" Sarah heard the phone drop and a cat cry out. "Sorry, for the interruption, Sarah. Scottie was just trying to relieve Kittybaby of his tail. Mercy! Okay, back to our conversation. You'll have to meet up with us at Stone Mountain Park. We've decided to spend a week there in our new RV. It does seem a bit strange to go camping so close to home, but with so much to do there, we thought the kids would have a lot of fun and learn some Georgia history at the same time. Colin is out loading our stuff right now. Thankfully, he has arranged to be off call at the hospital this week."

Pacing excitedly around the room, Sarah twirled with delight; her flannel nightgown wrapped momentarily around her legs. "Tess, you know I've always wanted to go there." Sarah took a deep breath, and her face lit up with excitement. She thought of the Civil War attractions and the carvings of General Lee, General Jackson, and President Jefferson Davis on the side of Stone Mountain. "Those men had such vision and strength of character to fight for liberty. They were much like the minutemen of our Revolutionary War. It is such a shame that General Jackson was shot by mistake by friendly fire in 1863 and died soon afterward. I've long believed that if he hadn't died, the South would have won the war. Jackson was a key strategist."

"Wow! I didn't know that. How awful for them all. If that hadn't happened, I wonder what our country would be like now," Tess mused.

"Well, I'll tell you what I think," Sarah said. "I think there would be two strong nations instead of one, the United States of America and the Confederate States of America. We'd all be much better off because neither nation would be overly large or powerful like our federal government is today. As you know, the Bible speaks of corruption in the world caused by man's conflict due to wanting his own will and not obeying God's will, right from the Garden of Eden. We can see on any given news segment that unfortunately our nation has become quite corrupt in so many ways, according to biblical standards."

Tess agreed, "Yes, I know. I can't believe some of the things I hear on the news. I wish things were different. As Christians who believe the Bible, we are strangers in a strange land."

"Well, for me, Philadelphia is a strange land now, and I am leaving. The house seems empty without Dad and Mom here. They have been dead four months already, and Lexi committed suicide five months ago." Sarah sighed deeply. "I miss them all so much. Joy has drained out of my life since they died. I don't know when I will stop grieving … maybe never. How do people get used to the absence of their loved ones?"

"Honey, time does help. Remember, they are alive with our Lord Jesus in heaven. Don't forget that for one minute. I know you miss them, and we do too. We will probably always miss them. And we want you with us, Miss Sarah Louise Gordon. How many times have we invited you to come live here and share our life? Everyone will be excited to learn you are finally moving down here."

"Please don't tell them I am coming. I want to surprise them."

A scream pierced the air. "Okay. Uh-oh! Gotta run! See you soon, Sarah," Tess interjected swiftly and rushed to see what mischief Scottie was into now. Sarah was left with her mouth wide open, and her next words were unspoken as the phone disconnected abruptly.

CHAPTER 2

Won't they all be surprised to see me!

Sarah giggled to herself as she shifted into fifth gear. Just hours ago, she had been talking with Tess on the phone. What luck to get a flight so soon! She wondered what other trouble Scottie had gotten into this day. He was all boy at two years old and into everything. She thought of one of her favorite Scottish fiddle tunes, "The Stool of Repentance," and knew her little nephew would find himself seated there quite often until he learned some self-control.

The thirty-minute drive from the Atlanta airport to Stone Mountain gave her time to review what lay behind and anticipate the joy of possibilities that could be just ahead. Sarah imagined the reaction at the museum when they received the resignation letter she'd dropped in the mail on the way to the airport. It would be entirely unexpected. Sarah contemplated that her twenty-eight years had been happy until death altered her path forever. At least her parents had died quickly and together in a terrible car crash, not knowing it was their last moment here on earth. Lexi's story was a tragic one and hard to think about, much less imagine happening.

Sarah recalled that she had been preparing Thanksgiving dinner with her mother. The kitchen had been warm and the aromas appealing. The football game was blaring from the living room, where her dad shouted out his suggested moves to the players. Lexi usually joined them for Thanksgiving dinner, but this year she'd said she wasn't coming for some reason. Lexi had no family left except for a distant brother.

The house phone rang. Sarah said, "I'll get it." She wiped her hands on the dish towel, then gave a swipe down the front of her apron before she answered the call. The wall phone was the same yellow push-button model with a long cord her parents had owned since she was a child. Her mother had scolded her as a teenager for stretching its extra length out of shape when she wrapped herself up in it while talking on the phone with her girlfriends.

Lexi's brother, Harry, was on the line. His call surprised Sarah because she had never met him. He explained that Lexi had given Sarah's phone number to him for emergencies. Harry said he had horrifying news and knew no way to break it to her except to directly tell the shocking report. With that introduction, Sarah held her breath to brace herself. Frozen in place, Sarah listened as Harry went on.

"Lexi has been found dead at the bottom of a steep waterfall. The officials who contacted me couldn't determine whether it was an accident or suicide." Harry's voice sounded strained. It was distressing news, even for this brother who had kept himself so distant from Lexi for unknown reasons.

Stunned as if in a bad dream, Sarah thanked Harry for calling her, then hung up the phone slowly. She knew the truth in her heart. Lexi had confided in her that she couldn't overcome her guilt due to something she had done when she was seventeen years old. Lexi had never told her what that "something" was, even when Sarah offered to listen and not judge her.

It hadn't been difficult for Sarah to guess what could have happened. Lexi had been involved with the wrong type of boyfriend when she was seventeen. No amount of reality about this guy, Alvin, swayed Lexi to break up with him. What she thought was love blinded her. Alvin came between them for a time, but Lexi finally broke up with him after a year. Sarah had been relieved when he no longer influenced her sweet friend.

Sarah was a person who wanted to help people, especially those she loved. Lexi was cheerful, but she would get into depressed moods at times. Devastated, Sarah thought, *Oh dear, dear, Lexi—gentle, quiet spirit, Lexi—why didn't you call me or talk to me about what you were thinking of doing? I could have helped you get through your darkest hours.*

They had been close friends for years. Sarah imagined Lexi climbing to the top of the waterfall all alone and in despair. She would have been shivering as the northwest wind whipped her last moments of heat from her thin body. Sarah could vividly picture in her mind's eye Lexi's final minutes during that dreadful late autumn afternoon. She'd probably stood there on the precipice, looking at God's beautiful creation but not focusing on it.

It was Thanksgiving Day, but Lexi wasn't focusing on thankfulness. She was overwhelmed with such turmoil that she could no longer deal with it. Guilt kept her prisoner, and it was the weapon that killed her. If only she had surrendered her guilt to Jesus and had forgiven herself. Lexi had been so full of self-blame that she wasn't thinking clearly. Sarah imagined her taking a weary, deep breath and then merely leaning over headfirst, falling unhindered to this life's end.

As the headlights washed over her face from passing cars, a change in Sarah's physical appearance was apparent. Thoughts of her parents, Lexi, and the gloomy North left her. The joy of embarking on her new life spread throughout her mind and body. Now with this decisive change, Sarah felt a surge of fresh hope. She didn't understand the purpose of her life ahead, but she trusted God. If her present happiness was any indication, she knew she was on the right path. Her lovely face reflected peace and delight that had been missing for some months now.

When Sarah pulled up to the Stone Mountain Park entrance booth to pay her admission, she felt like she was driving into her new season of life. After finding out the assigned space number for her brother's campsite, Sarah put all thoughts of her northern life behind her. She eased her car into the parking spot next to her brother's van. Sarah was amazed by the size of their new RV. It was one of the latest models with the living room and bedroom slide outs. They had plenty of room for her in this traveling house. Lights shined brightly from within as if welcoming her home.

Sarah gathered her unique presents for the children, which she had purchased at the Atlanta airport gift shop, then knocked on the door. As Colin swung the door open, Sarah shouted, "Surprise!" Colin jumped down the few entry steps and embraced his precious little sister in a big bear hug. How lovely it was to breathe in his familiar cologne and feel his strong arms around her!

"You are full of surprises, Friskie!" Using his childhood nickname for his energetic sister, Colin continued, "Oh, how great to see you, Sarah! Tess is bathing Scottie. Come in! Come in!"

As they entered the living room area, Sarah couldn't believe her eyes. It was like an actual house, so roomy, plush, and lovely. Everything was in different shades of neutral blues, grays, and browns. It seemed very well appointed. The design made great use of the space.

From a kneeling position as she bathed Scottie, Tess pushed open the bathroom door with her foot and shouted to Colin to please hand the baby shampoo to her from the kitchen counter. Sarah rushed to do the job at hand and entered the bathroom. Many shouts of greeting filled the air, and Sarah ended up wet from Scottie's splashing. The other two children were in their pajamas, combing out their damp hair, when Sarah surprised them. They had all been filthy from playing at the playground. The kids crowded into the bathroom and applied many kisses and hugs to a laughing Aunt Sarah.

Sarah joined Colin at the kitchen table until the rest of the family joined them. They were discussing the itinerary for the next day, planning to visit many of the Stone Mountain Park attractions.

Colin said, "I think you will like the carvings on Stone Mountain the best. It is quite impressive of the three key men of the short-lived Confederate States of America. I look at it in awe every time I get a chance to see it."

"Oh, I am certain it will be impressive. I have seen pictures, of course." Sarah dropped her eyes and thought for a moment. "You know, Colin, from what I learned in writing my thesis, I think I would have been called a traitor if I had lived during the Civil War. I came full circle in my thinking during my research. I wholeheartedly support the efforts and principles of the South for wanting to secede for states' rights and have the autonomy to rule themselves. Those are the very same principles our founding fathers took to heart. Freedom is vital to thrive as a person and a nation. All this became very clear to me during my research."

"I agree with you about freedom for all people. However, you wouldn't have been a traitor. Many families were divided then, and individuals had to follow the dictates of his or her own heart."

"Well, I've relinquished my northern citizenship, and as of this very moment, I'm proclaiming that I am officially a southern belle. With our mother being born in Macon, Georgia, and our father from Savanah, we actually are official." Mildly sarcastic, she continued in their mother's heavy southern accent. "Too bad Mama had to marry Daddy and move right away with him from Savannah to his new coast guard post in Philadelphia. You and I are Yankees only by accident of birth, don't you know. How sad to have to leave behind all this gracious southern charm!" Her arms swept wide open for emphasis.

They laughed, and Colin continued, "Yes, yes! That sounds just like Mama. And as she said countless times, 'You can take the southerner out of the south, but you can't take away their spirit.'"

Without warning, three enthusiastic children jumped on them. They spied their gifts on the table, which Aunt Sarah had brought, and she distributed them quickly into eager hands. Shelby, Ann, and Scottie proceeded to open their gifts with eagerness. The books and the pony collection met with approval, but the flashing, beeping toy robot brought a grimace from Colin and Tess.

Sarah shrugged innocently. "I know it is a little loud, but look how happy Scottie is to have it!"

Her brother and sister-in-law rolled their eyes in mock irritation. "You, my dear sister, do not have to live with the constant noise level of all these must-have toys you bring. How about choosing a stuffed animal next time?"

"Play a jig for us, Aunt Sarah!" Shelby demanded.

Sarah quickly tuned up her fiddle and launched into the upbeat Scottish tune "Middlin' Thank You." Colin and Tess laughed with delight as they watched their children dance a jig in their pajamas. Scottie was especially entertaining with his out-of-rhythm steps.

With the dance over, it was time to brush teeth and get the kids to bed. After the children were settled and asleep in their bunkhouse room, the adults decided on the schedule for the next three days of activities. The Stone Mountain Park activity map and information brochure were well laid out for efficient planning of all excursions. Their upcoming three-day agenda would be very full. Thankfully, the RV was just minutes away from all attractions within the park, so the rush of the Atlanta traffic wouldn't interfere with their plans.

Chapter 3

The exciting first-day excursion included a tasty picnic stop during the family's hike up Stone Mountain. They sat and ate next to an actual pirate's carving, with skull and crossbones and all. They were very creative in making up stories about the pirates who had once walked on that very same spot. They even acted out their imaginations. Sarah commented on how amazing it was that only space and time separated them from the pirates, yet the mountain of formidable granite was still the same.

They were hot and tired when they got back to the RV. Tess exclaimed, "I can't believe we walked to the top of Stone Mountain and back down again!" She gulped down an entire glass of cold water.

Sarah replied, slightly irritated at this point, "Tess, you've said that about one hundred times today. Just relax, and I'll supervise the kids' baths and get them ready for bed. And don't forget, it was Colin who carried Scottie in the backpack all the way up the hiking trail and back. He should be the one flopping down to rest."

Colin said, "I'm fine, I'm fine … not a bit tired out at all." However, Sarah noticed that her brother sat down on his reclining chair with some relief. He picked up the local newspaper and started to read it. Sarah knew that after he finished reading the paper, he would reward himself by working the crossword puzzle. He loved the challenge.

The air-conditioning felt divine to Sarah as well as to the others. Humidity was a constant unwanted companion in Georgia for most of the year. Sarah picked up the dirty laundry the kids were spreading around as they dropped their clothing. *At least everyone is cooling off and acting better now. How convenient that this camper has a stackable washer and dryer.* She put the children's dirty clothes into the washer and got it started. Ann had the use of the bathroom first, since she had "called" it on their way home. Shelby played his Bible story video game while he awaited his turn for the shower. Scottie was busy hammering the wooden pegs back and forth in the old cobbler's bench set that had been Colin's when he was a little boy. The color had faded, but it was durable.

They discussed their favorite attractions from the day. Sarah had been quite affected by the Confederate museum. The family agreed with her that it had been an emotionally moving experience to see the realistic life-size bronze statue of General Lee on his horse, Traveller. Their second-favorite historical attraction was seeing the figures of President Davis, General Lee, and General Jackson carved into the side of Stone Mountain. The Daughters of the Confederacy had sponsored the carving. It had taken years to complete, and the project had claimed some lives in the making.

Sarah had felt a deep sadness when she browsed the Confederate Museum and saw the actual uniforms, articles, and weapons belonging to the Southern men. *They fought with conviction and courage for their principles.* It was appropriate that the displays were on a background of red velvet, symbolizing the precious blood the brave soldiers had shed. She cringed to think of the agonizing deaths many of the young men from the North and the South had experienced. She remembered the haunting sound of the bagpipes she had recently heard on the Civil War documentary.

Oh, why does there ever have to be war?

Later at the RV, Aunt Sarah was on duty with the children for the night. She willingly accepted the task and enjoyed every minute of being with them. She shared a short Bible story about Jesus as she snuggled up with them on one bed. It was their favorite as Aunt Sarah dramatized it, and they imitated her. After bedtime prayers, the children fell fast asleep.

They play hard, and they sleep hard.

The adults munched on popcorn as they talked about possible plans for Sarah's future and reminisced about old times. They wanted to stay up later but decided to say good night to get a good rest for the next day. Sarah got busy converting the sofa into a sleeper. Tess gave her sheets, a blanket, and a pillow along with a tender hug. She said, "I am so glad you are here with us."

"So am I, dear heart." Sarah grinned. Being with family was the best medicine. Her discontent and loneliness disappeared.

With their bedroom door open, Sarah glanced in and saw her brother and wife cuddle, and she smiled. Then she overheard Tess sleepily ask Colin, "Do you think Sarah will meet her Mr. Right soon? She has much love and joy to share, and I know she will make an excellent wife and mother. I'm going to pray that God will bring the right man to her before too long."

A drowsy Colin replied, "Mmmmm."

Sarah settled into her bed with thoughts of meeting her Mr. Right. Would it be soon?

Chapter 4

The next morning, the excited children were up before dawn, wanting to go on the day's planned activities. They couldn't wait to get on the train ride, play mini golf, see the old cars, and pet the wildlife at the petting zoo. They would end the day at the huge playground. While driving to each activity, they could plainly see the magnitude of Stone Mountain. Almost from every vantage point, there was the natural wonder in the background or the foreground displaying its splendid bastion of sparkling grays and blues as if a representation of the gray and blue of the Civil War uniforms.

One of the group always commented, "I can't believe we walked up and down the whole of Stone Mountain yesterday!" They continually gazed up at the wonder of the granite God had created at the beginning of time. Sarah was awestruck time and again when she saw the carvings of Davis, Lee, and Jackson on the face of Stone Mountain as they drove by it.

Although they enjoyed all the activities, everyone was sweaty and exhausted from the heat and humidity. All were glad to be back to their home-away-from-home campsite. When Tess unlocked and opened the front door, the pleasant aroma of "chicken in a pot" greeted them. She exclaimed, "Oh, I am so thankful for Crock-Pots! After a tiring day, it is a real blessing to have dinner all ready for the family. A little extra work preparing it in the morning saves a lot of work in the evening."

On the third morning, everyone grew impatient while waiting in the van for Aunt Sarah to appear. Usually, she was the first one ready, so it was odd behavior for her to take so long. Ten-year-old Shelby kept busy playing with his action figure, and nine-year-old Ann occupied herself by singing her favorite songs. Pretending to drive with his little plastic steering wheel on his car seat, Scottie made revving engine noises. Saliva bubbled from his lips. Tess directed every vent on the front dash to blow AC directly at her, and Colin tapped his fingers impatiently on the steering wheel.

Sarah could hardly catch her breath. Though she had packed all her things in Philadelphia and sent them to storage, she had saved something special. She smoothed down the soft peach skirt, pulled on the fitted jacket, put her crocheted gloves on, and nodded her approval in the mirror. Her Civil War-styled outfit was beautiful. It was time to show the family. She patted her braids unnecessarily. They were looped and fastened perfectly underneath her snood. She opened the door and went outside.

Young Scottie broke the silence and said, "Peety Ah Sahrah!"

Sarah saw Tess's hair blowing from the AC vents. When Tess looked up, she gushed, "Oh, Sarah, you look absolutely gorgeous! I want a dress just like that too." She jumped out of the van and tenderly touched the creamy lace of the peach dress. Sarah smiled widely.

Colin nodded his approval of his sister's outfit and said, "Beautiful! But that overly stuffed leather knapsack and violin case on your shoulder detract a bit from the effect you want to create, Friskie."

Entering the van and buckling up, Sarah defended her knapsack. "As you well know, I always carry everything possibly needed on our outings, so match or not, I'm bringing it. And you know I always have to be ready to play a tune," she added matter-of-factly.

She glanced down at Ann, who was buckled up next to her, and smiled. Loquacious Ann remained speechless and awestruck as she stared at her Aunt Sarah. She looked at her as if she had never seen her before in all her life.

Shelby smiled his approval at his aunt, then asked his dad, "May we go to the Skyride now, please?" Colin drove off.

Sarah was thrilled that she had created this effect on her family and was enjoying every minute of the day in her beautiful dress. She was an attraction all on her own for everyone who saw her during the day's excursions. Sarah felt so right in her handmade outfit. The family knew that wherever Sarah went, her violin would be by her side. Ever since she had been three years old, she loved to play classical music, then sacred and Scottish fiddle music; and she delighted many audiences with her impromptu performances. Sarah even made a few dollars when people were passing by and dropped money in her open violin case.

Sarah created such an opportunity at the Skyride while they waited for their turn to board the exciting ride. When she noticed the many people waiting in line, Sarah tuned up her violin and began playing an upbeat medley of her favorite Scottish tunes. Once again, people dropped some money into her violin case. The spectators expressed their admiration and appreciation with a hearty round of applause. It was a great way to have fun while being stuck in a long line.

By afternoon, Sarah became a little concerned about whether the family was going to make it to the Antebellum Plantation. She was anxious to get there, but after Ann's skinned knees, Scottie's choking fit, and Shelby's disappearing act at the wildlife and petting zoo, much time was used up. Tess developed a headache and delayed them for a few more minutes when she asked Sarah for some aspirin and a bottle of water. It was a relief when Colin stared at his watch and finally said, "It looks like we'll have an hour left for the Antebellum Plantation. According to the brochure, it takes just forty-five minutes for the tour."

They entered the tour area and noticed with joy the lack of a crowd. Immediately, Sarah felt as if she belonged there and had come home. She looked as if she belonged too, in her stunning outfit and hairstyle. An avid time-travel novel reader and movie buff, Sarah could easily pretend she was back in time. Her vivid imagination allowed her to feel captivated by her surroundings. The plantation was beautiful with a multitude of flowers and neatly trimmed shrubs. The lawn was impeccable, much like the grass one would see on a golf course. The structures on the grounds seemed restored according to historical accuracy. They were so authentic looking that she could easily envision what the usual hustle and bustle would have been like there at its peak.

Touring the manor house was Sarah's greatest thrill. She hung on the tour guide's every word. She loved the white pillars at the entrance. The creaking wooden floors throughout the house were well worn, but they only added character. Sarah someday wanted to have the elegantly arched doorframes in her own home, and she made a mental note. She thought as she had so many times before, *My body is in 2018, but my heart is in the 1800s.* Sarah imagined herself entertaining guests in the ornate parlor by playing her violin while others played pianoforte, cello, viola, and harp. She could have stayed longer and dreamed, but the kids were getting fussy, and Ann had to use a bathroom, which of course was nowhere in sight. The family marched outside to find the restrooms. A gentle breeze cooled them momentarily as they walked.

No sense lingering when the kids are fussy, but really, I waited all day to get here. How disappointing!

Chapter 5

Approaching the stable area, Sarah said to her loved ones, "You go on to the restroom. I want to look in the slave cabin near the stables. I'll catch up to you in a few minutes." And with that, she walked toward the slave cabin. At the entrance doorway, Sarah stood very still just inside. After her eyes adjusted to the shadows, she could see the fireplace, eating area, sitting area, and sleeping loft. It seemed to be a workable arrangement. The accommodations were rustic but comfortable, which was a bit surprising to Sarah because she'd learned in the North about how deprived and mistreated all the slaves had been in the South. Although some no doubt were, this cabin reflected the possibly that everyone was well cared for on this plantation. She then turned and walked out of the cabin to look at the stables. In her haste, she crashed right into a very tall and formidable man.

"Oh, pardon me, sir! Excuse me!"

Quickly removing his hat, the man bowed and said in a rich, deep baritone voice, "Quite the contrary, I assure you, miss. Please accept my apologies."

Sarah adjusted the knapsack that had fallen to her elbow during the collision and hooked it back onto her right shoulder. On her left shoulder, the strap holding her violin case remained unmoved.

Getting a good look at the man, Sarah said, "Wow! What an authentic outfit!" The man merely looked blankly at her. "How do you like my dress? It's a copy of the original, of course. My family thinks me rather authentic looking." She curtsied for effect.

The man said politely as he bowed, "Yes, very lovely. Are you a guest of the manor, miss?"

Sarah frowned. "Guest? Well, yes, I don't work here, if that's what you mean. Do you?"

"Do I what, miss?"

"Hey, wait a minute! I just realized you're a great Stonewall Jackson."

Just then a woman's voice called out from a nearby brick building, "Thomas?"

The man turned and replied in his deep voice, which carried well, "Coming, my dear."

They heard the faint cry of a baby from a distance. He directed his attention again to Sarah. "Please do excuse me, miss. My family awaits my return."

He gave a slight bow to Sarah, replaced his hat, politely touched its brim, and walked over toward the redbrick guesthouse.

Sarah was wondering whether his thick, black beard and mustache were real. The stables forgotten, she set off toward the center brick kitchen building they had toured earlier.

Maybe the bathroom is on the backside of this structure.

As she approached it, she heard voices and pots and pans banging. She saw many black women dressed as old-fashioned maids in matching uniforms and caps; they were scurrying about, doing their chores. The door was open, so Sarah knocked on the doorframe, breathed in the delicious aromas, and asked, "Is there a reenactment dinner being served here tonight or something?"

The cook's face was flushed from bending over the open fire and stirring the contents of the huge cast-iron pot. With the back of her hand, she adjusted her cap and said in her thick Irish accent, "Six p.m., supper as usual, miss." Then she bent her knee in a quick bob.

Sarah raised her eyebrow at the "as usual" terminology but said nothing. She went on her way to locate the restrooms and her family. No bathrooms were on the backside of the building, and there was no sign of her family anywhere. Sarah decided to go to the entrance booth area in hopes that all her family were waiting for her there. The children must be very impatient by this point, so she quickened her step.

Hopefully, Tess's headache is relieved by now.

When she got to the entrance area, the ticket booth wasn't there. Sarah put her hands on her hips and wondered in consternation, *Am I lost?*

Fortunately, a beautiful horse-drawn carriage slowly pulled up and stopped near her. There was a driver in a livery outfit with ruffles at the cuff and throat, hat, knickers, socks and boots, and a similarly outfitted footman standing on the back, just like in the movies. A young lady of about Sarah's age and dressed much like Sarah, only all in white, leaned forward toward the open carriage window. She put her white-gloved hand on the window ledge and could just peek her head out so far because of the pretty feathered hat she was wearing.

"Excuse me, please. I do not believe that I have had the pleasure of your acquaintance. I am Miss Rebecca Esther Genalee Stuart, and you are?" she inquired formally in her silky Southern voice.

"I am Sarah Louise Gordon," Sarah responded properly, wishing she had a fourth name as well. She walked up to the carriage to continue the conversation. "I seem to have lost my family. I was looking for them at the entrance of the plantation, but I can't seem to find them."

"Perhaps they are at the manor's entrance. Please allow me to offer a ride to you, and we will try to locate your family."

"That would be great. Thank you. I've never been in a carriage like this before. What's happening around here tonight?" Sarah quickly asked as she boarded with the footman's help and settled down on the coffee-brown leather seat. It was soft, supple, and luxurious; and it smelled of freshly applied sweet oil. The driver moved on after the footman closed the door and repositioned himself.

"My father is having a political gathering, and people will be in and out constantly, I am afraid. I am trying to help Mother all that I can, but I do believe that sometimes I am more trouble than help." She grinned and fanned herself.

Nice touch, Sarah thought as she noticed the lacy, white fan. She nodded and said, "I know what you mean. I'm often more trouble than help too."

They smiled at each other with a knowing smile and felt instantly like kindred spirits.

Rebecca asked, "Is that why you and your family are here? For the meeting, I mean?"

"Oh, no, we're just here visiting and seeing the sights. I am so enjoying my first visit to Stone Mountain."

"Well, here we are, at the entrance to the manor. There does not seem to be anyone around." Rebecca glanced around at various areas of the property. "Do you see your family anywhere?"

Sarah looked out the carriage window, frowned, and felt confused. "This isn't the entrance ... at least, not the one where we came in today. Where's the ticket booth?"

Now Rebecca frowned and asked, "Ticket booth? Whatever do you mean?"

Just then, Sarah caught sight of a man in the distance at the doctor's cabin, which her family had toured a little while ago. She said with relief, "Oh, that must be my brother, Colin, just there at the doctor's cabin." She pointed in that direction and turned back to Rebecca. "Thank you so much for your assistance. I hope you and your family enjoy your party here."

And with that, Sarah disembarked with the servant's help, secured her knapsack and violin, thanked them all, and rushed the few hundred feet to the doctor's cabin. She called out with excitement and relief in her voice, "Colin!"

As she entered the open door area, she stopped dead in her tracks. The man inside was a stranger, and the doctor's cabin was all set up with apothecary jars, a table and chairs, and oil lamps. It had been empty when the family toured it earlier. Frowning, Sarah said unnecessarily, "You're not Colin." Then she turned and ran back swiftly toward the carriage. Before driving on, Rebecca had politely waited to make sure Sarah reached her family connection.

Winded, Sarah panted out her explanation. "That man is not my brother, Colin. He must be part of your party. The entire doctor's cabin is all set up."

The footman helped Sarah board the carriage once again.

Rebecca said, "Just come with me to the manor house, if you please, and we shall see if we can locate your family. I have an older brother. Samuel is quite older, as he was the firstborn of our family, and I am the baby." She grinned, indicating her delight in being the pampered youngest of the family. "There were also three other siblings in between us who died, but I never knew them."

Sarah interjected, "Oh, I am so very sorry to hear about your family's loss. I know loss myself. My parents died in a terrible crash a little over five months ago. I've just recently decided to live here in Stone Mountain with my brother and his wife and family. We are very close. Their daughter is Ann, and they have two sons, Shelby and Scottie." She then added sadly, "My best friend, Lexi, died not long ago too."

"Death is something we simply must accept, especially in these hard times. Thank God we have the hope of rejoining our loved ones in heaven one day."

"Oh, Rebecca, I am so glad to hear you say that. I believe that to be true too. I know that I could not have gotten through the tragedies in my life if it wasn't for the grace of God."

"I know what you mean, Sarah. I do not know how people who are not believers in Jesus ever get through life's trials."

The carriage stopped at the entrance of the palatial manor house. The footman helped the ladies disembark as the horses snorted and scraped their front hooves.

Sarah said, "I'm sorry I've lost my family temporarily, but I am delighted that I've met you, Rebecca. I'm enjoying your party very well already. How did you get everyone here so fast? Not half an hour ago, it was almost deserted here, except for the tour guide."

Rebecca raised her eyebrows and looked questioningly at Sarah. "Tour guide?"

"Yes, you know, the lady in the front hall who showed us around."

"You mean, you have been in the manor house not a half hour past?"

"Yes! And oh, Rebecca, I just love the manor house and would have given almost anything to have lived here myself. It is so beautiful with the ornate high ceilings and crown molding."

A butler, dressed in a crisp, black tuxedo, opened the door for them. A maid in a long navy skirt, white apron, and white cap stepped up to remove their jackets, hats, and gloves. No matter the weather, society rules required that ladies must wear expected finery and fashion.

Perhaps this is why so many women fainted back in the day.

Sarah felt relieved to remove the clothing items, but she kept her knapsack and violin close at hand.

"How kind of you to help me," Sarah said emphatically to the maid.

"Please accompany me into the parlor to have refreshments, Sarah." Addressing the servant, she continued, "Bessie, please bring lemonade and tea cakes."

"Yes, miss," replied the servant. With a slight curtsy and nod, she was off.

Sarah was quite impressed. Everyone was portraying his or her part in this Civil War period reenactment very well indeed.

The ladies chatted, ate, sipped their lemonade, and awaited the butler's response to Rebecca's order to find Sarah's family. While they waited, Sarah suddenly felt rather than saw a man's presence fill the room. As she looked up, a dashing, handsome, tall man entered.

Rebecca said in greeting as the ladies rose to their feet, "Oh, Samuel, come meet my new friend. Miss Sarah Louise Gordon, may I present my brother, General Samuel Benjamin Stuart."

General Stuart crossed the room in a few long strides and took Sarah's right hand into his. He bowed over it slowly and kissed the back of her hand. Her heart quickened at his touch. His light-green eyes and attractive masculinity created an unusual and unfamiliar tingling sensation in her stomach.

Sarah admired the man's distinguished looks. At first glance, the premature gray mixed into his hair and well-groomed beard gave him the appearance of an older man, but his skin was tight and youthful. She was to find out later that General Stuart was thirty-eight years old, just ten years her senior. He was a proud six feet two inches tall, lean and muscular. His Confederate general's outfit looked fetching on him. Sarah was enjoying herself with this strikingly handsome man, and as she assumed the role of a real Southerner, she politely curtsied and said, "Charmed, I'm sure, General Stuart." His effect on her lingered long after he released her hand and took his seat next to Rebecca.

Their eyes held a second longer than was comfortable for Sarah, and her stomach joined her heart in its flutters. She sensed her face blush and her skin grow moist. How could one man have this effect on her? Never before had she experienced such sensations. A quick glance at his left hand showed he wasn't married.

At that moment, the butler announced himself. He said no one had seen a man, woman, and three children anywhere on the premises.

Sarah stood up abruptly, distracted by this news, and began pacing. She exclaimed, "I don't understand. I left them near the stables, and I went to the slave cabin for a few minutes. When I came out, I bumped into one of your party who looks exactly like General Stonewall Jackson." She recounted, "Colin and Tess and the kids had gone off to find a restroom. Then, when I couldn't find them, I tried to find the entrance booth and found Rebecca instead."

Sarah stopped pacing and turned to face her hostess and host. "They have to be somewhere. Maybe they walked back to the van, thinking I would find them there since we missed each other here." She said with conviction, "Yes, that's it. I must get up to the parking area. It's been lovely to meet you both, and I hope you have a wonderful time. I wish I could stay to enjoy it with you. I feel very much at home here. But my family awaits, so thank you very much for your gracious hospitality. Goodbye."

Sarah picked up her knapsack, hooked her violin case strap over her shoulder, swallowed the last little bit of her lemonade, and whisked toward the front door in determined pursuit. She left behind a faint scent of her light lavender perfume.

Rebecca and Samuel Stuart looked at each other with frowns. Intrigued into immediate action by this mystery, Samuel called out in his gentlemanlike manner, "Wait one moment, please, Miss Gordon, and I shall escort you." Rebecca was at his heels.

Sarah heard General Stuart behind her and turned in the foyer. Just then, the maid appeared to swiftly assist Sarah with her light jacket, hat, and gloves. The butler opened the door and stood at attention. *I feel like I am in a* Downton Abbey *episode.* General Stuart caught up with her and firmly clasped her elbow. She acutely noticed his touch.

"My driver will take you to where you want to go, and my sister and I will accompany you. Do not be alarmed. We shall find your family." Rebecca quickly donned her outdoor apparel as well.

"I appreciate your assistance very much. Thank you for the refreshments."

Rebecca smiled in response as they embarked in the waiting carriage. Samuel tapped the roof to indicate they were ready to go. With a slap of the reigns, the horse began trotting. The sun was bright and the air hot and humid. Small puffs of breeze gave a little relief. The sweet oil fragrance on the leather seats filled Sarah's lungs as she breathed deeply. They headed in the direction of the doctor's cabin and down the gravel road for half a mile. No one spoke as Sarah anxiously watched everything that passed by while looking for her family. Politely patient, Samuel and Rebecca waited for Sarah to begin a conversation.

Turning toward them, Sarah said, "I know pavement is rough on horse's hooves, but would it be a problem if you took me to the parking lot or maybe just close to it so that I can find the van?"

Samuel and Rebecca stared at her, at each other, then back at Sarah.

Confused, Rebecca asked, "What manner of speech is 'pavement,' 'parking lot,' and 'van'? I have not heard of these terms before you spoke them."

"What? How can you not have heard of these terms before?" Sarah asked in disbelief. Then, with a look of dawning realization, she continued, "Oh! I see. You don't have to continue to stay in character with me. You are doing very well with your authentic Civil War period reenactment, and I don't mean to be rude, but this is serious."

Samuel spoke up. "I assure you, Miss Gordon, that we are quite serious as well. We are doing all we can to reunite you with your family. Perhaps you could explain yourself and your situation more fully?" His question had the distinct feel of a direct command. There was no spark between them at this moment.

Sarah felt threatening tears well up in her eyes. She was perspiring in the sweltering heat and humidity, and she felt miserable, which always put her in an ill mood. "Oh, for heaven's sakes! I thought you two were so nice, and I was enjoying your company and what you are doing around here. But now I feel that you are very unkind with your insistence in this charade when I am imploring you for your help." She continued in a slightly sarcastic, detailed explanation to impart her irritation more pointedly. "You know very well that *pavement* is the hard surface that covers roads in all fifty states of the United States of America. A *parking lot* is where people park their cars, trucks, and vans, in which so many families enjoy the amazing technology features of 2018."

Exasperated, Sarah stopped to catch her breath and compose herself. She was about to burst into tears.

Rebecca and Samuel stared wide eyed at Sarah. He sat erect and asked, "How can you speak of such things as these, and of such a time? Are you ill, or are you playing a charade with us, as you so charge that we are doing? It is the year of our Lord 1863. There are thirty-four states in the Union at present. However, if we Southerners have our way and win this War of Northern Aggression, the Confederate States of America will have victory and will begin its sovereignty with eleven states." His deep voice was low, pointed, and full of suspicion.

What has happened to our charmed beginning?

Just then, the first man Sarah had run into at the stables when she exited the slave cabin appeared on horseback and shouted to Samuel, "General Stuart, forgive my intrusion, sir, but might I have a word with you immediately?" He dismounted while General Stuart excused himself from the ladies and quickly left the now-stopped carriage. The two men saluted each other, then walked to a nearby shade tree, deep in conversation.

Sarah paled, stricken, as she comprehended General Stuart's words. She slowly turned her head away from the men and locked eyes with Rebecca. She kept her hands on the window opening. In a whisper, Sarah asked, "This … is … 18 … 63?"

With one assenting nod, Rebecca affirmed this fact.

Shocked, Sarah fainted and collapsed onto her new friend.

Chapter 6

When Sarah awoke, she felt disoriented and couldn't remember where she was or what time of day it was. By the look of the soft light coming in through the windows, she finally determined it was dawn. She saw a servant sitting near the window, staring at her. The servant silently left the room, and in a moment, Rebecca appeared, fully dressed in a yellow spring gown.

"Oh, Sarah, I am so glad that you have finally awakened. I was most distressed when you fainted and did not revive. Samuel assured me that you would be well after we had the doctor examine you, but one never knows."

Fully awake now, Sarah sat up in bed and noticed the lovely white lace cotton nightgown she was wearing. "What happened to me? Did I faint? I can't imagine doing so. I have never fainted before in my life. How long have I been asleep?"

"Ever since you fainted in the carriage early yesterday evening. You were saying the strangest things and acted so agitated, and then you fainted. I called to Samuel to assist me, and he and General Jackson carried you to the doctor's cabin. It was rather conveniently located nearby, you know. Then they brought you back to the carriage. Samuel kept you cradled in his arms on our way back to steady you. Occasionally, you opened your eyes, but you never said anything. Once home, Samuel insisted that he carry you all by himself to this room. I could not imagine why he didn't want to have the servants' help, but there you have it. Bessie and I undressed you and put my nightgown on you."

Sarah leaned back on the soft cotton pillow. "Your brother carried me the entire way? How gallant of him. He must be even stronger than he looks." She braced herself against the polished mahogany headboard and went on, "Rebecca, I feel strange in asking you this, but could you please tell me what year this is?"

"It is 1863, of course. Have you had a head injury?"

Sarah leaned her head backward, and with her eyes closed, she said, "Rebecca, I don't know how or why I'm here, but you must believe me." She opened her eyes and in earnest said directly, "I speak the truth when I tell you that yesterday morning, I was in the year 2018! What does all this mean?"

Rebecca frowned and stared at Sarah for a few moments. "Well, for all the things that ever were! As I live and breathe, I do not know why, but I do believe you, Sarah, as impossible as it seems. How did you get here?" Rebecca sat down on the nearby window seat.

"I can't imagine. Your home and property are a historical area open to the public for tours in my time. My family and I were visiting all the different attractions offered at Stone Mountain Park for the last three days. On the day we planned to visit this plantation, I surprised everyone with my authentic Civil War period outfit, which I was wearing yesterday. Then my family had to find a bathroom, and I told them I'd catch up. I wanted to tour the slave cabin and stable area."

Watching her movements in her mind's eye, Sarah continued, "I walked into the slave cabin and thought it to be quite nice compared to the impoverished quarters we learned about in the North. Then I walked out and turned toward the stables and ran right into the man who looked so much like General Stonewall Jackson." Sarah's eyes widened with realization, and she sat erect. "You mean … it was the *real* General Jackson?"

"The very same. General Jackson is a friend of Samuel's, and he and his wife and baby were here for a few days. It seems there has been some trouble someplace, and they had to leave immediately. Sarah, did you just say that you are from the North?"

Nervously clearing her throat, she replied, "Well, actually, originally, yes, but only by birth. My parents lived in Philadelphia due to my father's transfer to that coast guard station. My brother and I grew up in Pennsylvania, but my mother was from Macon, and my father was from Savannah. After my brother achieved his doctorate, he and his family moved to Stone Mountain, and he got an excellent job at the hospital. I quite recently left Philadelphia, and I plan to stay here in Stone Mountain. But ... how can I be in 1863? Maybe I'm just dreaming, do you think?"

Sarah pinched her skin to verify whether she was asleep. *I know. I will look out the window at Stone Mountain and see the Confederate memorial carvings. Then I will know something familiar to get my bearings.*

Sarah felt stunned as she gazed at the massive granite in her view. *What in the world? There are no carvings!*

"Oh, no, Sarah, this is real life, all right. There is a terrible War between the States going on that makes reality very harsh indeed at present. I hear of many people living near the battlefields, and they do their best to help the wounded. Food is scarce in some areas. So far we have not experienced any of that, and I pray the battle never takes place here."

Sarah silently processed Rebecca's description. *If you only knew what lies ahead with General Sherman's march through Georgia to the sea, but how could I tell her that? So much bloodshed and mayhem are ahead.*

After sitting quietly for some minutes, Rebecca restated, "For all the things that ever will be!" She put her hands to her cheeks and continued, "I am amazed that I do believe that you are from the future. God must be giving His grace to me to believe you, although I am not quite sure what I do understand." She frowned, stood up, thought for a few moments, and then said, "Wait a minute! If you are from the future, pray do tell. When do we win the war?" Rebecca looked joyfully expectant of Sarah's reply.

Sarah looked embarrassed, cast her eyes downward, and said in a small, whispered voice, "I am sorry to tell you that the South lost."

Gasping, Rebecca put her hand on her heart and went pale as she collapsed back into her chair. Then she jumped up and started rushing around the room. "No! It cannot be, Sarah. We must win this war. It is only right that each state has sovereignty to govern its people, not the Union."

Rebecca paced and paced. Her swishing silk skirt was the only sound in the room for a few minutes. Sarah silently watched the movements of her new friend. There was a faint distant chime of a grandfather clock from somewhere in the house. Rebecca stopped so suddenly that she almost lost her balance. She turned to Sarah and said emphatically, "I know why you are here, Sarah. God has sent you to help the South win this war. I just know it!"

Sarah sucked in her breath after Rebecca spoke her confident words. She joined Rebecca's pacing. She was barefooted, and her lovely cotton chemise flowed around her. Her expressive hands were flailing as she exclaimed, "Could it really be so? Is that why I am here? But how can that be possible?"

The two young women stared at each other.

Sarah continued, "Well, as I think it over, perhaps this is why I've always felt out of place in my time and wished I could have lived back then ... I mean now." The dawn of realization brought clarity to Sarah. "Yes! Yes! I've had a passion for history ever since I can remember, especially for the Civil War. I studied history at college, and my career has been as a museum expert on the War between the States. Also, I've always read time-travel novels and pretended that I was the main character. Now, here I am! Oh, Rebecca, I've been wondering what my life would become, and now here it is before me. My destiny is this changed purpose. I am to be God's instrument to change history and to help the South win this war and save many lives."

With the enormity of the task before her, she flopped down in an unladylike manner on a brocade cushioned chair near the window. Her flowing ruffled nightgown fluffed with the movement and slowly settled around her. The morning light was bright now, casting its gleaming rays on Sarah as if reaching down from the very heavens to touch this chosen one. The brilliant light created a glowing effect and highlighted her loose, gently curling waist-length dark auburn hair.

Rebecca came and knelt down in front of Sarah on the polished wood floor. She took her hands into her own and said genuinely, "Sarah, I know that I am to help you in your mission. As surely as I live and breathe, I know it is my destiny and purpose to assist you. Together, with God's help, we shall be His instruments to bring victory to the South."

Sarah clasped her new friend's hands tightly and said sincerely, "Thank you, Rebecca, for believing me and for being so willing to help.

God truly has brought us together." She thought for a moment, then said, "How God expects two young ladies to achieve this enormous task is beyond me. But we must remember the scripture that says, 'With God, all things are possible!' We shall trust Him and proceed one day at a time." They agreed with a smile and a nod. Sarah continued, "Now, tell me, what is today's date?"

"Today is the twenty-fifth of April."

Sarah gulped and squeezed Rebecca's hands. "Oh, no! I know what we must do immediately. Confederate soldiers will accidentally shoot General Jackson on the second of May, and he will die on the tenth of May. We must intervene!"

Chapter 7

With the hustle and bustle of two young ladies dedicated to the purpose of their shared goal—and with the help of Bessie, Rebecca's lady's maid—they were ready and on their way to Atlanta within the hour. They thanked Bessie for her assistance, and Rebecca gave a quick hug to her. She was like family to the Stuarts, as were all their servants. Sarah noticed this sweet relationship and wondered about it. She decided to discuss it with Rebecca on their trip.

During their swift carriage ride, Sarah questioned Rebecca about their slaves. Rebecca replied emphatically, "Oh! They are not slaves on our plantation. Well, of course, they were brought here as slaves, but once my father purchases them, he gives them freedom. Then he asks them to work for us for seven years, as indentured servants, to pay him back. We haven't had any of our servants leave us. After the seven-year indentured period passes, they choose to stay here on our plantation. My father continues to house and provide for them and also pays them a fair wage. My father is a wonderful man. He did this for years, long before Mr. Lincoln gave his Emancipation Proclamation on January first of this year. Interestingly enough, Mr. Lincoln only gave freedom to the Southern slaves during his speech. Why did he not include the Northern slaves as well if he truly wanted to free slaves in all of our country?"

Sarah knew the answer. "You are right, Rebecca. The Emancipation Proclamation did not free all slaves in the United States. Rather, Mr. Lincoln declared free only those slaves living in states not under Union control. In other words, he referred to the Confederate States. It tied the issue of slavery directly to the war, but as we both know, slavery wasn't the main issue of the war. If it were, President Lincoln would have set all slaves free in his Emancipation Proclamation on January 1, 1863. These are facts recorded in history from the mouth of Mr. Lincoln."

"I know. I read it myself in our newspaper a few months ago. We Southerners feel that in freeing only the slaves of the Confederate States, Mr. Lincoln was trying to ruin our economy and also prevent any more slave states in the North from joining our cause of states' rights. What Mr. Lincoln didn't realize was how absurd he sounded giving commands over states that were no longer under Union control. Our eleven states seceded and formed our Confederate States of America in 1860 and 1861," Rebecca explained.

"Yes, those facts are definitely clear in history. It is interesting to learn that your father has been freeing slaves and making them indentured servants for years on your plantation," Sarah stated.

"Yes, and my father has influenced many other plantation owners to do the same thing. When there is any news of mistreated slaves somewhere, my father or other plantation owners like him go to purchase them and save them from their plight. There are some very evil slave owners, to be sure, but there are many good Christian men who treat their freed servants with respect and are thankful to give them a better life. Like any human being, people respond to kindness."

"Kindness is always the best way to treat each other," Sarah agreed, then reflected aloud, "We read in the Bible of the Israelites serving Egypt as slaves for years. Unfortunately, slavery has been around in many cultures for generations and is likely to remain in one form or another in different countries. The reason slaves are here in America is because our nation started out as thirteen colonies of England, and in England, slavery was legal. I never give up hope, though, that people will come to terms with realizing that slavery is wrong in any culture."

Rebecca went on, "Years ago, my father organized a group of like-minded men to come together financially to purchase mistreated slaves and give them good homes. They even try to help train plantation owners to be kind and respect all human life. However, if they won't take the opportunity given to them to change their ways, my father's group purchases the plantations as well. We want our future generations to inherit a legacy of integrity."

Surprised, Sarah said, "What a wonderful idea! This plan and organization never got into the history books, as far as I can tell." Sarah grinned. "Even though I studied Civil War history in depth, I didn't read every single thing written, of course. But one would think that something this wonderful would have been accounted for, recorded, and published."

"Well," stated Rebecca, "as you can understand throughout history, many facts are left untold and even exploited. I am sorry to hear that my father's organization never made it into common knowledge of history."

"What is the organization called?"

"Redemption Liberty Warriors."

"Hmm, Redemption Liberty Warriors," Sarah repeated. "Thank God they existed—I mean, exist. It is difficult for me to speak of the past as the present. Sorry."

"Yes, they do exist, Sarah, and my highly respected father is their leader. One man can make a difference in this life, and my father is one of these."

"I can give account after account of how one person made a huge difference in the course of history. I am proud to know that your father is one of them."

Rebecca smiled and humbly stated, "God has blessed our family with my father being such a strong Christian leader in our home and community. My brother takes after him in every way too." Sarah was about to find out firsthand whether General Samuel Stuart possessed the integrity of his reputable father.

The carriage continued to jostle through the bumpy dirt road that carried these resolute ladies closer and closer to Atlanta for this fateful meeting. Dust was flying behind them because the weather was overly dry.

Almost shyly, Sarah said to Rebecca in a hushed tone, "May God make me one of those people who can make a huge difference in history, Rebecca. I humbly ask for His grace and wisdom as we speak to your brother."

Rebecca nodded assent, and the young ladies looked out the windows of the quickly moving carriage, lost in their private thoughts for a time.

While Rebecca prayed, Sarah reflected on the vast changes in her life in such a short time. She felt adrenaline causing a nervous type of excitement coursing through her. Finding herself on the brink of being part of historical alterations of this magnitude made her feel scared. She wondered whether she could fulfill this life-changing mission. She found comfort and strength when she recalled the scripture she had memorized in Philippians 1:6. "He that hath begun a good work in you will perform it until the day of Jesus Christ."

She couldn't understand why God would want her, just an everyday person, to be His instrument to change the entire outcome of this war. She considered the enormity of the tasks facing her yet had such an inner peace that comes only when a Christian knows, without a shadow of a doubt, that he or she is in the perfect will of God and is obeying Him. She began singing a praise tune in her mind as they approached the looming Atlanta headquarters of General Samuel Stuart.

Her thoughts were interrupted when Rebecca asked, "Sarah, have there been other time travelers in your family?"

Sarah answered immediately, shook her head, and pursed her lips. "No. Not that I know of anyhow."

Their carriage came to a halt, which announced that their journey had come to an end. The time it took to travel from the Stone Mountain area to the Atlanta meeting place seemed like only a few minutes to Sarah, not two hours. She concentrated on her presentation to General Stuart and decided to tell the truth. She knew from biblical principles that truth was her best course to follow.

Rebecca requested a private interview with her brother immediately. A soldier showed the ladies into a room that was apparently a man's study.

Noticing Rebecca's eyes sweep the room, Sarah asked, "You have never seen your brother's office until this moment, have you?

Rebecca replied, "No. There was never a need for me to be here before now."

Books, charts, maps, several tables, and a U-shaped desk filled the chamber. Sarah noticed a faint scent of leather from the three available chairs. Although not in use, the brick fireplace had a slight aroma of past fires burned there. No one was in the room, so the ladies sat anxiously on the edge of two chairs in front of the large desk. Since they were alert and prepared, their backs were as straight as could be. Sarah flipped the straps of her knapsack back and forth in the absentminded habit she had developed.

Both Rebecca and Sarah felt tense. They were well aware of the monumental task ahead of them to convince Samuel of everything Sarah had to tell him. They remained silently still for minutes. A ticking pendulum perfectly reflected the timing of their pounding hearts. Sarah could feel perspiration collecting above her upper lip and on top of her nose.

When the study door suddenly opened, they both jumped up to attention as if they were soldiers. In walked the commanding General Stuart. "Rebecca. Miss Gordon." He bowed as they curtsied. "What possible consideration has brought you both to seek me here urgently? Is something wrong at the plantation that could not wait until my return?" He had been interrupted from a meeting with President Davis.

Rebecca replied, "No. No. Everything is fine at home, Samuel. Please sit down, and we will explain why we are here."

They all took their seats. Sarah asked to open their meeting with a short prayer, which she did without waiting for their responses. God needed to prepare her as she launched into her story. As they sat, Sarah reiterated her entire story from start to finish, sparing no details. Both ladies stressed that Samuel's immediate action was critical to saving General Jackson's life. When they finished their appeal and fell silent, they waited for him to comment. He hadn't said one single word the entire time. He sat alert in his desk chair with his fingertips pressed together and waited. The atmosphere was thick with charged anticipation.

General Stuart at length glared straight at Sarah but spoke to Rebecca. His eyes never left Sarah's face. "Rebecca, this woman may very well be a spy for the Union and has been sent here to undermine us."

Sarah's reaction was swift in denial, and just as swiftly, she was silenced with a mere raise of General Stuart's hand to stop her. After some moments, Sarah requested permission to speak. General Stuart granted her request with a curt nod.

"Sir, I am not a spy. I speak the truth. There is something that may help you to believe me. On the thirtieth of April in Chancellorsville,

General Stoneman and his men will lead a raid on the Confederate Army of Northern Virginia. They will destroy portions of the Virginia Central Railroad and will cut General Lee's communication lines. Here is my proposal, sir. Do what you will with me until you see me proved right, but please, I implore you. Telegraph General Lee today. Tell him to expect destroyed communication lines on the thirtieth of April. When this happens, he is to get immediate word to General Jackson to report to him with his troops on the first of May. Forbid General Jackson to go into the section called the Wilderness, for this is where the Confederate soldiers will accidentally shoot him. If you do this, then you will know that I speak the truth, and this will save General Jackson's life. If you do not do this, General Jackson will be shot mistakenly by his men late in the day of the second of May in the Wilderness, and on the tenth of May, he will die."

With determination and courage, Sarah returned his stare steadily and waited for his reply. Her back muscles and shoulders ached from the stress.

Rebecca had been sitting stiffly on the edge of her chair, all the while silently praying for her brother to believe what he was hearing.

Suddenly, General Stuart stood up behind his desk and shouted in a commanding voice, "Lieutenant Smith! Enter!" Instantly, the door swung open, and a saluting officer was waiting to do his commander's will. "Take this woman," he said, indicating Sarah, "to the holding cell." The obedient officer approached and seized Sarah's right arm firmly but gently. She rose with dignity, fully cooperating.

Rebecca said in earnest, "Samuel, no! Please believe her! I do!"

Sarah knew her fate and tried one more time. She stared intently at General Stuart and implored, "I beg you to heed my warning, sir. Destroyed communication lines will offer no chance to send word to save General Jackson."

The lieutenant assertively pulled her through the doorway. Sarah had only a few remaining seconds in the room. She said finally, as she looked back over her shoulder, "General Jackson's life is now in your hands, sir. I have done what God sent me to do. I have carried the message to you. It is up to you now." Then the door closed.

Chapter 8

General Stuart kept his gaze on the door for a moment. He then beheld his sister and asked in an incredulous voice as he raked his hand through his hair, "Have you gone mad to believe this woman, Rebecca? She is a Union spy, and that is the only truth here."

Rebecca stood erect with conviction and lifted her chin. With the fire in her eyes her brother knew so well, she said, "No, Samuel, I have not gone mad. How dare you speak so to me! I believe Sarah, and I will tell you why. I do not doubt that she speaks the truth. Our God, Creator of the universe, granted me the faith to believe, and I do believe."

Her chin lifted again in affirmation. "Think for a minute, Samuel. God created all things, and by Him nothing is impossible. He created time, and He controls everything. Would it then stand to reason that He would and could use time for His purposes?"

Rebecca raised her eyebrows, then started pacing the room in front of Samuel's desk. He sat in his chair, leaned back, and watched and listened. Rebecca bent over the desk with both hands on it and continued, "With our own small, limited minds, even we can see that the people who lived before and will live in the future share a common bond. We all live on this earth, separated only by time. God created time, and He can certainly make it obey Him. He sent Sarah here to us so you can be His instrument to save General Jackson!"

Rebecca picked up Sarah's knapsack, then her gloves, and headed to the door. She hooked Sarah's knapsack on her shoulder, as she had seen Sarah do. Samuel remained silent. After slowly putting her gloves on, she placed her hand on the door handle. Hesitating, Rebecca turned to face her brother and said in a quiet voice, "Samuel, there's something else Sarah told me that she did not tell you." With a deep breath and eyes locked on her brother's, Rebecca said in a choked voice as a tear ran down her cheek, "Sarah said that the South lost this war of Northern aggression, Samuel. Unless you heed her warning, this will be our future."

Their gaze was unfaltering as the enormity of those few words struck their hearts. Then Rebecca exited quietly in pursuit of Sarah, leaving Samuel to his thoughts.

Sitting at his desk once again, Samuel picked up a pencil and tapped it rhythmically as he pondered all he had just heard. He stood, walked to the window, and stared at nothing for a long while. He couldn't imagine time travel to be real. It defied all logic and common sense. Could he take the chance of ignoring that it might be true? So much was at stake. Deep in thought, General Samuel Stuart decided to pray.

He knelt down on both knees, and the wooden floor creaked under his weight as he humbled himself before God. He bowed his head and said aloud, "Father, You know I am willing to obey Your holy will. If this woman has been sent here by You to help us save Thomas Jackson's life, the South, and this war, please, give me the faith to believe. Please give me Your peace that passes all understanding. Strengthen me, O God, and help me to believe and know what You would have me do. I need Your wisdom, Father. In the name of my Lord and Savior, Jesus Christ, I pray, amen."

Chapter 9

General Stuart rose to his feet after a long span of deep meditation. A gift of faith filled him so entirely that he felt as if he had to breathe very deeply for a few moments to steady himself. The sun was shining brightly, and his heart was full. He looked out the window heavenward and whispered, "Thank You, Father."

Turning with the resolution only a man with a new, urgent purpose would feel, Samuel marched directly out of the room and to the holding cell, dismissing the guard.

Rebecca stood there, quietly talking with Sarah through the small square opening in the wooden cell door. She turned and broke into a joyful grin as she saw the look on her brother's face. She took his hand, pressed it to her cheek, and smiled up at him. "Oh, Samuel! God has granted faith for you to believe. I can see it on your face."

With a smile, Samuel replied, "Yes."

While he unlocked the door of the holding cell and swung it fully open, the movement caused the metal hinges to squeak. Sarah moved back a few steps, then dipped into a deep, respectful curtsy.

"Thank you for believing me, General Stuart!" Sarah seemed to be glowing with joy.

He replied, "Thank our Lord, Miss Gordon, not me. God has opened my eyes and has given me this monumental task to change the course of history. You have done well, dear lady. Now, you will assist me on this mission, will you not?" He reached for her hand and escorted her through the threshold of the holding cell into freedom.

Sarah replied, "Most definitely I will assist you, sir!" She noticed his warm, masculine touch on her hand. The spark between them had returned, but she shook off the feeling for now and focused on what she needed to do.

Again seated in his office, the trio began discussing what Sarah knew to be true and what they needed to do to change current circumstances.

Sarah finally stated, "After General Jackson died on May tenth,

1863, there was much slaughter, especially at Gettysburg, Pennsylvania, on July first through the third, 1863. It seemed as if that was the turning point of the war. Weakened, the South continued fighting until finally, on April ninth, 1865, General Lee was forced to surrender at Appomattox Court House in Virginia to prevent any more loss of life."

"How is it that you, a young lady, know so much about military pursuits, Miss Gordon?" inquired General Stuart with raised eyebrows. It was a question of interest, not a command.

She chuckled, "Well, sir, I've always been interested in the Civil War ever since I can remember. I've studied it in depth and used my knowledge for employment. You see, I worked at a museum—up until last week, actually—and I have a confession to make. I grew up in the North. Unfortunately, they taught us that the main issue of the Civil War was about slavery." Then she added quickly, "But my heart has always been in the South, sir, with Southern values. My mother was from Macon, Georgia; and my father was from Savannah. After they married, they moved to Philadelphia because he was in the coast guard, and they transferred him. That is where my brother and I were born. However, we have come back to our roots. Just last week, I decided to move to the Stone Mountain area to be with my brother and his family to start a new life. Little did I know what that new life would be and where."

Sitting forward with animation, General Stuart said passionately, "You refer to this war as the Civil War, Miss Gordon, but it is the War of Northern Aggression. It is dividing families from the North and South because of their individual beliefs. The North is using slavery as a diversion to mask their true intentions. Northerners have slaves too, as you obviously well know. Slavery is a terrible issue, and all states need to address it and abolish it. We didn't fight the War of Independence from the English eighty-five years ago just to have another overly large political body subvert individual states' rights. The main issue of this war is the right of each state to govern itself."

"You will be glad to know that history recorded the courage of the brave souls in the eleven states who decided to leave the Union to form the Confederate States of America to this point in history. They are

South Carolina, Mississippi, Florida, Alabama, Georgia, Louisiana, Texas, Virginia, Arkansas, North Carolina, and Tennessee," Sarah recited from memory.

"Indeed." He nodded his approval, then excused himself from the ladies with a slight bow. He went first to order tea and a repast for the ladies to refresh them. Before it arrived, Rebecca and Sarah took advantage of Samuel's private outhouse, conveniently located just outside his back office door.

Samuel personally sent a telegraph message to General Lee. Why sacrifice the valuable lives of Southern men in this upcoming battle with the Union on April thirtieth in Chancellorsville? The telegraph included some strategy not only to prevent loss of life on both sides but also to enable the South to win the battle.

General Lee had finished eating his evening meal with his men and retired alone to his headquarters tent in Chancellorsville, Virginia. He was reading his Bible and praying for wisdom and direction when a voice called for his attention.

"Enter," commanded General Lee. A messenger came in with a telegram and handed it quickly to the general. He stood at attention, awaiting instruction. General Lee tore open the envelope in haste, glanced through the telegram, then dismissed the messenger. He studied the telegraph message for some time as he sat on his cot, deep in thought. He understood the contents but had no reason why these strategy changes had come to him at this late hour; nor did he have clarity regarding what new information had caused these changes.

General Lee stood up, went to his makeshift desk, and formed his reply. He had many questions, but answers would have to wait until a face-to-face meeting could be arranged with General Stuart. General Lee wrote his agreement to employ General Stuart's tactics. He called for the messenger to enter, handed the telegram to him, and gave a direct order to send it immediately. He set about planning the necessary maneuvers. General Lee would discuss them with no one until the time to give new orders to the men. They all needed a good sleep in preparation for what lay ahead.

General Stuart returned to his office after he sent the telegram. He offered his quarters to the ladies for the night. They dined together in his office and enjoyed a delicious stew, buttermilk biscuits, and sweet tea.

As strange as it seemed, Sarah particularly enjoyed the lack of electricity in this century. She had always liked candlelight and had often chosen to use candles and oil lamps at night in her own home in 2018. She considered how oddly prepared she was for this mission, even to the smallest details.

With the two Stuarts believing her and her campaign to save General Stonewall Jackson and the South underway, Sarah was able to relax for the first time in two days. She noticed most acutely how handsome General Stuart was, especially now that he wasn't thinking of her as an enemy spy. His face had softened, his green eyes were captivating, and his silver hair glowed in the candlelight in contrast to his tanned skin. They enjoyed some conversation about the present and the future, as Sarah had known it, and speculated on how it might be different after the South won the war.

Suddenly, Sarah's stomach lurched as she thought of her brother, Colin, and his family. She exclaimed passionately, "Oh, my heart! I just thought of something. My brother and his family are going to be so distraught when they can't find me. Surely there must be some way I can get word to them so they won't worry. We are very close, you see. I can't imagine God would call me to this mission, then cause my family lifelong grief of wondering what happened to me."

Sarah got up abruptly and started walking around the room. Her brow wrinkled as she began wringing her hands. "There is a lot of that in my time. Many children and adults are missing and hardly ever recovered. Pictures of missing loved ones circulate online, and Amber Alerts go out to the masses by texts when needed. Some thankfully are saved, but rarely, though, are the missing ever recovered."

Sarah could tell by the look on his face that Samuel suppressed many questions about what she had just said. He stayed focused and addressed himself to the main problem. "Well, Miss Gordon, there must be a way to get a message to your family, and we shall find it." He pondered the issue for a few minutes, then said, "Since your life drastically changed over the last few days before you came to us, tell me all about it in detail. I will see if I can help you in some way to get a message to your family."

Rebecca interjected, "Oh, yes, do tell everything you did from the time you left that horrid, bleak North to come to the beautiful, bright South!" Her arms opened wide with sweeping emphasis.

Sarah shot a glance at Rebecca with a wry smile. *She sounds like my mother.* She began her story slowly and thoughtfully. Sarah felt calm as she recounted her final hours before she left the future.

"Well, I took an afternoon flight from Philadelphia to Atlanta. Then I drove a rental car to the Stone Mountain Park, where my family was camping in their RV." Sarah stared at the candle flame as she talked but seeing these events in her mind's eye. She looked up to see the astonishment on the faces of her new friends, and she laughed. "Oh, dear! Let me interpret. A flight means just that—flying in a machine that is called an 'airplane' or a 'jet.' I boarded the jet in Philadelphia, and approximately two hours later, I was in Atlanta."

Looking at the amazement on their faces, she continued, "Then I drove a car, one I rented at the airport. A car is called an 'automobile,' but we future Americans like to shorten and abbreviate everything, so it's called a 'car.' It's a machine powered by a fuel called 'gasoline,' and it has four wheels and an engine. You'll find this difficult to believe, but the average speed is sixty-five miles per hour, a measurement you would probably relate to horsepower."

"Surely not, Miss Gordon!" Samuel Stuart exclaimed as he sat erect.

"Oh, yes, sir. You'd enjoy it very much too, General Stuart. I must admit it is fun."

"Not to me," declared Rebecca. "Four horses are quite fast enough for me."

Sarah laughed and explained, "Actually, a unit of power is called horsepower, and 'miles per hour' refers to a unit of speed. Physics tells us the equation. All we need to know is that the force exerted relates to its power and the speed it travels."

Rebecca felt totally lost. "You are a very educated young lady, Sarah."

"Excuse me, please, Miss Gordon," General Stuart interrupted, holding up the palm of his hand like a traffic police officer. "This is all very interesting. However, we are diverting from our main issue of getting a notification to your brother and family of your whereabouts."

"Yes, do go on with your remembrances of all of your activities before coming to us, and we'll get full explanations of future life later, Sarah," Rebecca said in agreement.

"Okay. We must figure out a way to get a message to them for sure." Sarah began pacing again. "Let's see, that night we planned our next three days of activities. Stone Mountain Park has all kinds of attractions to visit, so we did three or so each day. On my last day there, we planned a picnic on the Stone Mountain trail. It wasn't too far up the trail, and we ate right next to an ancient carving that was hewn into the stone, obviously done by some pirates. It had a skull and crossbones and date and everything. We made up stories about it while we picnicked."

Sarah went on to tell them every little detail about her last day with her family in the future. Her new friends promised to pray for wisdom to find a solution.

Chapter 10

After Sarah and Rebecca returned home the next morning from their meeting with General Stuart, Mrs. Stuart greeted them warmly. She stood on the front porch, all smiles and waves, wearing a lovely antebellum dress of pale lilac. The sun was shining brightly, and the day was already warm and humid. Mrs. Stuart flapped her white lace handkerchief in greeting.

"Welcome home, Rebecca. And this must be your new friend, all recovered and well. The last time I saw you, Miss Gordon, you were unconscious and gave us quite a fright." Mrs. Stuart hugged her daughter and kindly took the hand of her companion.

As if accustomed to doing so all of her life, Sarah dropped into a low curtsy and said, "Mrs. Stuart, I am so delighted to meet you. Please forgive my imposing upon you as I have."

"Think nothing of it, my dear. We are glad to be of assistance. It must be very distressing to lose one's family. Come! Let us sit in the parlor and have a cool drink of sweet tea and talk a bit, shall we?"

So sweet tea in the South has been around for decades. Hooking her arms into the crooks of the young women's, the older woman led them into the bright and airy parlor. It overlooked a beautiful sizeable ornamental garden.

They each took a seat, and the younger women respectfully waited for the elder to speak first. "Rebecca, how did you find your brother?"

"He is very well, Mama. In fact, I believe he is the best he has been for some time now." Rebecca glanced knowingly at Sarah.

Not one to miss any innuendo, Mrs. Stuart caught the look the young ladies exchanged. Turning to Sarah, Mrs. Stuart said, "Miss Gordon, how may I assist you in contacting your family?"

Sarah looked swiftly at Rebecca before answering, "Well, ma'am, you see—well, I'm not exactly sure how to get in touch with them."

"I see." Mrs. Stuart replied, but obviously she didn't understand such a statement. "Where is it that they live, Miss Gordon?"

"They live near Atlanta, ma'am," Sarah replied vaguely.

With a confident nod, Mrs. Stuart said, "Well then, I shall have my man ride there today and let them know you are safe with us. They must be anxious about you."

"Yes, ma'am, I imagine they are worried about me … yes, very worried indeed. It's just that, well"—Sarah cleared her throat and continued—"I don't think your man would be able to find where they live." Sarah started curling the corners of the linen handkerchief as her face blushed and her palms began to sweat. She commenced her unconscious habit of slightly shaking her left leg when she was stressed.

Mrs. Stuart noted the nervous behavior but continued the conversation. "Miss Gordon, I assure you that the man I will send shall be reliable enough and intelligent enough to follow your directions precisely."

Clearing her throat, again unsuccessfully, Sarah answered in a high-pitched voice, "Mrs. Stuart, my brother and his family will not be able to be reached for some time." Sarah cleared her throat yet again.

With a penetrating look at the young lady, and raising her arched eyebrows, Mrs. Stuart said, "Let me ascertain that I have your situation clearly in my discernment. You and your brother and his family came to Stone Mountain to see it, and you became separated and lost from them."

Avoiding the inescapable stare, Sarah averted eyes and quietly replied, "Yes, ma'am."

"Then just by chance, my daughter found you in our lane, and you became distressed and fainted. My son and the doctor helped you to our home. Then your unconscious state lingered into a night's sleep in Rebecca's chamber. Early the next morning, yesterday, you and my daughter rushed out in the carriage to my son's headquarters in Atlanta with important information he had to know immediately."

"Yes, ma'am."

"Rebecca left a note for me, explaining your whereabouts, and later in the day, I received a message from my son, stating that you two ladies would be spending the night at his headquarters."

Sarah replied in the affirmative, but she hadn't known about the note from Samuel to his mother.

"And now you are here, stating that your family is not only lost to you but also unreachable for some time."

"Yes, ma'am."

"I see." Mrs. Stuart pondered her words a moment, then continued relentlessly. "Did you attempt to contact them when you were just in Atlanta?"

"Umm … no, ma'am," Sarah mumbled.

"I see," Mrs. Stuart repeated. "Well, since I have my facts straight up to this point, please enlighten me further on two issues, Miss Gordon. First, what possible information could you and my daughter think you have that would be of such great importance to my son? And next, why is your family unattainable?" Mrs. Stuart's composure was kind and calm but steely, demanding the truth instantly. She took a sip of her sweet tea to give the girl a moment.

Sarah darted an inquiring look at Rebecca. The question in her eyes was understood completely. Rebecca nodded in agreement, rose briskly, and claimed her mother's attention.

"Mama, I am going to get Daddy, and then we will tell you both all there is to know." Rebecca left the room swiftly, and the rustling of the fabric of her dress faded into the dead silence.

Sarah studied her wrinkled, moist hanky and silently prayed that the truth she was about to tell Mr. and Mrs. Stuart would be received in faith, as it had been by their daughter and son. As she shoved the worn hanky into her pocket, she chanced a furtive glance at the older woman. Sarah found her eyes as she expected them to be, pinning her to her seat with their intensity. Mrs. Stuart looked like she never blinked, and her countenance, though softened with a smile, revealed a great determination to get to the truth of the matter. Sarah swallowed a sip of her sweet tea with difficulty.

How am I going to get through this?

Chapter 11

The atmosphere lightened for a brief moment when Rebecca returned with her father, and introductions were made. Sarah felt relieved to stand for a few minutes. Mr. Stuart dismissed the servants, and everyone claimed a seat.

He began the inquiry in a gentle voice. "Miss Gordon, I understand a mystery accompanies you to our humble abode. Would you do us the honor of allowing us to comprehend your visit here?"

Sarah coughed slightly, but it didn't help to relieve her dry, constricted throat. In an attempt to fortify herself, she took a deep, cleansing breath. It seemed inconceivable that the elder Stuarts would believe her story of being a time traveler. However, what choice was there but to tell the truth? Standing slowly and walking back and forth, Sarah pulled out her handkerchief and gave it a further workout as she collected her thoughts. Suddenly, she stopped, looked directly at her kind host and hostess, and told all. Her entire story gushed forth.

Mr. and Mrs. Stuart sat quietly and never interrupted Sarah as she related every event. Sarah thought it was clear that Rebecca, Samuel, and their parents were from the same family. They all absorbed her account silently, without interjection. She wondered whether it was the shock of what she said or whether they were just well-mannered, good listeners. After she finished, Sarah felt exhausted. She sat down, sighed deeply, took a gulp of her sweet tea, and waited. All eyes were on her, and she returned their thoughtful gaze without blinking. Then she looked away and asked, "Well, what do you think?"

Mr. Stuart turned to his wife. In their particular unity of spirit, they needed no words to communicate their feelings to each other. Mrs. Stuart nodded once, and Mr. Stuart rose slowly from his chair. He went to stand before Sarah, held out his right hand, and said, "Miss Gordon, please rise."

As she did, they all stood. Sarah felt as if she were a convicted criminal in a court of law about to receive a verdict of guilty and be sentenced to death by electric chair.

But wait! Electricity hadn't been invented yet, so what would happen instead?

Taking her shaking hand in his, Mr. Stuart pronounced, "Miss Gordon, think of us as your family now. God has sent you to us, granted mysteriously, but who are we to question the Almighty? May He be praised! The information you have brought to our son will save our dear friend, Thomas Jackson's life, and will enable the South to win the war." He held her hand tenderly in both of his and continued softly. "Rebecca has always wanted a sister like you." Then he lovingly stretched out his hand to his daughter.

As if on cue, everyone in the room was in one big embrace. Sarah said with thanksgiving and relief, "Oh, Mr. and Mrs. Stuart! I am no one special, and yet here I am. And to become part of this wonderful family—oh, it is all too much to take in." She started weeping; her tears overflowed as the joy did in her heart. She felt like collapsing right there on the spot with relief.

"Yes, Sarah, God is good. He is good to us all. He has not only sent you here to change history, but He has blessed us with the grace to believe you immediately. Now we have the joy of including you in our family. Welcome home, Sarah. Welcome home," Mr. Stuart said sincerely.

Mrs. Stuart embraced Sarah once again. "I say, welcome home too, my child. May we always have the strength and faith to obey, as you have done, Sarah."

Rebecca took Sarah's hand and said, "Come! We will get you settled in with me right now."

"Rebecca, you may have Sarah in the room next to yours, if you and she would prefer," Mrs. Stuart said.

"Oh, no, Mama! Sarah will share my room, won't you, Sarah?" Rebecca inquired the way a much younger girl would ask.

With a smile and a shrug, Sarah replied, "Whatever you like." And it was settled. They left the room as Rebecca called out for Bessie to assist them. She was there in a flash. They all worked together to organize it very well.

Bessie had a tepid bath ready for them in no time. Rebecca insisted that Sarah soak in the tub first. Bessie poured lukewarm water over Sarah's hair and helped her wash it with lavender-scented soap. It was luxurious and cooling. They chatted during the bath.

Bessie said, "Miss, I couldn't help but hear about you traveling through time. How can that be?" Without waiting for a reply, Bessie continued, "The good Lord knows what He is doing—that is for sure—but it just seems like such a strange miracle."

"I agree, Bessie. It has all been extraordinary indeed yet wonderful at the same time."

"What did it feel like to travel back in time to us, Miss?"

"Actually, I didn't feel anything at all. I was on this property in the year 2018, touring the plantation as a historical attraction. I walked into the slave cabin near the stables to look at it, and then when I came out, I was in 1863. It just happened. I didn't even know I had traveled."

"Well, miss. I won't tell the other servants because I know they would have difficulty believing in time travel. It is so strange, but somehow It seems like many things are uncanny, aren't they?"

"Very true. It is a blessing when God grants us an extra measure of faith to believe something that doesn't seem possible."

Bessie went on, "When I was a very young girl, I lived on a plantation with my family. We had a good life there until the master passed away. They taught me to read and write when I was young. I love reading the Bible."

Bessie lathered Sarah's hair for the second time and poured the now-cooling water over her to rinse it out. It was so refreshing.

Sarah said, "I detect your education by your speech."

The maid held a large towel for Sarah to wrap up in since she had finished her bath.

Bessie smiled. "Yes, correct grammar and only a slight Southern accent were allowed where I grew up. It reminds me of Phyllis Wheatley's life. I read about her in literature." She continued as she went about her duties with Sarah. "Phillis Wheatley was brought to Boston from Africa in 1761. She was loved and educated by the Wheatley family and given freedom from slavery. They treated her as one of their own children. She was the first African-American woman to publish a book of poetry in 1773. I memorized my favorite selection, "On Being Brought from Africa to America." With bright eyes, she said, "I will recite it for you!"

> 'Twas mercy brought me from my Pagan land,
> Taught my benighted soul to understand
> That there's a God, that there's a Saviour too:
> Once I redemption neither sought nor knew.
> Some view our sable race with scornful eye,
> "Their colour is a diabolic die."
> Remember, Christians, Negros, black as Cain,
> May be refin'd, and join th' angelic train.

Sarah said, "I know her story too and am familiar with her poetry. She was an amazing woman."

"Yes. And she is my inspiration to write poetry. I have several written already. I imagine the Stuart family is much like the Wheatley family was one hundred years ago."

Sarah replied, "Apparently so." Although this conversation was very engaging, it was difficult for Sarah to carry on her part of it with her chin on her chest while Bessie combed out her long, wet hair. Sarah made a mental note to ask her whether she may read her poetry sometime.

Bessie went on, her face suddenly troubled. "Then our kind master died. No one expected it. Our mistress had no choice but to sell everything and then go to live with her sister. A very evil man came and bought the plantation and all of us. I was just a new bride of one year when this happened, and I had a beautiful son. The new master sold my husband and son one day without any warning. It was the worst day of my life."

Bessie talked as she began to section Sarah's long hair into three parts. "Soon after, Mr. Stuart came to the plantation, and God performed a miracle. The evil man agreed to sell all of the slaves to Mr.

Stuart. Another kindly man bought the plantation and brought his people to work it. I will never forget getting on the open farm wagon and coming to the Stuart plantation. My heart was singing, except for the constant pain of missing my husband and son. Mr. Stuart told us right away that we were free, and he asked us to work seven years as servants to pay him back. After the seven years passed, we all began receiving a fair wage, and every one of us decided to stay here. It is home for us, and our quarters are very nice."

Bessie reflected a few moments as she stood still and remembered the fateful day. "My parents were old, but Mr. Stuart had compassion on them, and they stayed with us until they passed. Being educated, the Stuarts wanted me to be a lady's maid for Miss Rebecca, and that is what I have done for the past ten years." Loosely braiding Rebecca's wet hair, Bessie said, "I pray for my husband and son every day. God has given to me the assurance that one day I will see them again." Her face brightened with hope and faith. "I look for them daily to arrive here!"

Sarah was so glad that she had the opportunity to get to know Bessie and learn about her life. She seemed like quite a courageous woman with a heart for God.

Next, it was Rebecca's time for a bath. Bessie finished preparing the young ladies for bed, then excused herself. Sarah wondered where the house servants' quarters were located.

I'll ask Bessie to show me at a more appropriate time.

Sarah and Rebecca felt like young, giggly girls as they stayed up most of their first night together in their shared room. There wasn't much for Sarah to unpack, since she had only her knapsack, her violin, and the clothes on her back when she arrived. She had instructed Bessie not to go into her backpack, but she could launder her outfit if she wouldn't mind.

Rebecca was very gracious to allow Sarah to try on many of her outfits to see what would suit her. They were much the same clothing size, and they were surprised that even their shoe size was the same. Sarah enjoyed primping and preening in front of the large full-length mirror. Rebecca tried her hand at dressing Sarah's hair in the latest fashions. Sarah shocked Rebecca by fixing her hair in the future trends, mostly in styles hanging freely down her back.

"Oh, Sarah! How shocking for women to be so casual in the future! No self-respecting lady would be seen with her hair down in public in these days, I assure you. It just isn't done."

"You know, Rebecca, I agree with you that it is shocking. Well, maybe not shocking exactly but unfortunate that women in my time have become so very casual. I've always liked the rules of propriety of this time, and I like them even more now that I'm here."

Rebecca replied with certainty, "Rules give clarity, and they help us all to know our expectations. Society works well when everyone does their best in their station of life."

"Indeed." Sarah grinned. "I particularly like the slight bow your brother and father offer as we ladies curtsie. I also like how everyone dresses as if they care about what statement they are making in their mode of dress. It is lovely to dress in finery for the evening meal too."

"Certainly. This is how I grew up and how I expect it to always be," Rebecca said confidently.

"Well, in my time, women strive to be equal to men," Sarah simply stated.

Rebecca gasped. "Impossible! We are not all the same. Anyone can see that fact if they'll just open their eyes. Goodness sakes alive! God made us all different for a reason. It is ridiculous to think otherwise."

Rebecca replaced her silver hand mirror on her dressing table. She had been waving it freely as she talked to emphasize the points she was making with Sarah. "Just read Proverbs 31, for example. There are many important things a woman can do as a helpmeet, according to God's design. I have seen my father and Mama discuss issues, and my father listens to her opinions. Mama gives Father respect, and he gives her value, worth, and security, as they both should do. It is all right there in the Bible, if anyone would care to read it."

"Yes, well, I wish there were more women like you in the future. Things would be much better if we still embraced the values of this time."

Rebecca said thoughtfully, "I like being provided for, yet I do expect to have my thoughts and opinions taken seriously. I may be a bit outspoken for a lady, but it's how I feel. We need to be respected and honored for our intellect. Some men do have a different opinion on the subject of what a woman thinks and where a woman's place is in society. I believe, as a lady, that I hope to be valued for who I am."

"Well, as I think of it, the women from 2018 and prior years wanted the same things—to be valued, feel worthy, and be recognized for their capabilities. They achieved this in various ways too."

"What about the men in the future? Don't they want to provide for their wives and families?"

"Well, yes, most of them do, but it's mostly expected by both men and women in my time to have two careers and two incomes."

"Well, what about the children? Who takes care of them?" Rebecca asked in a concerned voice.

"Many go into day care in infancy, some have private nannies or family members to care for them, and some women decide to make their careers as stay-at-home-mothers. Many help out with the family income through a cottage industry."

Rebecca listened to this and then replied, "I couldn't conceive of such a lifestyle being common. It is so different from what I know."

Rebecca paused, smacked her hand down on the bed, and brought the conversation back to her reality. "Well, wouldn't it be wonderful to be included when the gentlemen take their leave from the dinner table and withdraw to their smoking and billiards room? They may be surprised by how lively the conversation could get."

The ladies laughed, talked into the wee hours of the night, and then finally collapsed on their respective beds and fell into a deep sleep.

Chapter 12

After their family breakfast, Sarah asked to be excused from the table to take a walk by herself. She needed some time alone to think. They respected her request and warned her not to go too far from the manor house. If Samuel had been home, he might have offered to escort her, but he was in Atlanta.

She strolled along the edge of the lawn, where the thick woods began near the stately manor. As she walked, she reflected on her new life and how grateful she was for God's will for her.

It's a miracle that this family truly believes I am from the future. God works in mysterious ways, she thought. *How true that is!*

She twirled in her joy and chuckled as her new, beautiful, full skirts whipped around her legs. *If my brother and Tess could see me now, they'd say I have finally come into my own. I must say that I was born for these clothes and this lifestyle.* She twirled around in glee and made her skirts swirl out as she had loved to do since she was a child. *Now, if only I could invent air-conditioning, life would be perfect.*

Sarah reached down and pulled a long piece of sweet grass from its base and put it in her mouth to nip at its freshness. She liked the taste and found comfort in its familiar flavor. As Sarah bent down to break off the stem of just the right piece of a broader blade of grass to blow on and whistle, something caught her eye at the edge of the woods directly in front of where she stood. The morning sunshine filtered through the trees, making odd-looking patterns. She frowned and thought, *That looks like a man's boot.*

Sarah dropped her blades of grass and stepped forward to pick up the boot. It was black leather and quite worn. As she began to lift her find, she felt resistance, then heard a loud moan. She sucked in her breath, dropped the boot, and took two steps backward. She lost her balance and fell rather ungracefully with a jolting thud. Her arms stretched behind her for support, and her heart beat wildly, but she sat stunned for only a few seconds.

She promptly knelt and approached the boot cautiously. She entirely forgot what she was wearing. Her clothing was getting soiled and stained by the grass and earth as she inched her way on her knees. Sarah pressed her lips closed with her left hand and courageously but slowly reached toward the boot again. When she touched it lightly, nothing happened. Moving her hand upward, Sarah felt a leg attached to the boot. She pulled back quickly and thought for a moment about what she should do next. Standing tall, Sarah shook out her skirts and then plunged into the shadows to see what enigma she had found.

As her eyes adjusted to the instant shade of the thick foliage, she saw a tall man dressed in a Union soldier uniform. He lay prone and unconscious on his back. His right leg had oozed jellied blood all over his thigh. This dark red, blackish gel had attracted many flies. Sickened to the point of barely containable nausea, Sarah flicked her handkerchief in the direction of the smelly wound to shoo the flies away. Their annoying buzzing was very loud in the silence as they swarmed around the injury.

She bent cautiously over the man to discern his features. He had a thick, black beard that covered most of his face, and he looked to be a compelling individual, even in his state of unconsciousness. She noticed the soldier's uniform to be that of the rank of colonel. He looked as though he were peacefully asleep. She flipped her handkerchief near the wound once again to chase away the persistent flies and thought, *Now what do I do?*

She decided to get help and stood up straight with determination. Sarah reasoned that the man might be the enemy, but he was still a man, and God says to do good to your enemies.

Suddenly, a firm handclasp gripped her ankle. Sarah shrieked and fell backward again. She stared in disbelief as the colonel tried to hold her ankle but couldn't do so because of his weakened state.

His brown eyes, now widely open, drilled a hole into her. With a cracked, hoarse voice, he managed one word: "Water."

Sarah ran as fast as she could to the small stream nearby. She cupped her hands to scoop up water and carried it to the dehydrated soldier. Sarah slowly moistened his cracked lips. He opened his mouth for a trickle of the fresh water, which flowed onto his parched tongue. She dashed back to the stream and repeated the process several times. Then she told the soldier not to worry. Help would come momentarily.

Sarah ran to the manor house. The first person she saw in the hall was Mrs. Stuart, who exclaimed, "Why Sarah! Whatever is the matter with you, my dear? You look as if you have seen a ghost." Looking her up and down, she continued, "How did you get so soiled?"

Catching her breath, Sarah said in a rush, "Yes, ma'am, Mrs. Stuart, I practically have seen a ghost. I fell backward. Then I crawled forward." Her statements made no sense to Mrs. Stuart. "Please! Come with me instantly! Hurry!" She unceremoniously grabbed Mrs. Stuart's hand, pulled her out of the house, and rushed with her to the edge of the woods.

Mrs. Stuart was so startled that she wasn't able to speak. She willingly allowed herself to be pulled along into the yard. She was perspiring from the unexpected exertion and said, "Oh my! I'm not as young as I once was. What is this all about?"

Reaching their destination, Sarah released Mrs. Stuart's hand and led her into the woods. She exclaimed, "Look!" as she disclosed her find with her finger pointed in the direction of the soldier.

Mrs. Stuart's eyes quickly adjusted to the shadow of the woods, and she gasped as she saw the wounded man. Without requiring an explanation, she said, "Quickly, Sarah, run and get our men who are working on the barn. Tell them to bring planks to carry an injured man. Have Bessie bring some hot water and clean rags from the kitchen and some water to drink. Make haste! And pray, child!"

The servants quickly obeyed and already had the soldier in a sitting position when Sarah and Bessie returned with hot water, clean rags, and a dipper full of cold water for the colonel. First, Mrs. Stuart gave the man a drink, and he gulped the water as if his life depended on it, which it most likely did at that moment. His head fell back with relief, and a thin ray of sunshine glistened on the droplets of water clinging to his unkempt beard.

The water droplets were the only things sparkling about this man. He was filthy from head to toe, but Mrs. Stuart went about her work uninhibited. She tore open the man's already-shredded pants and applied sopping wet, warm rags to the wound to soften the congealed blood. Mrs. Stuart wiped it repeatedly. She spoke soothing words to him the whole time, as if he were a young boy, telling him not to worry or be afraid. She assured him that they would help him.

Mrs. Stuart cleaned the worst of the filth away, then announced matter-of-factly, "I shall have to take that bullet out, son."

The colonel spoke slowly with a hoarse voice, "Yes, madam, I expect you will ... if I am to live, that is."

"Oh, you shall live, son. With God's mercy, you shall live. Why do you think the good Lord sent you to us?"

The colonel's head straightened as he looked directly into Mrs. Stuarts's eyes and said, "I made it this far without God, madam, and I expect I will make it the rest of the way without Him as well."

Mrs. Stuart returned the wounded soldier's stare and said with fortitude and assurance, "No, son, God has been with you all along and always will be. You just do not know Him yet. He is the reason you are here in my care; you may count on it. Even though you are the enemy, I will care for you first and foremost because you are God's creation. I will do all I can for you because I am a Christian lady."

Weakly, the colonel replied bitterly, "So they can hang me or imprison me when I am well?"

Mrs. Stuart glanced at Sarah before answering. "We shall see about all of that later, son. Right now, we have to get you to the manor and get that bullet out."

Even with the help of the male servants, Sarah could tell that the distance to the manor seemed like miles to the struggling, injured officer.

Dear Lord, please help this man.

Mrs. Stuart directed them to lay the colonel on a wooden table in a small room off the butler's pantry area. Preparations for the surgery began.

The male servants held the colonel securely, and as soon as the first cut sliced his wounded flesh, the soldier thankfully fell unconscious again. The operation went well and quickly. Mrs. Stuart displayed skills that showed she had a natural talent and some practice in healing. Sarah stood by, assisting and learning. She was very impressed with the accomplishments of the women in this century. While maintaining the art of femininity, they possessed a strength of steel.

After having the colonel bathed, put in a clean nightshirt, and placed on a soft bed, the women retreated from the room to allow the wounded man time to rest. A servant girl spooned broth into his mouth very slowly, and a manservant was posted inside to tend to him when he fully awoke. Then Sarah and Mrs. Stuart went about their somewhat-altered day's plans.

Chapter 13

Later that day, General Samuel Stuart returned to the estate and was informed in detail about all that had taken place. In full uniform, General Stuart entered the colonel's chamber. Having just lit the oil lamp on the table, the servants quietly left the room and gently closed the door. Many tense moments passed as the two men stared silently at each other across the distance. It was dusk, and they could just make out their facial features.

Finally, Samuel walked over to the bed and said sternly, "I wasn't certain until this very moment what I would say to you or do with you. You are my enemy." They gave each other hard looks, knowing the duty of each to be loyal to his respective side. "I am a godly man, sir, and above all, I seek to serve Him. The Bible says to love your enemies, to do good to those who hate you and despitefully use you, and if your enemy thirsts, to give him drink. I shall offer protection and care to you until you are fully recovered and then a safe escort to the place of your choosing."

Astonished, the colonel eyed him suspiciously and croaked out a reply from his parched throat. "Why would you do this for me, General?"

Samuel looked him straight in the eye and replied, "Because it is the will of God."

As Samuel exited the room, the colonel said sincerely, "Thank you, General."

Samuel nodded and went out of the doorway, leaving a most relieved Union colonel to his thoughts. The guard posted outside the sickroom door saluted General Stuart.

Samuel rode hard to get home from his Atlanta headquarters after receiving the urgent message from his mother concerning the officer. This wounded enemy was now their God-given responsibility. He couldn't imagine what God's plan was at the moment, but he knew with certainty that God had one. In faith, the Stuarts all believed that nothing happened by chance. They all trusted God on a daily basis and purposed to please Him with their lives.

Samuel retired to his room to bathe and change for dinner. He hadn't expected to be home for days yet and relished this unanticipated time with his loved ones. His man, Joe, assisted him.

"It is good to have you home, sir," Joe stated. "We were all wondering how this situation would turn out with the wounded enemy. Of course, your mother was as staid and stoic, as usual, under a crisis."

Checking himself in the full-length mirror before exiting the room, Samuel replied, "Yes, my mother is strong and courageous. She is the most capable woman I have ever known. She is the epitome of a Proverbs 31 woman and a wonderful example for us all."

Joe nodded in agreement as he slipped Samuel's dinner jacket on him.

"I have decided that we will minister to this injured colonel, then see him back safely to his territory." Samuel noticed that Joe seemed quite surprised by that answer but went on. "We have no other choice, Joe. God sent this Union colonel to us. There must be a good reason. I walk by faith and trust God." There was no arguing with that statement.

When Samuel entered the dining room, the feelings Sarah experienced sweeping through her astonished her. She felt secretly delighted to have him home for dinner. Feeling her face redden and her palms sweat, she glanced furtively around, hoping no one else noticed her reactions.

Composing herself, Sarah asked Samuel about the Union soldier. He had little to say in reply except that the wounded man would stay under their care and protection until he recuperated. He further commanded that no one in the family was to attend to him or converse with him. Samuel had assigned specific servants to his care and a twenty-four-hour guard posted at his door. He was, after all, their enemy.

Even though some rationing had begun to take place at this point in the war, the cooks made meals stretch without anyone noticing a lack. Flavorful shepherd's pie helped to stretch the meat with it mixed into the plentiful mashed potatoes. Cornbread and corn muffins were an easy substitute to their dwindling whole wheat flour supply. Homemade jams, jellies, honey, and plenty of canned garden vegetables still lined their pantry. Chicken and rice soups, beef broth, and dried pea soups were a creative way to extend their hearty feasts. Their smokehouse still had a good supply of hanging smoked hams and bacon. Fortunately, the Stuarts ate dessert only on occasion, so the rationed sugar lasted a long time. Everyone on the estate ate heartily since he or she was mostly self-sufficient and didn't depend on very many food shipments.

Samuel smiled at Sarah as he took his last bite of shepherd's pie and excused himself from the table. To her consternation, she felt herself blush, but she smiled back.

Later in the evening, Sarah's curiosity about the soldier's condition clouded her better judgment. She reasoned within herself that she wasn't a member of the family, only a guest; therefore, Samuel's command about not conversing with the colonel, she thought, didn't directly apply to her.

She crept to the sickroom door and rapped lightly. The posted guard didn't question her as she nodded at him with authority. Hearing no reply from her knock, she slowly creaked the door open and entered. She found the colonel lying in bed on his side with his back toward her. Silently approaching the bed, she held the candle up higher to cast more light on him.

Suddenly, he turned over and asked, "Who are you?"

Sarah took a step backward when he turned so abruptly. She quickly lowered her candle and said, "I'm Sarah Gordon. I'm the one who found you this morning. Please forgive me for disturbing you, but I am wondering how you are feeling. I assisted with your surgery."

He replied, "I thank you for finding me, miss, and for helping to repair my leg. I am in pain, but it is bearable."

"What is your name?"

"I am Colonel Joseph Scott Jenkins."

"Jenkins? I had a friend named Jenkins where I used to live. Her name was Lexi Jenkins, and she died a few months ago. Where are you from, Colonel Jenkins?"

"Philadelphia, Pennsylvania."

Sarah sucked in her breath and felt a bolt of shock run through her. She put her free hand to her mouth, then said in a whisper, "That's where Lexi and I lived!"

The colonel looked perplexed and said, "You are from Philadelphia? How did you come to be part of this Southern manor, Miss Gordon?"

"Well, it is a long story, really, and I don't want to tire you, Colonel Jenkins. However, I would appreciate it if you'd tell me something. Are you married, and do you have any children?"

A bit surprised by her personal, direct questions, he answered, "Why, yes, I am married to a fine lady, and we have one daughter and another child on the way. I thought I'd never see them again, but now I have hope."

"Colonel, what are the names of your wife and child?" Sarah held her breath while she waited for his answer.

"My wife's name is Rachel, and our daughter's name is Mary Beth. We are hoping for a son this time. We will name him after my father, Jeremiah James Jenkins."

Overwhelmed by this revelation, Sarah had to sit down and did so immediately in a straight-backed chair near the bed. Lexi and Sarah had been most interested in their family genealogy and had spent several years researching their ancestors. Now here before her in flesh and blood was Lexi's great-great-great-grandfather.

Sarah recovered a bit and said with new interest, "My, my, my, the Lord does work in mysterious ways, doesn't He?"

"I never had much time for such thoughts myself, Miss Gordon. I don't consider God at all. My mother died when I was a lad. No God who was the loving type my mother told me about would have taken a mother away from her needy six-year-old son." He spoke in a monotone, evidence of his broken heart.

"Oh, Colonel Jenkins, I am so sorry to hear you talk like that. God is loving and merciful. He has a special plan for all of our lives. God didn't promise that bad things won't happen to us in this life, but He does promise that He will never leave us or forsake us. Why, just look at how God has taken care of you—sending you here to be cared for and returned safely to your family instead of dying in the woods alone from your wound. Do you think for one minute that it was chance that brought you wandering so far to this particular destination?"

With bitterness of spirit, he replied, "Save your breath, young lady. I have no use for this kind of talk." He then turned his back on her.

Sarah felt disturbed and excused herself, then slipped out of the room. Preoccupied and thinking of their conversation as she walked down the corridor, she unexpectedly collided with Samuel Stuart as he was leaving his study. Wax spilled over the edge of the candle holder, and a large splatter of it burned her hand as it clung to her skin. "Oh!" she cried out in pain, completely surprised to run into the object of her secret affections.

Samuel steadied her and sincerely apologized for their collision. He noticed the melted wax on Sarah's hand and quickly took the candle and led her into his study. After removing the wax with haste, he applied a wet cloth from his washstand to her burned skin. She sat during his ministrations and expressed her thanks.

"Miss Gordon, I do hope you are feeling a bit of relief now. Hot wax can produce a nasty burn if not attended to directly."

Her heart fluttered wildly at his touch. Trying to control her voice, she answered, "Yes, sir, I am feeling the pain ease a bit already. Thank you. You are most kind."

"You are easy to be kind to, Miss Gordon," he replied, locking eyes with her for a seemingly endless moment.

Sarah couldn't breathe or think. She felt lost in his striking green eyes. In that brief moment, both of them acknowledged their attraction to one another. Sarah felt her cheeks burn more than the actual burn on her hand.

Sitting in the matching chair opposite Sarah's, Samuel asked her whether she had been on her way to retire for the night but took a wrong corridor.

The enchantment of the last few minutes seemed broken when she admitted to what she had done. "Well, not exactly. You see, I have just come from a visit with Mr. Jenkins. I found out the most exciting news.

He is my friend, Lexi's, grandfather, three times removed if my memory serves me correctly. I am so thrilled to meet him."

The atmosphere in the study turned intensely uncomfortable. Samuel pointedly inquired, "Who is Mr. Jenkins?"

Uh-oh! I'm in for it now. He isn't accustomed to his orders being disobeyed.

"Oh … well … uh … you see," Sarah stumbled, "he is the injured colonel … but don't get angry with me, please. I know at dinnertime you forbade the family to converse with him, but after all, I'm not family, so … technically, your command didn't apply to me, right?" she asked feebly, knowing in her heart the answer.

Samuel stared at her with his right eyebrow raised and finally said, "That is very good, Miss Gordon. Perhaps you missed your calling, and you should now be studying the finer points of law and how to evade the truth by employing far-reaching technicalities."

Sarah, now flaming red with embarrassment, hoped the orange glow of the candlelight hid that awful fact. She dabbed intently at her burn, hoping to distract Samuel's penetrating gaze—to no avail.

Finally, she said, "I apologize, sir. I should not have ignored your command to the family. There. I said it." With a huff, she continued, "But you must understand my curiosity. After all, I am the one who found the man, and look how it has all turned out." She went on brightly, "Now I know he is my friend, Lexi's, grandfather. There must be an answer here. Maybe I can prevent Lexi's death somehow."

Then Sarah told Samuel the entire story of Lexi's horrible death. He agreed that perhaps she could indeed do something to help her friend, and he promised to ponder the situation as well.

He then slowly escorted her to the bedroom she shared with Rebecca. He held her elbow firmly and gently the entire way. Sarah wished his touch would never end.

At the bedroom door, she looked up and stared deeply into his green eyes. Sarah felt a longing begin. *Does he feel it too?*

He smiled and said tenderly, "Good night, Miss Gordon." They shared one last captivating moment before he bowed and turned away.

She curtsied and then went slowly into her room, careful not to disturb a sleeping Rebecca. She paused behind the closed door and listened as Samuel's footsteps faded into the distance. Sarah spent the remainder of the night dreaming the dreams of a young woman in love.

Chapter 14

"A carving on Stone Mountain! Of course!" General Stuart stood abruptly from the wicker chair on the front porch. He raked his hands through his thick, salt-and-pepper hair and said triumphantly, "Miss Gordon, we are going to carve a message to your family on Stone Mountain, directly next to the pirates' carving. They will see it when they go there to picnic."

Sarah broke into a Christmas morning gleam, jumped up from her chair, clapped her hands, and exclaimed, "Oh, General Stuart! Thank you! Yes! Yes! That is a perfect idea." She began pacing in her excitement. "A message carved into Stone Mountain would certainly withstand the ravages of time." She abruptly turned to face him with suddenly a deer-in-the-headlights expression on her lovely face. "Do you think my family will still go there for a picnic? But I was there for the picnic. How can it work? Maybe they'd miss it." Sarah went from elation to worry in one second flat and plopped down unceremoniously in the vacant wicker porch chair.

"My tenacious sister, Rebecca, assures me that our God, who created the universe and all things in it, can certainly work out any logistics, and that would include getting your message to your brother and family. Please write out your message, Miss Gordon, and I shall implement it immediately. We shall leave the rest to God. Agreed?" He took Sarah's warm hand into the two of his with gentleness, strength, and comfort; and he smiled his marvelous, winning smile.

Sarah felt his exhilarating closeness and was cheered and hopeful. She also realized she was increasingly attracted to this charming man. She knew intuitively that all would be well. She said quietly, while looking at him in admiration, "You are remarkable that you remembered the details about my family picnic when I described to you my last day in the future."

Samuel Stuart smiled lovingly down into the pretty face he had come to cherish and said quietly, "You would be further surprised at what else I remember about you and of how often I think of you, my dear." As he raised her scented, gloved hand to his lips, he bowed gallantly. Their magnetism deepened as their eyes searched each other for confirmation of their growing attraction.

A week later, Sarah awakened with an unexpected but understandable deep longing for her brother and family. She could scarcely stand the weight of it in her heart. At breakfast, she was uplifted a bit when General Stuart asked her permission to escort her to an undesignated destination. She was intrigued and agreed without hesitation. They hadn't seen each other for several days, and she looked forward to a bit of time with him.

Sarah smiled widely with realization as the couple approached the path of the Stone Mountain hiking trail. "You've done it, haven't you?" she asked with expectation in her voice.

His only answer was a sly smile and a raised eyebrow as he took her elbow and gloved hand, and assisted her up the trail. Sarah was dressed in the fashionable lavender of the day. Her dainty slippers were hardly appropriate for the hike. However, with General Stuart's attentive assistance, they climbed easily.

The one thing that looked much the same in the future as it did now was Stone Mountain itself. The carvings of Davis, Lee, and Jackson were obviously missing from the north face of the mountain. Sarah knew they wouldn't be a finished work of sculpture until 1970, even though the project would begin about 1923. There were no painted yellow lines to indicate the pathway like there were in the future and no handrails, but the path was obvious. As her anticipation grew with each step, Sarah didn't even acknowledge the sweltering heat, humidity, or irritating insects.

"Well, here we are." He let go of her hand and forearm and allowed her to walk forward toward the indicated spot. He removed his crisp linen handkerchief from his inside jacket pocket to blot the perspiration from his forehead and face.

Sarah sucked in her breath with an audible gasp, and her eyes widened in amazement. There, next to the pirate's carving, was her message to her brother and family. "Oh, Samuel! I pictured the carving exactly this way." She stooped down, removed her right glove, and lovingly traced each letter of the new carving. She read the message aloud.

> Colin, Tess, and kids, God sent me to 1863 on a mission.
> I am well. I love and miss you all! Prayers, Friskie Sarah.

Tears fell uninhibited from her eyes as she whispered a prayer of thanksgiving to God.

Sarah hadn't realized that she had called General Stuart by his Christian name, but he noticed it. He was most pleased to discover that she thought of him in this intimate manner. She looked up at him and said, "Thank you," then covered her face and broke into choked sobs.

Quickly, Samuel was on his knee beside her and took her lovingly into his arms to comfort her. He held her close until she cried out her loneliness and grief for her family. Finally, reaching into his back pocket, Samuel brought forth a clean handkerchief and offered it to her. He seemed to have an endless supply.

With a deep breath and an attempt at self-control, Sarah wiped her eyes, blew her nose as delicately as she could, and sat directly on the carving. She willed her family to feel her presence on the engraving in 2018. After some moments, in a voice much higher than usual, Sarah asked, "Do you think they saw my message?"

"Miss Gordon, I do not doubt that they did see your message and, furthermore, had a full understanding of its content. Obeying God is not always easy, and your course has been particularly challenging. The Bible tells us He will reward those who are faithful and obedient. You, Miss Sarah Gordon, are that!"

He waited while Sarah blew her nose again. A flock of birds in a V formation flew above them. He continued, "I feel certain that your family found your message very quickly after your disappearance, and although they miss you, as you do them, they are content in knowing that you are well and about God's work."

He spoke with such confidence that Sarah's doubt evaporated with his certainty, and God gave her complete peace in her heart. They lingered a while until Sarah felt ready to go. She talked about her family and described each one to Samuel. She shared some happy memories, and Samuel listened attentively. Sarah felt valued and respected. Now comforted, she was ready to go to her new home.

Sarah felt resolve replace her grief. Whatever God had planned for her, she was most willing to accept. Would this handsome, intelligent man be part of her future? As they descended the mountain, Sarah was acutely aware of everything about "her General Samuel Stuart," as she thought of him. Sarah astonished herself with the realization that she had already claimed him in her heart.

Is he thinking of me in the same way?

Before she knew it, she said, "You know, my family would love you." Then she blushed at her blunt statement. It seemed most premature in this society, and she hoped Samuel didn't think her too forward.

He looked surprised but said tenderly, "I would be honored to meet them and get to know them. Perhaps God has that planned in our future somehow."

Sarah smiled.

He is thinking about our future. Oh, thank You, Jesus!

Chapter 15

2018

Colin, Tess, Shelby, Ann, and toddling Scottie walked toward the restrooms behind the carriage guesthouse, just over from the stables at the Antebellum Plantation.

"Mommy, me first!" rushed Ann as she dashed inside the single potty and closed the door.

Shelby stated, "I can't wait, Mom." He walked quickly over the soft grass toward the thick woods bordering the property, then disappeared. He was no stranger to using nature for his immediate need.

Sarah said, "You all rest here for a bit. I want to look around the grounds a little bit." She walked off by herself, her ankle-length dress still looking fresh and lovely. She was careful to hold up the skirts so they wouldn't drag on the ground and get dirty.

Tess replied, "Okay, Sarah." Tess rubbed her index finger inside the front top of the toddler's disposable diaper, "I wish there was a place to change Scottie. He's soaked through."

Colin pointed across the lawn toward the kitchen outbuilding. "How about that bench over there, Tess?"

"Okay. Will you please wait here for the kids while I go change Scottie?"

"Of course, my dear." They exchanged a knowing look. Tess was overly cautious in public, determined never to have any of her family on the missing person's list. She never let them out of her sight unless she knew Colin was watching.

Walking across the lawn, Tess felt a strange sensation that caused her to shiver, even in the oppressive heat. She frowned and thought of that saying that someone had walked over her grave … or something like that.

After finally changing her active son, Tess stayed on the bench and nursed him. Being a modest person, she tastefully always used a cotton receiving blanket to cover her skin. She reflected on how many people thought she was strange for still nursing her child when he was two years old. Tess was a firm believer in letting each child wean himself or herself when ready. She'd studied up on how important it was to complete the first sucking stage of life. At this point, Scottie nursed only when he was tired ... mostly at nap time and bedtime. He was on his way to weaning himself, for sure. Tess always had to pray for people when they asked her, "Are you still nursing?" as if it was a horrible thing. Many women had her same philosophy of letting their children wean themselves. At any rate, it was her conviction, and she lived by it.

It was late afternoon and especially lovely with so few people touring the plantation. The intense heat of the day would soon be waning a bit, Tess mused. When it got close to those sweet times of the early evening, the trees took on a particular cast, as if expecting the sunset to clothe them in evening attire. Twilight was her favorite time, but she was often too busy with the children to enjoy it. She enjoyed special moments like this and relished them.

Shelby and Ann started to play tag in the expanse of the freshly mowed grass. There was nothing like the smell of newly cut grass.

Once the rest of her family had reassembled, Tess wondered why Sarah hadn't appeared. She asked Colin, "What do you think is keeping Sarah so long?"

Colin shrugged. "You know Sarah, the history buff. She's probably inspecting something that caught her attention."

With slight irritation in her voice, she said, "Well, I wish she would hurry up. The kids are hot, tired, and beginning to get grumpy." She turned her attention to the children. "Shelby! Stop pushing Ann like that!" Tess looked pointedly at her husband. "We need to get back to the camper."

Colin thought but didn't say, *Someone else is getting grumpy too.* He said, "You stay here with the kids, and I'll go find Sarah."

A few minutes later, Colin returned alone. "I didn't see her anywhere. She must have already gone to the van. Let's go."

Tess felt further annoyed at Sarah for doing such a thing without letting them know. She gathered the diaper bag, blanket, and camera.

They all headed back to the van. Colin carried Scottie on his shoulders, and the family enjoyed his little squeals of delight.

When they got to the van, Sarah was nowhere in sight. Feeling somewhat alarmed, Tess explained, "Colin, this is weird. Sarah would never give us cause for concern, and surely she would have told us if she were going scouting around. We'll wait here while you go back to find her." Trying to lighten her encroaching fear, she said in a forced, cheerful voice, "Thank goodness we parked under this wonderful old shade tree."

The late afternoon sun was still bright and hot in the parking lot, though. Tess went about keeping the children occupied with singing and games while Colin went back to inspect the plantation grounds and locate his sister.

The children were busy playing a game of "I spy" when a half hour later, Tess saw Colin returning. He wasn't alone. Next to him walked an official Stone Mountain Park guard. The pit of Tess's stomach turned to stone, and she felt the blood drain from her face as she watched the men approach. In a defeated voice, Colin said to her, "We couldn't find her, Tess. This guard has sent out an alert throughout the park. Let's get the children back to the camper; then I'll go back out and look for Sarah." His face now held the same expression of his wife's grave concern.

Restrained only by the presence of her children, Tess was barely able to control her panic. She loved Sarah so dearly. She nodded in agreement, not able to speak. For once, the children quickly entered the van and hooked up their seat belts without objections, while Colin fastened Scottie into his car seat. Tess was grateful for the children's cooperation because she couldn't have spoken a word at that moment without crying. Her fear was as real and oppressive as the heat and humidity.

Colin got into the van, started it up, and turned the air-conditioner to the high setting. He directed the front dash vents toward Tess, as was his habit. The refreshing cold air brought some relief. He looked at his wife and said, "I know what you're thinking, but I wouldn't worry. Somehow, Sarah probably missed us and got a ride back to the camper. You just wait and see." He patted her shaking hand to comfort her.

Changed Purpose

She didn't believe him and said quietly, "She would never do that." They both knew it to be true, and they drove back to the RV in silence, praying in their hearts more fervently than they had ever done so before.

Colin parked and rushed to unlock the RV. He called out loudly inside, "Sarah?" No one answered.

As Tess got Scottie out of the car seat, Ann asked her mother, "Where's Aunt Sarah?"

Having cooled off in the air-conditioning and being strengthened by her prayers, Tess was more in control of her emotions. Brushing her daughter's silky bangs out of her eyes, she said, "We missed our meeting place with Aunt Sarah. Daddy is going back to get her while you help me get dinner ready, okay, darling?"

Dear Lord, please let Sarah be safe. Please help Colin to find her right away.

Chapter 16

Colin was already out the door and back in the van. It was difficult for him to drive within the speed limit, but he did. He hadn't wanted to alarm his wife, but he was quite concerned now. Sarah was a responsible person and would have never willingly caused her family a moment's worry about her whereabouts. He retraced all their excursion spots, except he didn't walk up the Stone Mountain hiking trail again. Colin checked with the park officials. They were still looking for Sarah but had yet to see any trace of her.

He returned to the RV alone, feeling distressed. The children were just finishing eating their supper. Colin noticed that Tess hadn't eaten a bite. Worry was written all over her lovely face. All the family members were now profoundly concerned and couldn't imagine what had happened to Sarah.

Ann suddenly changed the atmosphere by saying brightly, "Daddy, I think Aunt Sarah is playing a trick on us. Since the only place you didn't look for her is the hike up the Stone Mountain trail where we had our lunch picnic, I'll bet that is where she is right now, waiting for us to find her. She loves to play hide-and-seek with us."

Shelby interjected enthusiastically, "Yes! At the pirate's carving. She's at the pirate's carving, I'm sure of it. Remember how cool she thought it was?"

Having their silent doubts but wanting their hopes to be true, they all agreed it was a possibility. Then, joining hands, they had a family prayer to ask God to protect and take care of Aunt Sarah, wherever she was. They also asked God to help them find her before nightfall.

They all rushed out to the van, buckled up, and drove to the entrance of the Stone Mountain trail. Filled with hope, they walked quickly to their picnic spot. It was about one-third of the way up Stone Mountain. Shelby and Ann hurried up ahead, calling, "Aunt Sarah! Aunt Sarah!" When their parents and Scottie arrived, not far behind, they found their eldest children standing as still as the Civil War statues. They had stopped dead in their tracks and pointed, dumbfounded.

Shelby said, "Mama, Daddy, look! There, next to the pirate's carving!"

Colin watched the color drain from his wife's face. Tess looked at the ground, where her children were pointing, fully expecting to find Sarah collapsed, injured, if not murdered.

Colin said in consternation, "Sarah is not there. What are you pointing at, Shelby?"

Everyone gathered around. Sarah's message to them, which General Stuart had prepared over a hundred years earlier, was discovered.

They all just stared at it in silence and blinked in disbelief. Confused, Shelby asked, "Dad, what does this mean?"

"I am not sure, Son," Colin replied. He kept staring at the carving, trying to make sense of it.

Tess finally whispered, "But that wasn't there when we had our picnic here earlier today."

Slowly, realization of what had happened came to Colin, even though it made no logical sense. Colin took his wife's hand in his, kissed it, and said gently, "No. It wasn't here earlier today. Sarah was with us today during the picnic, but now she's in 1863!"

Shelby said, still pointing, "I don't understand."

Now with confidence, Colin replied, "Neither do I, Son, but God understands. He has a mission for Aunt Sarah, and somehow He made her travel back in time to fulfill her purpose."

"Cool beans! I wish I could go too. That would be so cool!" cried Ann.

Tess said with great feeling, "Oh, no, you don't, young lady! You are staying right here with me. What do you think I'd do without you?" She hugged her precious daughter close to her and cried tears of relief. They now knew where Sarah was, and God was protecting her and using her for His purposes. It was a different kind of mission trip to be sure but one they knew Sarah was well qualified to perform. Tess lovingly ran her index finger across the carving, as if caressing Sarah's cheek, and read it aloud.

Colin, Tess, and kids, God sent me to 1863 on a mission.
I am well. I love and miss you all! Prayers, Friskie Sarah.

Colin took a picture of it with his cell phone.

Feeling the incredulous shock of the miracle they now understood, they slowly headed back to the van. Colin speculated on what God could be using Sarah for back in 1863. In one way, it was strange how they all so readily accepted her destiny. But in another way, it wasn't a bit surprising, for they had an inner assurance that Sarah was where she belonged.

Approaching the parking lot, Colin frowned and said, "Tess, did you buy a Confederate license plate at the gift shop today and put it on the van?"

"No, darling, I didn't. Why do you ask?" Tess had calmed down significantly now that she knew no harm had come to Sarah.

"Well, look at the van," Colin replied as he pointed at the back of it.

They all surrounded the rear of their vehicle and studied the Confederate license plate that had replaced their Georgia one.

"I didn't notice it earlier," he said. "It must be a prank. I'll have to report this to the guard. This license plate isn't a legal plate, and we need ours back that matches our registration. I also need to let the guard know we found Sarah ... sort of." He smiled and squeezed Tess's hand.

Tess nodded in agreement, then said wryly, "Leave it to Sarah to make such a grand exit. I wonder if we'll see her when she completes her mission."

Colin said, "Only God knows that, my dear. We'll trust Him to do what's best. Of course, we'll spend all eternity with Sarah in heaven, so the answer to your question is definitely yes. We will see our Sarah again." Colin smiled his most loving smile.

As the family loaded up in the van, Shelby expressed all their feelings entirely by saying, "Wow! Time travel! Cool beans!"

As Colin buckled an unusually cooperative Scottie into his car seat, Tess said, "I feel so much better now that we know where Sarah is, but it's going to be very difficult to live without her near." Colin saw her blink back tears.

"Daddy, how did Aunt Sarah go back in time?"

"Well, precious, I don't know the answer to that question."

"It is a wonder, though, isn't it?" Tess asked.

Colin replied to his wife as he got into the driver's seat. "It is a mystery for sure. Perhaps God will send her back to us when she has completed her mission in 1863. You know," he went on thoughtfully, "it is so interesting how God prepared Sarah for this trip. She has been absorbed in history and especially so in the Civil War era since she was a young teen. She always dreamed of wearing clothes of that period and romanticized the qualities of honor and noble character. She thought everyone back then daily dressed as if they were going to church … and perhaps they did."

"Well, she's finding out now. That outfit she wore today surely was just right, wasn't it?" Ann remarked.

"The Lord works in mysterious ways," commented Tess, using their family's favorite saying.

Driving by the playground area, Colin saw the guard in the parking lot, the man he had talked to earlier about Sarah's disappearance. He turned in, parked in the shade, and left the air-conditioning running for the family. As he approached the security guard, he noticed the man wore a different uniform, but he was the same man. The guard had been wearing a khaki-colored uniform, but now it was light gray. Colin glanced at the patch on the guard's left shirt pocket and wondered what CSA meant, but he didn't ask him about it. Colin explained to him that the family had located their lost sister.

The guard replied politely, "Sir, I am sorry, but I have no idea what you mean. When and where did you report your sister lost, sir?" He flipped open his notepad and manned his pen, waiting to write down Colin's reply. He reminded Colin of an anxious reporter on the trail of an exclusive.

Colin frowned. "I made my report to you personally at the Antebellum Plantation at about five o'clock this afternoon."

Now the guard frowned, lifted his eyebrows suspiciously, and scratched furiously on his notepad. "This is quite interesting, sir, as I have never seen you before this moment. Would you care to elaborate on our supposed meeting?" The guard's radio hanging on his belt interrupted their conversation, demanding him to answer the call. Colin listened carefully and was astonished at what he heard.

"Confederate Guard Lowe here." answered the guard into the radio.

He had to respond quickly to the call to another park location. Clipping the radio back onto his belt again, he looked at Colin and said, "Sir, I don't understand your implication that we have met earlier this day at a nonexistent plantation here on the grounds. However, since your problem no longer exists, I won't investigate. I would appreciate, however, if you would show your driver's license to me if you don't mind, sir."

Colin pulled out his wallet, removed his license, and gave it to him.. The guard commented that it looked in order, handed it back, and left for his next destination. However, Colin didn't move. He stood there so long that Tess finally called out to him. When he didn't respond, she turned the van off. Colin heard Tess warn the children to sit still, then get out of the van. He heard her footsteps approaching, but he couldn't take his eyes off his driver's license.

Curious, she put her hand on his shoulder and asked, "What is it, Colin?"

"Tess, something strange is going on here. That guard didn't remember me at all, and he called himself the "Confederate Guard." He said the Antebellum Plantation doesn't exist and that my driver's license is in order. But look at it!" He passed it to his wife.

"Confederate States of America?" Tess incredulously read aloud. "And there's no picture of you on it. How can he say this is a valid license? Honey, this is weird!"

A thought struck him. "Honey, I have a strange feeling, and it may explain why Sarah is gone. Let's get back to the camper and discuss this."

But they didn't make it back to the camper immediately. Instead, they drove around the entire Stone Mountain Resort grounds until dark descended, amazed by the changes. So many things were different. The guard had been right. There was no public tour for the Antebellum Plantation because there was no such tourist attraction. The estate was still there, but it was apparently privately owned. Stone Mountain Park's lawns looked precisely mowed and edged daily. The shrubs were all trimmed and shaped and decoratively pruned, and the houses and buildings looked freshly painted. The Confederate flag flew everywhere. Not one bit of litter could be seen anywhere, and the edged grass of the sidewalks was immaculate. It looked like the town in the movie *Stepford*, where everything looked so perfect.

Shelby observed, "How can everything look like this so fast?"

Ann whined, "I'm tired. May we go home now?"

Scottie was already asleep in his car seat.

Tess said again, "This is weird." She always lost the command of her advanced vocabulary when she was under stress or in shock. "Weird" became her only available descriptive word. "I feel like I'm in the twilight zone. This is weird, but you must admit it is very nice."

After a few minutes of looking at all the changes as they slowly drove to their RV, Tess took her wallet out of her purse and pulled out her driver's license. It was identical to Colin's. No personal information was listed; there was just the plain card stating the Confederate States of America Driver's license with her name on it and the fee of five dollars. That was all. No picture, no address, no number, no fingerprints—no height, weight, or date of birth.

"I am stunned!" she said.

When Colin pulled up to their RV, Tess was afraid to look at it, and she covered her face. Colin saw her look through her splayed fingers, though. "I am so relieved, Colin. Our RV looks the same." She breathed another sigh of relief. All would be well.

"I am going to have a talk with God about my fears because I know God doesn't give believers a spirit of fear. I want to be free of all my worries and trust God in all things. It would take time and effort to focus on God's promises, but I'm determined to get rid of all my fears as soon as possible."

Colin kissed her hand and said, "I love your determination, sweetheart."

They all went inside their RV and rushed the tired children through a quick snack and into bed.

Colin and Tess sat across from each other at the kitchen table, holding hands. "What do you think this all means?" asked Tess in all sincerity.

"Honey, the only explanation I can see is that Sarah's mission trip included a much broader scope than we could have ever imagined. Tess, I believe God used Sarah to change the outcome of the Civil War. I believe the South won the war."

Staring at her husband, repeatedly blinking as this assumption sunk in, Tess finally replied, "The South won the war? How could our Sarah do that?"

Colin smiled. "Sarah didn't do that. God did. He just used Sarah as His instrument to make it all happen. Don't ask me why or how. I just know it is so."

Thinking for a bit in silence, Tess said excitedly, "Oh, Colin! We must go to the Confederate Museum tomorrow. First thing." And they did.

The entirely different history tour and the altered program they witnessed that morning amazed the whole family. There was no mention of General Sherman's march through Georgia. Georgia hadn't been destroyed or burned.

Shelby commented, "Aunt Sarah would love this. She'd be so happy to know the South won."

Colin replied, "I am confident that she is happy, Son. She knows all about it; you can be sure."

Ann wandered around the corner of a glass display, only steps in front of her family. She cried out with an anguished sound, and her parents and brother were at her side within seconds. She pointed at the glass display area. All eyes turned and beheld a mannequin dressed in Sarah's peach-and-cream lace outfit. Was it only the day before that they saw it on her? It seemed like weeks had passed. Next to it was a man's Confederate general's uniform. The identification card in front of these articles of clothing merely stated the year 1863. The family instinctively held each other's hands, including little Scottie's from his stroller, and they whispered a prayer of thanks to God for this further confirmation about Sarah.

Ann began to cry, with silent tears pouring over her cheeks. "Aunt Sarah looked so beautiful in that dress. I want her!" And she clutched her mother's skirts and hid her face.

In hushed tones, Tess comforted her grieving daughter. The family slowly moved away from the clothing display and shared mixed emotions. It was difficult to think of Sarah living so long ago and that she would now be dead, but how could she be? She had left just yesterday. It was all too taxing emotionally.

Colin noticed another glass case display. "Tess, look at this!" he said urgently.

They crowded around the glass countertop and stared down at some old papers. One document was the Declaration of Independence of the Confederate States of America. President Jefferson Davis had written another missive, which lay next to it. Colin read it aloud to the family.

> To the future generations of the Confederate States of America: it is my privilege and responsibility to inform you of one woman's great effort and sacrifice in aiding our nation in winning the War of Northern Aggression. This young woman wishes to remain nameless but allows me to record her initials: S. L. G. I can tell you that she sacrificed her entire family and left her home and all familiar surroundings to do the will of God. She assisted the Confederacy at a crucial point during the war. Without this young woman's purposeful dedication in obedience to God, I can assure you the Confederacy would have lost many more lives, which could have ultimately resulted in the South losing the war. Although unknown to you, God knows exactly to whom I refer, and I charge you now to take a private moment and thank our heavenly Father for this courageous young woman and her family in all future generations. Pray for them to have God's peace, which passes all understanding. Pray for abundant blessings

for them all. With heartfelt gratitude and thanks, I leave this tribute to this brave young woman.

Faithfully yours,
President Jefferson Davis,
Confederate States of America

The date was faded, but May 26, 1863, was still legible.

Stunned, the family looked at one another and instantly felt the peace the honorable President Davis had requested for them. It was nothing short of another miracle, and they all knew it.

The children were hungry, so the family departed and went to the Stone Mountain Grill for lunch. It was a fast-order cafeteria-style restaurant with large windows all around. The nearby Skyride attraction to the top of Stone Mountain was visible, and so was the historic carving of Davis, Lee, and Jackson.

Colin said, "Well, the sculptured carvings are still there, but it makes sense that they would be." Everyone looked and nodded in agreement.

Tess felt overjoyed as they sat to eat their lunches. "You know, Sarah would be so pleased to know that she not only helped the Confederates to win the war but also changed fashion for all time. Look at all of these people in here. They all look like they are going to church."

The family noticed how well dressed and mannerly everyone was, and they thoroughly enjoyed the effect. Everyone looked like he or she cared about his or her presentation. The women dressed in skirts, dresses, or dress pants, and the men wore ties or casual collared shirts tucked in. The children also looked comfortable in their dressy-casual finery. Southern gentility was the norm, and average people obviously had high standards for their appearance.

Tess said, "It is a good thing that we all like our classic style of dress, isn't it? We fit in just fine with everyone, don't we, even though we are just a little more on the casual side?" Everyone agreed as Shelby tucked his shirt in a little tighter. Colin bent over to quickly wipe dust off his penny loafers with his napkin. Tess continued, "Now you can see why I don't allow you to go to events in your playclothes, children."

On the way back to the van, Colin stopped at the sidewalk vending machine and purchased the *Confederate Daily Newspaper*. Throughout the paper were beautiful color pictures.

After reading the entire paper in silence in his comfortable camper living room recliner, Colin crumpled the paper into his lap as his arms relaxed. He announced, "I feel like I have just read one of the greatest happiest-ever-after stories imaginable."

Tess asked, "How do you mean, sweetheart?" She was busy in the kitchen, preparing her homemade buttermilk biscuits for the family.

"Well, the last paper I read a few days ago was full of reports of death, violence, drugs, political struggles, immorality, and financial burdens. This paper is unbelievable. There were only two reports of minor violence and crime. The entire rest of the paper was about how the Confederate States of America is flourishing by the grace of God. Incredibly, people help each other in all aspects of life now. I read about the laws of the land, and they have direct quotes from the Holy Bible. Can you imagine? The Confederate States of America obey and serve God Almighty openly and thoroughly."

Tess placed her tray of biscuits into the oven. "Wonderful! Praise God! Do you think the United States of America has also improved?"

"Oh, yes, I'm sure it has improved and benefitted. There are some articles in here about investment opportunities in the USA and trade deals. What wonderful liberty and blessings we enjoy by being submissive to God! Think of the grace He has given to us right now by allowing us to know of these changes. I suspect we're the only living creatures on earth who know about Sarah's time travel and what things were like before she left."

"Dad," Shelby began, "do you think people won't be as sick as they were before this happened? What about your practice? What if no one needs a doctor anymore? What will you do?"

Colin smiled and answered, "Son, if no one is sick, God will direct me to another line of work. Don't worry a bit. However, I suspect that even though things have improved greatly in our new nation, people will still be subject to illness and injury at times."

"Won't it be great if your schedule is less hectic, Colin? We would be thrilled to have you around more," stated his loving wife.

He smiled thoughtfully. "We'll see, we'll see."

Chapter 17

1863

Colonel Joseph Scott Jenkins stood silently at the entrance to Samuel's private study. The morning sun streamed through the windows and revealed his commanding stature. He was a striking man, tall and muscular, standing there in the new clothes the Stuarts had provided for him. The Stuarts had supplied everything for him over the weeks of his convalescence. He was now fully recovered from his injuries, and he felt burdened with the debt he owed them.

He cleared his throat, and Samuel looked up from his writing. He invited the colonel into his study and offered the chair in front of his desk.

Colonel Jenkins sat down and began earnestly, "Sir, I owe my life to you. I will spend the rest of it repaying you."

"Colonel Jenkins, you owe nothing to me. It is God to whom you owe your debt. Because of His will and direction, you have been in our care."

Nervously clearing his throat again, Colonel Jenkins said, "Yes, so you have told me ... but how do you know?"

With conviction, Samuel said, "I know because of this book right here." He held up his worn King James Bible. "I read God's Word daily, study to know His will, and purpose to obey Him."

"All God's done for me is take my mother when I was six years old," Colonel Jenkins retorted.

"Sir, bad things happen in this world because of evilness. Adam and Eve disobeyed God first, in the Garden of Eden, and there has not been a perfect person or perfect life ever since ... except for Jesus. Jesus is God's Son and was sent by God to us to save whoever will believe in Him. Jesus taught people God's wisdom, commands, and will, and He healed many people. But they betrayed Him. Jesus foretold all that would happen to Him. Nailed to a cross, He died for us. He sacrificed

His life to pay for our sins, so that we, who believe in Him, are forgiven, and we don't have to pay for our sins. As He said, He came alive again on the third day when God resurrected Him, and He lives."

General Stuart could tell Colonel Jenkins was truly listening and searching, so he continued. "The Bible says anyone who believes in Jesus and asks Him for the forgiveness of their sins, He will come into their lives and hearts as Savior; they will be with Him forever in heaven. The Bible also says that anyone who does not have Jesus as his or her own personal Savior will go to hell. Hell is total separation from God for all eternity. It is all right here in the Bible, Colonel Jenkins." Samuel held his Bible up again to emphasize his point. "All anyone has to do is read this to see the truth for himself." He waited a moment and then continued. "Let me ask you something, Colonel. Did your mother ever talk to you about the Lord Jesus?"

"Yes, sir, she did. She talked about Him a lot and always had me say my prayers at bedtime and mealtime. She told me the streets of heaven are gold and that there are many mansions. She told me Jesus was coming again to the earth one day too. But when she died, my interest and what little faith I had died with her." He paused and shifted in his chair uncomfortably. "I have been thinking about this all of these days of my convalescence, sir. Your servants read the Bible to me and prayed for me. They didn't know I was awake a lot of the time. Sometimes I just listened and didn't make any comment. It brought back much of what my mother told me, and I started to feel more open to God as I heard His word spoken aloud."

Colonel Jenkins coughed, trying to clear a nervous throat. "Thank you for allowing me to write to my wife. I received a response from her, and she said she is praying for me. She said she has been praying for me to find my way back to God. But I have been angry at God for so long that feeling open to Him now feels strange to me."

"Changing, even for the good, is often difficult. We have to be willing to let go of our old ways. Any man is blessed to have a praying wife."

"Oh, yes, sir. She is the best of women. I have respected her religion, but I haven't joined her in it. But she has never failed in inviting me to go to church with her. She has quietly encouraged me, and she has such a sweet spirit. Really, my wife is a lot like my mother," Colonel Jenkins stated as if he just realized that for the first time.

Samuel gave the man a few moments, then said, "It sounds to me like your mother was a Christian, and you can be sure that she is alive in heaven. She has been there since her last breath here on earth. Don't you want to see your mother again, Colonel? You can, you know."

"How do you figure that?" he asked in a strange voice.

"If you pray and ask Jesus to be your Savior, you can have your sins forgiven and be sure that you are going to heaven."

"I have a great many sins to be forgiven, sir. Is there a limit?"

Samuel smiled at the question. "No, Colonel Jenkins. God is not limited in forgiving your sins. He does require that you confess your sins and repent of each one and purpose to follow Him. You will also be required to teach your family and all whom God brings into your path about Him and His ways and to speak the name of Jesus with reverence."

Colonel Jenkins straightened his back as if in full alert. "Well, sir, how do I confess my sins?"

Feeling sure this man had made his eternal decision, General Stuart bowed his head and began a prayer. "I'll pray with you, and you can repeat this prayer after me. Dear heavenly Father, I confess my sins to You now, and I am very sorry for them. Forgive me, please God, for being angry at You all of these years. I believe that Jesus is Your Son. Please send Jesus into my heart to be my Savior. Thank You for His sacrifice for me so that I may come to heaven one day. I'll purpose to read Your Word and obey it and teach others about it from this day forward. Thank You, dear Jehovah God. In Jesus's precious name, I pray, amen."

Colonel Jenkins echoed the prayer, then added, "And if it isn't too much trouble, dear God, please tell my mother that I have prayed this prayer. I know she will be very happy. Thank You."

As the men lifted their bowed heads and opened their eyes, Samuel was astonished to see the change on his face. The broad smile illuminated his face and made him look much younger and healthier.

Colonel Jenkins expelled a deep breath and felt new and clean; his prior burdens instantly lifted from his heart. He stood, offered his hand, and said, "Thank you, General Stuart. I shall never forget you."

Samuel smiled, stood, and shook hands with his new brother in Christ. He said, "May God bless you and yours, Colonel Joseph Scott Jenkins. Please accept this Holy Bible as a gift from me." He handed a new Bible to Colonel Jenkins, who accepted it with joyful thanks.

"As I promised, my men will safely escort you to your choice of destination. Of course, I request that you return them to me unharmed."

He agreed; then as he was leaving the room, Colonel Jenkins turned back to face him for one final look at this kind man. Samuel said, "Joseph, you are now my brother in Christ. I will see you in heaven."

Joseph replied in the familiar in kind, "Samuel, my brother, I shall introduce you to my mother one day." They both smiled. Elated by what had transpired between them, they shared a bond at that moment that indeed went with them throughout eternity.

Colonel Joseph Scott Jenkins exited the office and gently closed the door. He walked down the hallway and out into his new life, his steps lighter than ever before.

Chapter 18

Sarah, Samuel, and Rebecca strolled through the family's lovely ornamental garden. It was beautifully landscaped and so very colorful with all sorts of blooming flowers. The sweet fragrance of her favorite gardenias filled Sarah with joy. She felt she belonged. Amazingly, she was even beginning to adjust slightly to the humidity and heat but only a little. She still longed for air-conditioning.

The trio sat comfortably on the white wrought-iron benches situated in the middle of the aromatic garden. A lively trickling stream flowed nearby, entering into a small pool. Colorful flower petals floated, scattered on the water's surface. The shade from the tall sculpted hedges, combined with the nearness of the water, gave a cooling effect, which Sarah most certainly welcomed.

They were grateful for the day of rest, the Sabbath. Their morning had been spent learning God's wisdom from the local Methodist pastor. As was their custom, the family invited the pastor and his wife to come home with them for Sunday dinner. The buffet-style feast was piled high with cold ham, turkey, and beef slices, rolls, biscuits, apple butter, corn, vegetable relishes, salads, and cheeses. Several pies, cookies, tarts, and pastries with clotted cream were kept cold in their springhouse for a delicious dessert. Mr. and Mrs. Stuart's house rules included preparing the entire Sabbath meals on Saturday. They purposed to obey the commandment of the Lord to remember the Sabbath day and keep it holy. They required no work from their servants on this particular first day of the week. The entire estate worshipped God together in their chapel. Then the family helped themselves to the already-prepared foods, and the servants enjoyed time away from their usual duties.

During the meal, Samuel could tell his father suspected the growing undercurrent of attraction he had with Sarah. Samuel asked to be dismissed from the gentlemen's debate and said that he wanted to escort the ladies to the garden to find some relief from the heat of the day.

Mr. Stuart replied, "Certainly, Samuel. Pastor Ross and I have plenty to talk about on our own." They headed to the library.

Mrs. Stuart said, "Thank you for including me, my son, but I must excuse myself for an afternoon nap." Samuel gratefully thanked her with his smile.

Now, the younger trio escaped all eyes and ears. Samuel and Rebecca were ready for Sarah to tell them details about the future. They settled in the coolest part of the garden.

"How can I begin to describe the United States of America as it was when I left it?" she mused. "It had great privileges and great evils." She went on at length, telling them of the many medicines, childbirth care, surgeries, transportation, shopping malls, electricity, appliances, TV, radios, cell phones, home computers, Internet, and electronics.

Rebecca was most interested in hearing about the central air-conditioning. "Now that I would like immensely. Oh, to be cool at any time I choose with just the push of a button." She imagined this while cooling herself with her lace fan, which matched her beautiful pale-blue gown.

"One other thing you may like equally as well is frozen yogurt!" Sarah went on to explain refrigerators and freezers being standard in each household.

Samuel announced, "Even King Solomon in all of his glory had nothing such as this. I wonder how much of his kingdom he would have given in trade for a refrigerator and a freezer."

"And air-conditioning!" Rebecca added quickly. They all laughed.

Suddenly, Sarah remembered her knapsack. "Wait right here. I have to go get my knapsack." She quickly went to get it from her room. After just a few steps away from the shady garden spot, she felt assaulted with the heat and humidity of the glaring afternoon sun. But she didn't notice it as much as usual because she was so excited to be sharing her items from the future with her new friends. She had kept her prizes tucked away until the proper moment.

Within minutes, Sarah was back, toting her beloved brown leather knapsack. "Here! Look at these things I brought with me from the future." She showed them each one, and they marveled as they touched and examined the objects. Sarah took them out one at a time and passed them around, explaining them all. She had disposable diapers, baby wipes, diaper rash ointment, infants' ibuprofen, and peanut butter crackers. She showed them the boxed apple juice with the little straw kids loved to squeeze and spill out from the microscopic hole in the top. Her kit included oatmeal cookies, small bottles of Coke, lip balm, aspirin, bandages and ointment, acetaminophen, tissues, nose spray, cough medicine, mints, safety pins, a pair of nail clippers, a sewing kit, trail mix, sunglasses, a camera, a wallet, and a cell phone.

She grabbed the cell phone and exclaimed, "The cell phone! Do you think it could work?" Her captive audience stared at her blankly. "I'm going to give it a try." She turned it on, and the screen lit up. Encouraged, she put in her password, swiped the screen to dial, and pressed her speed dial for her brother. She held her breath, amazed that the battery still worked. Nothing happened, of course.

"Oh well, it would have been too good to be true to think I could talk on the cell phone over a hundred years away." She chuckled to herself. "Finally, a good reason not to have clear cell phone reception." She giggled, then explained about cell phones.

"Oh! And just wait." She moved her arms in animation. "The most delicious beverage is on the horizon." She handed two small bottles to them. "It will be called Coca-Cola, and it debuts in Atlanta in the year 1884. I know because I studied up on it. I usually research things that interest me, and this is my favorite drink. We call it 'Coke' for short. Try it!" She showed them how to twist off the plastic top. They hesitated to put the unfamiliar bottle up to their mouths. Sarah demonstrated for them. They copied her then and took a drink. Their eyes widened and revealed their delight.

Rebecca squealed, "Oh! It makes my tongue all fuzzy!"

"That is the carbonation."

Samuel and Rebecca tried their best to take in everything Sarah said, but so much was foreign to their thinking. Grasping an understanding was difficult. However, Samuel said, "Well, I shall make a note to look for an opportunity to invest in the Coca-Cola Company when it becomes available. This is delicious."

Reaching into her knapsack, she saw a wrapped gift. She frowned. *What can this be?* She pulled it out and saw her brother's familiar handwriting on the fancy gift wrap in bold black marker, "To Friskie. Love, Colin." Tears welled up in her eyes and spilled quickly down her cheeks. She lovingly held the present to her heart and whispered, "It's a present from my brother. He must have slipped it into my sack the night before we set off for our last day together."

Wiping the tears off her face with a handkerchief Samuel had offered, she reverently unwrapped the paper to reveal a history book. Sarah leafed through it and saw It was a day-by-day account with pictures of the significant details of the unaltered American Civil War. Sarah closed her eyes for a moment and hugged the book to her heart. She silently thanked God and Colin, then offered this unexpected treasure to General Stuart. "This is for you from my brother and me. It is up to you to change this outcome."

With a raised eyebrow, Samuel accepted the gift and looked through it for a few minutes. He stared at Sarah with gravity on his face. "This will be our future if I don't do something about it immediately?"

Sarah nodded.

He stood up, alert, as if ready for battle. He said earnestly, "I must rush this book to President Davis. Thank you!"

Looking at his sister, Samuel said, "Rebecca, please inform our parents that I have urgent business with President Davis. By the grace of God, this war will soon be over victoriously for the South."

Ever the gentleman, he gallantly took Sarah's hand and bowed over it. Their eyes held briefly but with significance. Then he turned abruptly and was off.

In less than one month, the War between the States was over, on May 26, 1863.

CHAPTER 19

After the meeting with President Davis, General Stuart was dispatched directly to General Lee's camp in Fredericksburg, Virginia. With haste General Stuart rode as he had never ridden before and arrived in record time. They rested during the heat of the day, then traveled at night. His faithful horse lathered in sweat even in the cool of the night. President Davis and General Stuart decided at the meeting that only they and Generals Lee and Jackson would be privy to how God had used Mistress Sarah Louise Gordon as His instrument to travel back in time to assist the Confederate army. President Davis would personally convey these details to Generals Lee and Jackson at a later date.

The history book about the Civil War, which Sarah had given to Samuel, remained with President Davis to study and keep under lock and key. The substance of the book swayed President Davis to believe in Sarah's time travel. He couldn't deny the proof and didn't doubt Miss Gordon's mission.

It was late in the night when General Stuart arrived with the password "Victory," which gained him immediate entrance into General Lee's tent. Lee was reading his Bible by the light of one single candle while he sat on his cot. The glow of it set off the white of his hair and beard in contrast to his gray uniform. General Lee rose quickly and greeted his friend warmly with a firm, receptive handshake and pat on the shoulder, formality dispensed between them. With questions in his eyes and voice, General Lee asked incredulously, "What did President Davis find out that changed our plan of attack in the Wilderness? I was so sure of my strategy."

General Stuart hesitated. "All I am at liberty to divulge at this moment, my friend, is that God has blessed us with certain information that is going to assist us to win this war." He went on with great feeling, "Praise God!" As he removed his leather riding gloves and slapped them against his thigh, he assured his friend, "President Davis said that he wants to inform you directly of the detailed facts at a later date."

General Lee stared at his long-time friend. Samuel could tell from the look on his face that he was disappointed. However, Lee's respect for President Davis and his years of professional training prevailed. He said, "I thank the Lord Jehovah God for His mercy to our cause of states' rights."

General Lee called for some refreshments for them. The generals talked well into the night about strategies planned to implement immediately and in the near future. General Stuart had with him an outlined plan for all the Confederate states forces to meet in Fort Victory, Virginia, and to win the war with one final battle. This plan spared the lives of many men both from the South and from the North. The Southern men were gentlemen to the core, and they were going to prove it even in victory. As God was showing mercy to them, the South in turn would show mercy to the North.

Scouts were sent out in every direction to the leaders and commanders of the various posted Confederate armies so that in twelve days' time, all troops would be united at Fort Victory, Virginia. The determined scouts were exhausted after riding hard and long to the farthest troops. They obeyed and delivered the president's commands.

Most of the soldiers felt their spirits rise during their long marches by singing their favorite tunes, "The Battle Cry of Freedom," which William H. Barnes gave Southern lyrics; and "The Bonnie Blue Flag." Robert E. Lee was often quoted, "I don't believe we can have an army without music."

It was a sight to see as all the Confederate troops entered Fort Victory, Virginia, seemingly as if on cue. They approached from all directions—some on horseback, most on foot. The townsfolk heard the troops singing long before they saw them arrive. Cheers and celebration greeted them. Excitement charged the atmosphere the way only the victorious know and share.

The residents of Fort Victory, Virginia, would share with their descendants for all time their exciting stories of experiences with the Confederate army and how they had helped them. Men—black, white, and some Native American—were camped everywhere, awaiting the scheduled battle to begin in two more days. States' rights were as important to these men as independence from England had been in 1776 for those who fought for liberty.

President Davis had alerted the townspeople when he dispatched General Stuart to visit General Lee. With almost two weeks to obtain the necessary supplies to feed the troops, President Davis granted all money needed for preparations. The folks of Fort Victory, Virginia, were ready and able to do their duty to their president and their soldiers. The townspeople opened their homes, properties, rations, and hearts to the very thankful armies. History was being made and recorded, and they all had the joy and satisfaction of knowing they were a part of it.

President Davis dispatched the first ambassador of the Confederate States of America at the same time the scouts had headed to the troops. Highly recommended by General Stuart, formidable Mr. Robert MacClayne was most pleased and honored to represent the Confederate States of America. Passionate about his mission, MacClayne gained an audience with President Lincoln without delay.

Standing at attention in his formal Highland regimental regalia, Ambassador MacClayne hand-delivered the "Challenge to Battle" from President Davis. Mr. Lincoln sat at the conference table and silently read the document. Only the slight tapping of his two fingers on the table betrayed his fury.

The periphery of the conference room held several guards and officials, who were required to protect and advise the president. MacClayne glanced at them while he awaited Mr. Lincoln's response. He saw some of the men eyeing his kilt with a sneer. He silently scoffed at their ignorance of his honorable attire. The Scots had been some of the first people on American soil, and fight for it they had while holding dear their heritage through the wearing of their clan tartan kilts. Under different circumstances, he would challenge any of them to a toss of the caber.

Aye! That would test their strength.

As the silence thickened, MacClayne stared hard at his enemy. The room felt hot but not only from the midafternoon sun shining through the windows. Mr. Lincoln gravely read the challenge to meet the Confederate army with his troops at Fort Victory, Virginia, for the "last battle of the war." He looked up silently at Mr. MacClayne and returned his stare while he slowly stroked his full, black beard. Finally, he said in a stern voice, "How is it that Mr. Davis is so presumptive to send this challenge to me?"

"With all due respect, Mr. Lincoln, President Davis intends to win this war, sir, and with it the states' rights to govern themselves. President Davis has chosen the location to be the last battle fought in this war, thus producing two separate nations. The South shall be known as the Confederate States of America and the remaining Union, the United States of America. We do not want Union land; nor will we force any states into the Confederacy. We demand respect for our states' rights to secede from the Union to govern ourselves. I will not elaborate as to the terms and details of peace at this time. However, I assure you, Mr. Lincoln, that your treatment as the defeated of this war shall reflect true Southern gentility and generosity.

Sitting rigidly, leaning forward, and narrowing his eyes, President Lincoln said, "Mr. MacClayne, there is no possibility that the South will win this war." Mr. Lincoln rose from his chair and stood to his full height with determination in his eyes. "I accept Mr. Davis's challenge and will send my troops to battle with your rebels at the appointed time. You will have safe passage back to the enemy lines, Mr. MacClayne, and then that will be the last protection I offer. We shall stop your rebellion, and you and your people will abide by the laws of the Union!"

Ambassador MacClayne took two deliberate steps forward and looked squarely into the eyes of Mr. Lincoln. The guards were at attention and on alert with MacClayne's movement. Intimidating to anyone nearby, taller and broader than Mr. Lincoln, he thrust out his hulk of a chest and lifted his chin. With fire and passion in his eyes and voice, MacClayne said, "Do you so easily forget, Mr. Lincoln, of the quest of our forefathers to seek freedom and liberty to govern themselves? Do you fail to remember the not-so-distant history of this country and the founding principles? Remember the fervent words of Patrick Henry when he said, 'Give me liberty or give me death!' England could not stop our God-given choice to be free to govern ourselves, and neither shall you!"

"This meeting is over!" shouted Mr. Lincoln, his right fist hammering the table as sharply as a judge's gavel. He abruptly turned and left the room. His retinue divided; some stayed with the president, and some remained in place. As stiff as statues, their anger was controlled but physically sensed.

Ambassador MacClayne turned with dignity. Within a few strides, he was swiftly out of the office and on his way with his waiting Confederate escort to report to President Davis, joined by those assigned by Mr. Lincoln.

The single sheet of parchment with the challenge from President Davis in his own hand to President Lincoln was the only thing on the highly polished table. A direct ray of sunlight from an upper window seemed to pierce the paper as if a sword impaled the center of it, proclaiming Southern victory.

Chapter 20

While Sarah and so many were home diligently praying, dawn at Fort Victory, Virginia, brought the promise of clear skies for the imminent battle. President Davis, mounted on horseback, went trotting down the lines, shouting to his amassed troops, "Men of the Confederate States of America, this day we shall win and end this war!"

The troops cheered and whistled for many minutes before silence fell for President Davis to speak again. "United we stand and fight for our liberty ordained by God!" More cheers filled the air. "Go forth in the strength of our Lord Jesus Christ. Fight for the Confederate States of America and all future generations!"

Hats and a thrilling rebel roar filled the air. Finally, silence fell once again, and President Davis prayed with his men. "Dear Jehovah God, our heavenly Father, we thank You for the responsibility that You have given to us to fight and win today. It is in Your Name that we go forth to do Your work. Protect these men, dear Lord, and lead us to victory. We dedicate the Confederate States of America to You, Jehovah God. In the name of Jesus Christ, our Lord and Savior, we ask, amen."

The soldiers and townspeople who were watching from the sidelines gave a collective "Amen." The men replaced their hats and dispersed; the feeling of victory clung to them like droplets of baptismal water, pure and sure.

"Now men, fortify yourselves with a hearty breakfast, prepared and served by the generous hospitality of the Fort Victory folks. We shall assemble for battle in one hour."

The aroma of freshly baked bread, biscuits, ham, sausage, bacon, eggs, coffee, and woodsmoke from the many campfires around the fields filled their senses. The townspeople had been making the food preparations long before dawn. The Confederate army made their way to the many campsites serving various foods. They ate their fill and relished each bite, knowing full well it could be their last meal. That feeling was the only shadow on the celebration. Anticipation of victory prevailed.

After finishing a fortifying breakfast and thanking their hosts, the soldiers quickly assembled in their designated units under the expert command of Generals Jackson, Lee, and Stuart. Many of the men carried goodbye letters to their loved ones in one of their pockets, just in case. The troops marched, and the mounted soldiers rode proudly to the battleground a half mile away. The approach seemed perfectly choreographed as the Confederate and Union troops neared their strategic positions at the same moment. Two rolling hills filled with soldiers, their respective banners waving. A mantle of quiet fell throughout the ranks as the opposing troops took their positions in their areas. The Union soldiers were so vast in number that their blue uniformed movements resembled surging dark ocean waves brewing in a storm. All the men felt the stark reality of the forthcoming battle.

One Confederate flag bearer began to sing at the top of his voice as he waved the Bonnie Blue Flag. The lyrics fortified them as they all boldly sang together.

> We are a band of brothers and native to the soil,
> Fighting for the property we gained by honest toil.
> And when our rights were threatened, the cry rose near and far,
> Hurrah for the Bonnie Blue Flag that bears a single star.
> Hurrah! Hurrah!
> For Southern Rights, hurrah!
> Hurrah for the Bonnie Blue Flag that bears a single star.

At the conclusion of the singing, the Highland Regiment immediately began the last verse with their inspiring bagpipes and drums. President Davis saluted, then commanded General Stuart to lead the men into victory. General Stuart returned the salute and humbly received the honor as President Davis passed the crowd of men to him.

Claiming the soldiers' attention, General Samuel Stuart shouted in a loud, commanding, confident voice, "Courage, men! We fight for our freedom, for our families, for our homes, and for our futures! Go with God! Defeat this War of Northern Aggression! Give it everything you have! Victory is ours! Claim it!"

Leading the men in the bone-chilling rebel yell, General Stuart dug the heels of his black leather boots into the sides of his best stallion, Little Man, and charged straight at the enemy on the battlefield. The mounted soldiers quickly followed while the men on foot raised their weapons and joined the charge at full speed. Confederate flags waved proudly during the attack.

The eerie sound of the rebel yell momentarily shook the Union troops. Even so, their commanders didn't hesitate and led their charge with bugles blasting and the Union flags waving. The two armies poured straight down the hills and into the valley like a rush of floodwaters from bursting dams. Everything seemed to happen at once.

The scent of sweat and blood almost immediately thickened the air, along with ear-splitting screams, battle cries, and orders shouted in every direction. The perfect formation of the soldiers' approach ceased to exist, and the battle raged. The pipers and drummers of the Highland Regiment continually played rousing tunes and marched forward with their fellow soldiers. Battle cries didn't cover the resonance of the bagpipe and drum music. Some wounded men from both the South and the North glanced up at the pipers and drummers, their last connection here on this earth as they fell. Gunpowder, sweat, and blood assaulted and replaced the lingering smell of ham, bacon, and biscuits in the air.

The townswomen, children, and elderly retreated into the woods or to their homes. Some wanted to see the battle and stayed, but others were afraid. They all knew the cost of victory would be the lives of some of the young men they had just fed and befriended during the breakfast they had served. Had that been only a few hours ago? The womenfolk kept dabbing at their eyes with their aprons or hankies, remembering the sweet faces of the brave teenage soldiers who could have been their sons, and some were. Children cried in fear as the din continued.

Vibrations of the cannonballs hitting the earth and echoes of the battle were lingering sounds never to be forgotten.

General Stuart rode hard toward the right flank at the top of the hill for a better view of the battle. As he came through the shade of the trees at the precipice, there sat Colonel Joseph Scott Jenkins on his horse with his Henry rifle pointed straight at him. General Stuart shouted his name just in time. As Colonel Jenkins recognized who the rider was, he lowered his gun. The two men stared at each other, incredulous of their separate meeting amid the tumult. They realized it wasn't by chance. It was a brief moment of assurance that God was near.

Colonel Jenkins shouted back, "Now it is my turn to save your life, sir." General Stuart saluted with respect and honor, and Colonel Jenkins returned the salute. They paused a moment, then resumed their respective paths, never to see each other again. Their encounter gave them inner peace and strength while surrounded by the pandemonium of war.

General Stuart rode on to the appointed place to meet with General Stonewall Jackson. Under the command of General Robert E. Lee, Jackson continued to build his reputation as Lee's right-hand man. Jackson's courage and resolve, as well as his skillful battle tactics, made him indispensable. It was time to show his grit, and his men were alert and ready.

After several hours of intense fighting, General Stuart returned to his troops, who were engaged in battle in the valley, and commanded them, "Retreat! Retreat! Follow me!" Without question, the Confederate soldiers began to run after General Stuart as he rode hard to the east. They disappeared behind a hill, and the Union soldiers pursued them. The feigned retreat was the signal for General Jackson and General Lee.

At that moment, General Jackson led the surprise attack from the upper-right flank. At the same moment, General Lee brought the final flanking maneuver from the left with his unexpected charge of the Army of Northern Virginia troops attacking from higher ground. The deafening rebel yell sealed the victory as the defeated Union soldiers were surrounded and pushed into each other so tightly they could no longer move. There was no escape for them. The victory was even sweeter because the Union soldiers had outnumbered the Confederates four to one, but there they stood, helplessly pressed into a strategic cleft of the mountain. The Union couldn't regroup to fight again. The commanding officer of the Union troops, General William T. Sherman, stepped forward with his empty hands in the air.

Sherman gave his last battle command to his men. "Disarm!"

A perfect picture of the victor, General Robert E. Lee trotted over on Traveller to this now-historic and hallowed ground. General Sherman looked up at the man he had hoped to defeat. After a moment, Sherman said the most disheartening words of his life. "I surrender the Union army to you, General Lee."

As he raised the Bonnie Blue Flag in his right hand, General Lee declared in his clear and commanding voice, "On behalf of the Confederate States of America, I accept your surrender and declare that the War of Northern Aggression is now over!" The Confederate army cheered and whistled. The Union army remained surrounded and mute, yet a look of relief was on many of the soldiers' faces. The war was indeed over.

General Lee remained on Traveller and called for a horse for Sherman. General Lee escorted the defeated General Sherman to President Davis, who was nearby in a wooded area. President Davis wanted his brilliant and brave generals to experience the full effect and reward of their tireless efforts. After the two men dismounted, it was General Lee's honor to hold the "Document of Surrender" as General Sherman reluctantly signed his name. A drop of ink fell from the quill tip onto the parchment paper before Sherman signed it, forever recording his hesitation.

Then, standing at attention, in turn General Lee, General Jackson, and General Stuart eagerly and boldly signed as witnesses. President Davis dismounted, then signed the "Document of Surrender" last. With a flare, he underlined his name for emphasis, as significant as an amen at the end of a prayer, and added the date, May 26, 1863.

The Union soldiers observed the surrender in silence, unsure of their fate. The Confederate soldiers' cry of victory blended with their rebel yell when President Davis trotted toward the troops, the surrender document waving in his hand. The townsfolk of Fort Victory joined the celebration.

Requesting silence, President Davis dismounted and commanded his men to kneel as he did. They all listened to the most soul-stirring prayer of thanksgiving they had ever heard him pray. With their hats over their hearts, their faces expressed their thanks and gratitude to almighty God.

President Davis stood, then turned to the defeated and downcast General Sherman. He announced in a clear voice, "General Sherman and soldiers of the Union army, you are free to go to your families. The War of Northern Aggression is now over. Go home and leave us in peace. We wish you Godspeed and a bright future with your families." Stunned by these words, no one moved.

General Jackson commanded one of the soldiers to bring a choice horse to General Sherman to keep as he departed. As General Sherman mounted, President Davis said, "Tell Mr. Lincoln that I will send a delegation to meet with him tomorrow to discuss the peace agreement between the Confederate States of America and the remaining United States of America." General Sherman touched the brim of his hat in salute, then turned to head north with his troops.

In one swift movement, President Davis mounted his dependable horse, Blackjack, and rode at a slow trot toward his camp. General Robert E. Lee, General Stonewall Jackson, and General Samuel Stuart were President Davis's retinue. They were a sight to behold, and none ever forgot the moment. Their men parted as if on cue and applauded, cheered, and whistled. After their leaders disappeared, all soldiers began helping each other, attending to the wounded of both the North and the South. They were at peace. All rejoiced that the war was finally over.

The townspeople had earlier decided to create a cemetery for the brave soldiers. More than one hundred older men from the town came to assist in the process of identifying and burying the men in their designated plots. It took some time, but the preplanning had helped create both Southern and Northern cemetery areas. Logbooks kept a record of each soldier's identity and location in the cemetery. For generations to come, people from the North and the South would visit these graves and be thankful for the forethought and kindness of the Fort Victory residents. Many commented on the tactical plan of the Confederates to fight the final battle of the War between the States at Fort Victory. "Victorious at Fort Victory" became a well-known slogan passed down through the generations in story and song.

    Samuel sent a telegram to his parents, Rebecca, and Sarah. It simply said, "Victorious at Fort Victory! Praise God!" Hearts were light and soaring with joy at the Stuart Plantation on May 26, 1863.

Chapter 21

Just ten days later, President Davis and Generals Lee, Jackson, and Stuart were in a meeting at their headquarters in Atlanta. Sarah had been requested to appear before them.

As she entered, she curtsied low with respect and awe. Standing, all the gentlemen waited for her to take her seat. She felt a bit nervous, but she didn't show it at all. General Stuart, in particular, thought she looked radiantly beautiful in her deep-burgundy gown, matching gloves, and veiled hat. Sarah had taken great pains in deciding what to wear for this historic meeting.

President Davis said, "Miss Gordon, we owe you the victory of the Confederate States of America. You are to be richly rewarded and recorded in history as an integral part of the war effort."

Sarah blushed and respectfully stated, "Thank you, President Davis, but I wish no reward nor acknowledgment. Sir, I am truly humbled and thankful that our Lord God chose me to assist you, and I look forward to earning my reward in heaven. I know I fall short so many times, sir, but I aspire to hear these words from Jesus when it's my time to stand before Him: 'Well done, good and faithful servant.' I thank you for your noble gesture, Mr. President, but that is the high reward I seek." Sarah looked demurely down toward her folded hands after she spoke.

The four men glanced at each other and nodded assent. When President Davis cleared his throat, Sarah looked up at him again. "Well, Miss Gordon, a woman with such a goal as this will surely earn it. If you ever need my assistance in any way, you shall have it immediately. I make this my lifelong commitment to you." He bowed deeply, and the generals joined him with their respectful tribute to this remarkable lady and bowed also.

Sarah rose, curtsied to them low and long, and relished the moment shared with these excellent men. She briefly caught the eye of General Stuart, and her heart fluttered as she took her leave.

After the door closed, President Davis reverently picked up a book from his desk and said, "We won't be needing this anymore. Gentlemen, I suggest that we burn it. Do you agree?" He held up the copy of the Civil War history book Sarah had given to General Stuart in the family garden. "General Lee and General Jackson, there are good reasons why I didn't give you free access to this book. What I showed to you was enough for you to understand how God helped us to change the outcome of the War of Northern Aggression and to live in peace with the blessing of our Confederate States of America. It is vital for you two to know just how important your leadership and bravery have been to our success."

President Davis and General Stuart exchanged glances. Only they knew of the full account in the Civil War book. After prayer and discussion, President Davis and Samuel Stuart had decided to never speak of what would have been their future had Sarah not come back through time to fulfill her God-given mission. They thought it best that General Lee and General Jackson celebrate their victories and their prospects with their families without the shadow of knowing what might have been. It was kindness and respect that inspired this decision.

The generals agreed, and in a solemn ceremony, they witnessed President Davis place the book into the fireplace on the low-burning fire. Flames engulfed and surrounded the book, much as the Confederates had surrounded the Union soldiers at Fort Victory. In the intense silence, the crackling fire seemed quite loud. President Davis said in a hushed, reverent tone, "Thank our merciful God that Gettysburg never happened!"

"Yes, indeed. Amen!" the Generals replied. Generals Lee and Jackson knew only that Gettysburg would have brought great slaughter, and they joined in thankfulness that it had never happened.

They all stood in their private thoughts until the book turned into ash. General Stuart silently thanked God for saving the life of General Jackson. He also felt so thankful that General Lee would never be in a position to have to surrender the Confederates' great cause of states' rights. All their lives now had changed purpose because of God's intervention. General Stuart picked up the iron poker, stirred the ash of the book past recognition, then stood tall. With his left hand on the mantel and the fire poker still in his right, he smiled and looked at them.

He said, "I would have liked to save the photograph of your three images on Stone Mountain. Do you think the future generations will still immortalize you with the carvings?"

They raised their eyebrows, shrugged, and glanced at each other. General Jackson replied, "Only time will tell."

Sarah had quietly slipped into the room's back hallway entrance used by the servants. With her violin in hand, ready to be played, she silently stood as she watched them. They had no idea of her presence. "Excuse me, please, gentlemen." They all looked in her direction and bowed as she entered the room and curtsied.

"If I may, I would like to play 'Amazing Grace' for you on my fiddle. It seems a fitting conclusion to this meaningful ceremony." They nodded in agreement.

After checking her tuning quickly, she launched into four verses of the beloved hymn. She played expressively from her heart. The men sang along reverently in their low voices as her bow and fingers played in the Scottish style with ornaments and double stops. The last note faded and lingered before anyone could move. It was indeed a fitting conclusion.

Sarah packed up her violin, then asked Samuel to escort her to her waiting conveyance. He carried her violin case for her, and she appreciated his attentions. By his demeanor, Sarah could tell Samuel felt proud of her. As he assisted her to board the carriage, he handed her violin case to her. Sarah felt him squeeze her hand. and they smiled at each other. Their bond deepened in these unspoken gestures. "I will see you at home as soon as I can."

Sarah nodded and said sincerely, "I shall look forward to your return." The carriage ride back to the plantation in Stone Mountain was a sweet time of reflection and gratitude.

Chapter 22

Sarah turned one last time to Rebecca as they stood at the top of the staircase.

"Do I look presentable?" she asked for the tenth time. "I've never been to a ball before."

"Indeed, you do! You look absolutely gorgeous," Rebecca said patiently. "We just need to wait for our names to be announced, and then we will make our entrance."

Sarah looked out the window. She could tell the leaves were just beginning to change, signaling autumn. They had decided to wait until autumn to have the Victory Ball to give everyone time to grieve and adjust.

All conversation died as their lifelong butler announced Sarah and Rebecca at the head of the wide fan staircase. The guests turned their gazes expectantly. Sarah was sure that in the sudden silence, everyone could hear her heart beating wildly. Her eyes locked with those of Samuel Stuart, who was waiting for her on the bottom landing. Candles blazed a lighted path and made dancing wisps of light on the wall.

Sarah and Rebecca descended the wide curved stairs slowly, gracefully, and with the air of dignity that only ladies portray. Sarah was on the right, her formally gloved hand barely trailing the banister with a fingertip, while Rebecca matched her in beauty, poise, and step.

Sarah wore a forest-green satin dress, in the latest style made just for her. Her green eyes and artfully arranged ringlets of auburn hair made her a striking sight. She enjoyed the feel of the formal gloves reaching above her elbows. Rebecca, too, was at her very best in a jeweled rose silk, also newly fashioned for her, with her light-brown hair puffed and curled into a beautiful upsweep.

Sarah saw Samuel whisper to Luke but didn't know that he said, "Such youth and beauty deserve appreciation. Let's go!" He walked forward in confidence, bowed, and took Sarah's gloved hand in his. The soft linen didn't shield the electricity between them. Sarah saw

Samuel take a deep breath and hoped he noticed her lightly scented rosewater perfume. He smiled his most charming smile and asked, "May I have this dance, Miss Gordon?" Sarah nodded and followed him to the dance floor. The crowd applauded the couple as they began to dance the first dance together. Sarah felt that Samuel had never looked as handsome and distinguished as he did tonight in his Confederate general's uniform.

Rebecca's attractive uniformed gentleman also met her at the foot of the stairs, and she shared a mischievous smile with him. As Sarah turned around on the dance floor, she glanced at Lieutenant Luke Carnegie and Rebecca. He looked like he was the happiest man alive. Soon all would know their secret. When they began to dance, another round of applause welcomed them. As hosts of the first ball of the season, they were the two honored couples, and everyone waited for their first dance to be finished.

Stone Hill Manor Plantation was lit up to glory visible for miles around. There were so many candles; no one could even guess their number. The weather had blessedly changed into an unusual early touch of coolness, announcing the beginning of autumn along with the colored foliage. The oppressive hot and humid air of summer was gone, and the gentle breezes brought delight and comfort this evening.

The elegance of the plantation manor house was at its height under the care of General Samuel Stuart. After the war was over, his father had given the responsibility of running the plantation to his only son. Samuel had a class and unmatched distinction in his choice of understated sophistication combined with simplicity. As carriage after carriage of guests approached the main entrance, their elegantly dressed occupants were quite impressed with the grand manor house.

The elder Stuarts entered the dance floor with a bow and curtsy. Welcoming applause burst forth to honor them. Sarah noticed this time that the ladies' applause sounded like doves' wings because of their gloves, but the gentlemen applauded with strength. Mrs. Stuart's sparkling jewels in her hair were almost as bright as her charming smile. Mr. Stuart was as dashing as ever in his Prince Charlie jacket and kilt. Many more couples joined them on the spacious ballroom dance floor.

Even in their joy, the participants thought of the precious lives lost in the war. Every man who had died was a gift of love and loyalty, freely given in sacrifice for the victorious South. These sons were memorialized and revered in the heart and spirit of the Confederacy. Each step taken, each breath breathed, each child born in the Confederate States of America would be a testimony to these brave men and lads who had fought for states' rights, freedom, and principles. They bought with their lives the victory they sought. How they must be rejoicing in heaven, knowing their sacrifices gave liberty for all future generations and improved life significantly.

As the dance ended, General Stuart led Sarah off the dance floor. He looked deeply into the eyes of his partner and said softly, "I have never before met anyone like you, Miss Gordon."

Leaning toward his ear, Sarah whispered and laughed a little. "Sir, meeting a time traveler is not an everyday experience, I'll grant you that."

He smiled, "Miss Gordon, you are a unique young lady, and I have very much enjoyed getting to know you these past months."

"I, too, have had a most enjoyable time getting to know you, sir, and I hope to get to know you much better yet." Her lacy fan added a demure, feminine touch as she created a faint coolness with it.

"That is my wish as well," he said in his deep, rich voice. The way he was looking at her was quite intense, and Sarah felt a bit self-conscious but thankful for his focused attention on her. Her blush betrayed her composure.

Maybe he will think I'm just flushed from the dance.

Rebecca and Luke joined them, and the gentlemen gallantly offered to obtain some punch for the ladies, which they gladly accepted. While they were alone, Sarah noted, "You look very pleased with yourself, Rebecca. Lieutenant Carnegie is certainly impressive tonight." Their eyes followed the gentlemen's progress.

"Oh, yes, he is indeed." Rebecca beamed and fanned herself. "He is the most handsome of men that I have ever seen or ever will see."

Her friend's face glowed. "I can see how much you like him, Rebecca. Does my face shine like yours when I look at your brother?"

Rebecca snapped her fan together into her palm, turned her face to Sarah, and exclaimed, "Sarah Louise Gordon! Are you telling me what I think you are telling me?"

"Yes, I am," she admitted, smiling widely. "Do you have any objections?"

"None whatsoever! I am thrilled! I can see that you two will suit each other very well indeed. I confess that I have thought that for these past months." Rebecca noticed someone, then smiled at Sarah and added, "You may have a bit of competition to overcome first." She nodded in the direction of the piano.

In a moment's glance, Sarah assessed the situation. There, seated on a Victorian velvet bench near the grand piano, was an unattractive woman who was hard to look at, in Sarah's opinion. Her hair was coarse and in no particular style. Her eyes were buggy wide and her demeanor unseemly. Standing next to her, engaged in conversation with her, was General Stuart, two punch glasses in his hands, looking most uncomfortable.

Sarah could tell instantly that the ugly woman had grand designs on Samuel by the way she was flirting. The nerve! Sarah determined to change that fact immediately. She walked straight to the piano, stood next to General Stuart, and unceremoniously interrupted their conversation. "Oh, there you are, my dear. Thank you ever so much for getting our punch for us." She took a punch cup from Samuel's hand, then took his arm to escort him away. "Rebecca and Luke are waiting for us to rejoin them."

Sarah glanced down at the scorned woman on the piano bench as if she had just noticed her and said, "Oh! Excuse me, madam. I am Sarah Louise Gordon, and you are?"

The woman answered in a miffed tone, "My name is Mrs. Blanche Tarte. I am a close friend of the Stuart family, Miss Gordon, for these past five years." Blanche was all prickles in her response, as her name suggested. She instinctively knew Sarah was her rival. Blanche hadn't missed the familiar "my dear" term Sarah had used for her Samuel.

It was all Sarah could do not to burst forth in an unladylike laugh or snort. Thank the Lord her parents had taught her self-control. Blanche Tarte! *She must be kidding.* The name fit her perfectly.

Sarah, taking on a distinctive air of significance, raised herself to her full height of five feet two and a half inches and said, "Well, it seems we have something in common, Mrs. Tarte. I am a very close friend of the Stuart family as well. In fact, I live here at Stone Hill Manor!" she added triumphantly.

General Stuart was standing there, mute. Sarah could tell he wished he was anywhere else at the moment.

Noticeably surprised, Blanche added, "Well, my late husband—God rest his soul—was an excellent acquaintance of General Stuart's ever since we moved into the area." She put her wrinkled lace handkerchief to her eyes for effect and went on. "Alas, my poor Robert died suddenly a year later, and General Stuart transferred his friendship to me." She smiled triumphantly and didn't hear the groan that came from Samuel's throat in response, but Sarah did.

Just then, thankfully, a lady approached and engaged Mrs. Tarte in conversation, which left Sarah and Samuel free to politely excuse themselves.

They hurried back to Rebecca and Luke, who had observed the entire altercation with Blanche. They didn't hide their amused grins. Everyone knew Blanche had her sights set on Samuel but to no avail. He had been kind to a neighboring widow, and that was all.

After a time, needing a word with others, the gentlemen respectfully bowed to Sarah and Rebecca and took their leave. Rebecca got all the details from Sarah as to what Blanche had said. Rebecca apprised her of Samuel's real motives. He'd pitied Blanche and escorted her to various events so she wouldn't be alone. Blanche apparently had gotten the wrong idea. Thus, Samuel had put distance between them over these last months. She was far too old for him at any rate. There was without question no attraction on her brother's part. Rebecca assured Sarah's heart, then excused herself to mingle.

Blanche, having had her eyes pasted on the interaction, saw her chance when Sarah was left alone. Blanche straightened herself but had a rather unattractive slump for a woman and approached Sarah with the determination of a lioness after its prey. She pounced on an unsuspecting Sarah. "Well, Miss Gordon, you certainly are making a spectacle of yourself this evening."

Sarah had watched Mrs. Tarte approach and thought, *What an ugly orange gown the woman chose to wear.* Sarah casually sipped her punch, frowned, and with her head cocked looked at her questioningly with a raised eyebrow. "Spectacle?"

"Why yes, you poor young thing. Everyone is talking about how you are throwing yourself at General Stuart," she lied as she unnecessarily adjusted her gloves. *Her body heat must elevate when she lies.* Sarah could smell the unwashed aroma of Mrs. Blanche Tarte mingled with scented powder. Why do some elderly people tend to think they can cover up any body odor with perfumed powder, she mused as she stepped away slightly to breathe fresher air.

Blanche continued pointedly, "Since you are new here, one must make allowances, I suppose. But you should know it is common knowledge that General Stuart and I have an understanding."

The audacity of this woman! Sarah wasn't going to make it easy for this aggressor. She nonchalantly finished her remaining punch. "Whatever do you mean, Mrs. Tarte?"

Blanche coyly flicked open her fan and began fanning herself and smiling as she said, "May I speak plainly? General Stuart and I have been friends these past five years since my husband died. Why, we have been almost constant companions, and I have been able to fulfill his needs." More lies and innuendos spewed from her mouth.

Not one to back down from an altercation, Sarah confronted her squarely. "What needs might those be, Mrs. Tarte?"

All the reply Blanche gave was flicking her fan closed shut with a snap. She tapped it in the palm of her left hand and offered a smug, knowing look. She then whisked away, leaving her unpleasant body odor trailing behind her in the whirl she'd created.

Sarah felt the intended strike. She was stunned. Surely there had been no intimacy between this horrid woman and Samuel. Before she could recover, Samuel approached with more cool drinks. His bright smile faded as he noticed Sarah's distress.

"My dear Miss Gordon, whatever is the matter? Are you ill? He placed the fruit punch down on a nearby table and took her elbow.

"No. I ... yes, rather," Sarah stumbled.

"Here, allow me to escort you to the verandah for some fresh air." He took her elbow and guided her skillfully through the crowds. They sat on a bench in a semiprivate area, the music of the string quartet and the drone of the guests left behind.

"Thank you, General Stuart. I am not ill, just shaken a bit. Mrs. Tarte just injected me with some of her venom, and I was caught off guard."

General Stuart frowned. "Blanche injected you with venom? I do not understand."

Sarah looked at him and held his gaze while she explained. "Apparently, she thinks you are going to marry her, and she feels threatened by the attention you are giving to me. She implied that you two are already intimate."

General Stuart stood up, raked his hand through his hair, then faced Sarah to explain. "Surely you know that her words are not true. Blanche is the widow of one of my late friends. He asked me to look after her. We have suited each other's needs as escorts to a few functions, and that is all. I never thought she expected to marry me, nor anyone else, for that matter!"

So those were the needs! Sarah knew in her heart that Samuel was a pure man, but it felt good to hear him say it. "Well, she wants to marry you, and she implied that it is a well-known fact that the two of you are practically promised."

"She is gravely mistaken. I have no intention of marrying her."

Sarah also stood with her hand on his shoulder and gently said, "Perhaps you could advise Mrs. Tarte sometime of your feelings, for I assure you, she has claimed you as her own. Now, shall we go back inside for that delicious cool punch we abandoned?" She took his arm and gave him her most winning smile.

Later in the evening, General Stuart asked Mrs. Tarte to dance. She looked at him and chided, "Samuel, I have been waiting all evening for you. Whatever has kept you from me?"

He loosely held her gloved hand and turned to face her at an acceptable distance as the dance began with a bow and a curtsy. After a few moments, he said, "Blanche, this may not be the time or the place to discuss what I have to say, but I feel it cannot wait another minute."

Blanche had the grace to actually blush as she thought, *He is finally going to propose!*

"Blanche," he tried again and cleared his throat as he looked straight into her eyes. "I want you to know that I have looked after you since your husband died because he asked me to do so."

Misinterpreting what he had said and hearing only what she wanted to hear, she inappropriately burst out, "Oh, Samuel! I've waited so long for you to declare yourself."

Samuel continued, nonplussed, and restated his words. "Robert was my dear friend, and I promised him I would look after you after he died. I feel that I have kept that promise and more, don't you?"

"Oh, yes, yes, I do, Samuel. You have been most attentive, and we have grown so close these past few years since dear Robert passed away." She smiled lovingly into Samuel's perfect green eyes as the beautiful music filled the room and they danced around the crowded floor.

Samuel continued, "Yes, well, Blanche, what I want you to know is that you can always count on me to help you at any time. However, there seems to be a misunderstanding that I need to clear up with you. I am not in love with you, Blanche, and I have no expectation ever to marry you. I am sorry if I did anything that gave you the impression that my intentions were more than they are. Would you forgive me, please?"

Expecting his proposal of marriage, Blanche stopped dead right in the middle of the dance floor and let out a shriek. "What? What are you saying? I have loved you and have been patient for you to marry me all of this time! How can you say that you have no intentions of marrying me? We have been everything to each other!" Her eyes bulged out of their sockets, and her face and neck were flushed red in rage. Her features were distorted and even uglier in anger. She looked like an evil witch, choking on her own poison, and she was.

Everyone in the room had stopped dancing and conversing. They all stared at the strident couple. Even the musicians had stopped playing. General Stuart tried to console her, to no avail. "Blanche, please."

"Don't you ever say my name again, you contemptible scoundrel," she hissed, then slapped him so hard across his face that he had to take a step backward to regain his balance. Immediately, her handprint appeared on his cheek in red-and-white welts. She picked up her skirts and ran from the room, sobbing.

General Stuart removed his handkerchief and dabbed at his cheek and forehead, then said to the room at large, "Please, forgive me, everyone. This public display was most badly done by me, to be sure. Mrs. Tarte had unreasonable expectations of our relationship, which I just attempted to set straight. Please, please, continue the dance, everyone. I do apologize." He bowed slightly and left the room as the musicians began the next dance tune. A murmur of conversation resumed as the guests discussed what they had just witnessed.

Rebecca and Sarah, enjoying a bit of refreshment, were amazed at the scene. Rebecca looked shocked and shared a look with Sarah, who just realized she had a mouthful of biscuit in her gaping mouth. She quickly chewed and swallowed it but had never tasted anything so dry in all her life. She regained her composure rather quickly and said to Rebecca, "Excuse me" before Rebecca had even closed her mouth.

Sarah quickly caught up with General Stuart in the entrance foyer. They were blessedly alone. She touched his left arm, and as he turned to face her, she said, "Oh, General Stuart, I am so sorry. I had no idea such an ordeal would develop from our conversation about Mrs. Tarte. I am truly sorry."

Folding and putting his linen handkerchief in his inside breast pocket, General Stuart said, "Miss Gordon, I assure you that you have no responsibility at all in the matter. In fact, I am most grateful to you for bringing the situation to my awareness. What just happened needed my attention. I dare say Mrs. Tarte will not trouble you again with her spite. I had no idea what her true character was until this moment past. In fact, I owe you a debt of gratitude. How my dear friend Robert ever survived the tongue on that woman is beyond my imagination. No wonder he went to an early grave."

"I am glad to have been a help in your life. However, the public spectacle must be terribly embarrassing for you."

"Think nothing of it. Blanche indicated to you that general society knew of our supposed understanding. Everyone needed to know the outcome. People would have found out eventually through gossip. This way, all knew firsthand, and they no longer need to imagine anything."

Samuel offered his arm to Sarah. "Care to take another stroll with me in the gardens, Miss Gordon? I believe this one will be peaceful, and I could use the air myself."

"I shall be delighted, sir." Sarah locked her arm into his elbow, and they very much enjoyed their pleasant walk.

Chapter 23

Two weeks later, Sarah and Samuel were sharing a private moment by the creek, soothed by the rushing sound of water flowing over the rocks. For an autumn day, it was cool but not brisk, and there was no wind. Sarah thought it was perfect weather and company. They spoke for hours, covering countless topics and enjoying the small fire Samuel had built. She liked to watch him move as he fed the small blaze as it lit up the late-afternoon shade.

After stirring the embers again, he turned and stared at her for some moments with an unusual look on his face. He seemed suddenly nervous and uncomfortable. Sarah couldn't understand this abrupt change in his manner. He approached her and held out his hand, apparently wanting her to get up, so she complied. Shaking her skirts out, she frowned and asked with concern, "What is it, Samuel?"

He held her gaze for some moments without speaking. Then he knelt on his right knee in front of her, lightly kissed her ungloved hand, and said, "Sarah, I have grown to love you deeply. You are the most wonderful lady. I know you love God first, and I am hoping that you may love me next. Sarah Louise Gordon, will you do me the honor of becoming my wife?"

Sarah was surprised for only a half second. She had hoped for this moment for some time now and placed her free hand on his warm cheek, then smiled. Expelling a deep breath, Sarah answered, "Samuel, I have loved you from our very first meeting. Yes, my darling, I shall gladly be your wife."

She could see relief flood his face. All at once, Samuel was on his feet. He swiftly pulled her into a firm embrace and whispered, "Oh my dear, beautiful Sarah." He gently tilted her chin to the perfect angle, then kissed her lightly. Sarah's eyes closed in pure pleasure, and she let out a deep sigh. His kiss deepened, and their embrace tightened. She had no idea how long they stood there in each other's arms, not wanting the moment to end. The long kiss felt sacred.

Samuel then slipped his mother's diamond ring on her finger, and it fit perfectly. They kissed again, awakening the natural longing for each other to be man and wife. After their kiss ended, Sarah opened her eyes to find his, dark and intense. She was still clinging to him, waiting for the dizziness to pass.

"Sarah, I love you, and I shall live my life showing my love to you in every possible way. God sent you here to me, through time, which makes our love a miraculous gift. I thank Him, Sarah. I'll thank Him every day of my life for you." She felt the warmth of his firm hand on the small of her back. He breathed in the softness and scent of her beautiful hair. A symphony of bird songs mixed with the cascading waterfall caressed her senses, along with his touch. Surrounded by his loving arms, she felt secure and confident of her future.

The coolness of the autumn day chilled her as Samuel stepped away to extinguish the fire. While they began packing up their few refreshments, Sarah tucked a wayward hair behind her ear. She exclaimed, "Oh, Samuel! How differently I feel as we turn to go home. I am now sure of your love for me, of the promise of our life together, and oh, I love you so very much!" They stopped to embrace and kiss again. Sarah's cheeks hurt from smiling so much. She held her hand up to admire her diamond as it sparkled in the sunshine.

"I know that my parents and family would be pleased with our plans. Will your parents be happy, do you think?" Sarah asked her betrothed as they folded the quilt together.

Samuel smiled. "Yes, sweetheart, they shall be very pleased. They already love you as a daughter." He put the folded quilt and the picnic basket in the carriage and then said, "You have made me the happiest of men. My life has been full of military pursuits, yet my few quiet moments were painfully empty. You have now filled my life and heart to overflowing." He put his arms around her again. Sarah smiled as she sensed his warmth and firm muscles. She rested her head against her beloved's shoulder. They then took their first few steps together into their future as they strolled arm in arm to the carriage.

As they entered the manor's parlor, Mrs. Stuart looked up from her book. She was reading Jane Austin's *Pride and Prejudice* again and was coincidently at the part where Mr. Darcy was proposing to Lizzie. When she saw her son and Sarah, she put her book down and said, "Well, by the looks on your faces, some good news is forthcoming, I predict."

Samuel walked over to his mother, bent to kiss her cheek, and said, "Yes, Mother, the most welcome news is about to be yours to share." Walking over to Sarah and lifting her hand with the family ring on it, he said, "Mother, I have asked Sarah to be my wife, and she has consented."

Mrs. Stuart was out of her chair with the spring of a young girl and embraced them both, saying, "Oh my dears! How happy I am to hear this wonderful news! I am not one bit surprised." She took Sarah's hand and admired how well the family ring looked on her finger. "Now I understand why Samuel was never seriously interested in any one girl before. He was waiting for you." She took both of her hands in hers and continued, "In these past months, I have grown to love you as my daughter, and now you will truly be so." Mrs. Stuart leaned over and kissed Sarah on her cheek, then kissed her son's. They all sat together, cherishing their moment of joy.

"Your father will be so pleased as well. He has long felt you needed a wife, Son, and with your choice of Sarah, I know he couldn't be happier."

"When will Father be returning from his railroad meetings in Atlanta, Mother?"

"He should be home tonight by suppertime. Let's make tonight special in your honor, my dears."

A beaming Sarah replied, "Thank you, Mrs. Stuart. You are most kind."

"Well, now we shall have none of that, my dear. You shall start calling me 'Mother' this instant!" She smiled to soften her words so they didn't appear as a command. "Oh! When are you planning on setting the date? The sooner the better, I think. We have so much to plan and do. Let's see." She pondered a moment with her finger tapping her chin. "Three weeks could just be enough time. Granted, they would be days packed full, but we could do it, don't you think?" She waited for the betrothed pair to answer.

Samuel and Sarah looked at each other. Both were amused, thankful, and willing to fit into the schedule Mrs. Stuart had so quickly outlined. They agreed, and with the clap of her hands, a light in her eyes, and a hurried sentence reflecting her rush to get started, she was gone from the room, calling, "Bessie! Bessie, I need you, quickly." Then the attendant closed the door behind her.

Samuel and Sarah momentarily stared at the closed door, then at each other, and burst out laughing. "Do you mind, my darling, Sarah? Mother has been waiting for this occasion for so long. I hope her taking over does not offend you in any way."

"Oh, Samuel, quite the contrary. I am thrilled that she is so delighted. How sweet of her to want to do everything and to get started immediately. No doubt Bessie will be in a whirlwind too, but I think we shall all enjoy the plans immensely." She paused a moment and continued, "You know, I have no family here with me, so it is wonderful to enjoy your mother and what she is willing to do for us. I owe her and your father so much for taking me in and caring for me. They could never offend me. I have grown to love them dearly."

Samuel swept his beautiful fiancée into his arms and thoroughly kissed her. She felt transported to their own, exclusive world where everything was beautiful and overflowing with love. Bessie quietly knocked on the parlor door with a grin. She was sure the couple inside were kissing just as sure as if she were looking through a window directly at them. Reluctantly parting from their loving embrace, Samuel said his usual command. "Enter."

Bessie entered and swept in with hearty congratulations to them both. Sarah hugged her with appreciation.

I could only be happier if my family could share in my joy too.

Chapter 24

Later in her room, sitting at the task Mrs. Stuart had assigned to her, Sarah was at her desk, writing a list of everything she thought she might need for her wedding and trousseau.

The door flew open, and in rushed Rebecca, exclaiming, "Sarah, you are going to be my true sister! Oh, I am so thrilled!" She practically knocked her out of her chair in her enthusiastic embrace.

"Yes, sweet Rebecca, I am going to be your sister forever truly. Although let's not forget that this occasion also requires notice of the fact that I am to be your brother's wife as well." She grinned broadly.

Rebecca looked blank for a moment, then laughed.

"Oh, details, details!" Rebecca said with a smile and a wave of dismissal. "I have always wanted a sister like you, and now I have one." She reflected a moment, then looked instantly sad, with an exaggerated lower lip pursing outwardly. "Only three more weeks to share our room together. Oh, how I shall miss you, Sarah!" And they embraced again.

"I won't be so far away, you know. If you recall, your brother's quarters are just on the other end of this very floor."

Rebecca replied, "Yes, but you know what I mean. It just will not be the same for us." They looked at each other with the realization that their relationship would grow and deepen but change as Sarah became Samuel's wife.

"Well, we all must adjust to changes, dear Rebecca … even when they are wonderful and joyful. There are times and purposes for every season."

Rebecca agreed, "Yes, that is what my dear friend Pauline Hendricks says. She is like a second mother to me. I look forward to having you meet her soon. She lives nearby, but this isn't the time to discuss neighbors, however dear." She flew into the task of helping Sarah plan her wedding clothes, and they acted like young, giggling schoolgirls for several hours. Bessie came in with some mint tea and fresh buttermilk biscuits with honey. The ladies invited Bessie to stay and join in the conversation for a few minutes.

Rebecca confided in Bessie that she had hopes of being married in the not-too-distant future as well. Bessie said, "Your feelings have been transparent, Miss Rebecca. I am not one bit surprised." Sarah had a smug look on her face that Bessie missed entirely.

I already know Rebecca's secret. In fact, I was the first one to know.

Sarah and Rebecca held glances, and Rebecca nodded to the silent question. Hesitantly, Sarah asked Bessie for details about what they should expect on their wedding night. "We know what is supposed to happen, but what is it really like, Bessie? Do you remember?"

Bessie smiled and said, "Of course I remember! Land sakes! A woman doesn't forget her wedding night." She tried as delicately as she could to describe what it was like between a husband and wife when they became one flesh. "Since there is nothing else to compare it to, it is difficult to explain. But fear not, my ladies. I am here to tell you that it is wonderful."

Sarah and Rebecca giggled and blushed. Bessie grinned as she remembered.

An unexpected knock came on the door. Sarah opened the door.

Samuel said with love and tenderness in his voice, "May I speak with you privately?"

I am thrilled this handsome man will soon be my husband.

"Of course, Samuel." Sarah shot a glance back at Rebecca and Bessie, and raised her eyebrows. They all giggled, acutely aware of what they had just been discussing.

Chapter 25

Sarah's mood changed instantly to seriousness as she heard Samuel say, "Darling, there is something we must discuss before any more time passes. Please, come with me. I have something for you to see." Offering his arm, Samuel led Sarah to a far wing of the house, which was separate from the family quarters.

Pausing with his right hand on a door latch, Samuel looked at Sarah and said, "This may come as a shock to you, but I have another sister. I should have told you about her earlier, but as you will see, it's not something easily discussed. There is something wrong with her mind, Sarah. I thought you had a right to know this before you marry me." And with that he opened the door.

Inside was a large room that appeared to be a nursery, yet the inhabitant wasn't a child. A young woman sat on the floor with her nanny, an older servant woman, and they were building with wooden blocks. The young woman looked up and grunted her delight. A smile lit her pretty face. The family resemblance was unmistakable. She looked so much like Rebecca and their mother.

She got up, ran to Samuel, and flung herself around him while she made sounds of joy. After an affectionate hug, she put her face up and pressed her flat lips against his in her version of a kiss. She did this repeatedly until Samuel said, "Go build with your blocks now, Posie." He used this particular term of endearment for his sister and steered her back to the colorful wooden blocks and her nanny.

In low tones, Samuel said to Sarah, "Joanne Louise was born this way. We don't know her affliction, only that she cannot speak. Joanne has a very short attention span and little understanding. She has learned some obedience and self-control, but at times she has dark moments where she strikes herself and cries. I imagine she becomes frustrated, but I don't know for sure. Nanny has taken care of Joanne since birth, and we are grateful for her loyalty and dedication. I come here and spend as much time with Joanne as I can, and I am devoted to her, Sarah. I am committed to caring for her and protecting her all of her life. I know this certainly may come as a shock to you."

Sarah listened and watched Joanne in silence. She replied, "I am not shocked, dear Samuel. Bless her heart. She can't help the way she is. I respect you for your commitment to care for her." She smiled up at him and touched his face with her hand. "Why has Rebecca not mentioned Joanne to me?"

"Rebecca has a hard time accepting her. When Rebecca was just a toddler, Joanne was about eight years old at the time. Rebecca kept after Joanne, wanting a stuffed doll that Joanne did not want to surrender. Not knowing how to control herself, Joanne flew into a rage, picked Rebecca up by the hair, and threw her several feet across the room. Rebecca screamed for hours, frightened to death. Petrified, she never came to this room again. When mother or I tried to bring her here, she would cry and run to the safety of her bedroom. We finally stopped trying to make her visit Joanne. Rebecca has coped with her by ignoring her existence."

"Oh, dear me. How sad for everyone."

With a deep sigh, Samuel said, "Yes, I hope that one day she will change toward her. No one blames Rebecca for how she feels. We are all patiently waiting for her to grow through it."

Sarah nodded in understanding while she observed Joanne.

"Does she know she is limited, Samuel?" Sarah knelt on the floor and smiled. She gently stroked Joanne's blond hair and face but got no response from her.

"As far as we can tell, she is unaware of her lack. We had hoped and prayed she would get well in time or that God would grant us a miracle for her. However, she is as you see."

Sarah spoke quietly to Joanne for a few minutes, then introduced herself to the nanny. She learned that all the family called this woman Nanny, even though her name was Jane. They had a short conversation, and Sarah liked Nanny instantly. She could see her heart for Joanne and the entire Stuart family in all she said. Nanny was a treasure to this family, and Sarah told her so.

Her short observation of Joanne brought her to the conclusion of what her affliction most likely was, and she proceeded to tell Samuel. Rising and approaching her betrothed, Sarah took Samuel's hands and led him to the corner of the room. Joanne seemed unaware of their movements.

She spoke in a hushed tone. "Samuel, I have seen this condition before. It is called PKU, which stands for phenylketonuria. I had a friend who had a sister with it. PKU is now actually curable in my time. However, to my knowledge, before the 1950s, the doctors didn't know about it or how to diagnosis it. My friend's sister was exactly like Joanne in behavior. She also had the blond hair that is a characteristic of the condition. I believe there is some imbalance of the amino acids in the system of those afflicted with it. We can and shall continue to pray for a miracle because that is the only way Joanne will be set free from her condition."

Samuel listened intently, and a look of great sadness reflected on his facial features. He stared at Sarah for a few moments, then let go of her hands. Samuel walked over to Joanne and sat on the floor with her, just as Sarah had done. He stroked her hair, and Joanne smiled and put her face to his lips for repeated kisses. She let out happy sounds. He felt his heart breaking for his beloved sister. Samuel had long held hope for her recovery. This new information was quite difficult to bear.

Sarah encouraged him as she went on. "One good thing to know, Samuel, is that Joanne's severe brain damage prevents her from understanding that she is not normal."

Samuel continued to sit with his sister. He looked up at Sarah and was thankful for her kindness and knowledge. *But knowing what she knows, will she decide not to marry me?*

He kissed his sister on the cheek and thanked Nanny. As he got up, he beckoned Sarah to go out of the room with him.

Joanne broke free of Nanny's grasp, ran to Samuel, and threw herself on him before he was able to close the door. She clutched him with superhuman strength to keep him with her.

Sarah said, "How remarkable that Joanne understands that you love her. She wants to be with you and is having no trouble expressing that for sure."

Samuel had to gently but firmly tell Joanne no. He removed her grasp on him and took her back to Nanny. As they were closing the door, Joanne made unhappy sounds as Samuel and Sarah left the room. It would be some time before she settled back down, but sweet, loving Nanny knew what to do to soothe her. As they began to walk down the hallway, Sarah could hear the older woman softly singing to calm her charge.

Nervous to learn the answer, Samuel asked, "So, my beautiful Sarah, does this situation in my life give you pause for thought about marrying me?" He continued quickly, "Before you answer, let me assure you that I completely understand if you feel you must change your mind about accepting me." Samuel held his breath until she replied.

Looking directly into his eyes, she said with great feeling, "In no way would I think any such thing, my beloved." She took his hands in hers and continued, "Joanne is precious, and I will learn to love her too, as you do. Along with you, I shall care for her and protect her."

Samuel resumed breathing as Sarah squeezed his hands in affirmation.

Chapter 26

Later that night in their shared room, Sarah took the plunge to ask Rebecca about her view of Joanne. She said only, "I met Joanne today."

With her back to Sarah, Rebecca was as still as granite and said nothing. Sarah felt her tension. She continued directly but tenderly, "What makes you ignore her, Rebecca? You are a grown woman now, and she can't throw you across a room by your hair anymore. It is not her fault to be as she is, you know."

Rebecca turned suddenly and asked incredulously, "Ignore her and fault her? I did fear her when I was little, but fear is not what keeps me from her now." She bit her bottom lip and said in a whisper, with tears in her eyes, "It could have been me, Sarah. And I have been afraid all of my life that one day I might lose my mind too. What if being around her somehow makes me sick, like she is? I am sorry for Joanne, but I do not want to become like her." Rebecca hid her face in her hands. "I never have told anyone of these feelings that I hide. I am ashamed to say it."

Sarah went to her friend, put her arms around her, and said softly, "Yes, it could have been you. But it wasn't you, was it?" Sarah lifted Rebecca's chin and moved her hands away from her tear-stained face. She continued, "I know what affliction your sister has, Rebecca. I have seen it before, and I assure you that you cannot become like her by being around her."

Rebecca's eyes widened, and she gasped as Sarah explained about Joanne's condition. "If you had PKU, you would have had the same brain damage from birth. Rest your mind and heart, dear Rebecca. The affliction is not contagious. You have nothing to fear."

They hugged again as this truth seeped into the very soul of Rebecca. She took a deep breath to calm herself and breathed a prayer of thanks to God for showing her that she didn't need to be afraid.

Sarah said gently, "God allowed Joanne to be as she is for His purpose. We cannot understand it now, but when Jesus comes back again, or when Joanne goes to heaven, she will be made whole and well."

She smiled. "We will have all eternity to spend with Joanne. She will talk to us then and laugh with us."

Rebecca felt elation renew her. "You are right, Sarah. Our Joanne will be whole and well then." The idea was obviously a new one to her. She hugged Sarah tightly and said, "Oh, thank you for that hope. I must go see her immediately and beg her forgiveness."

They went together to Joanne's room. She was already tucked into bed for the night but not yet asleep. A single candle illuminated the soft light. Nanny was in her adjacent room. While Sarah stood back and watched, Rebecca knelt by the bed and held her sister's hand. As she stroked Joanne's hair off her forehead, Rebecca's tears flowed.

She held Joanne's uncomprehending eyes in a locked gaze and said to her, "Please forgive me, Joanne. I could have been a good sister to you all of these years, but I was not. I was afraid that your illness might become my fate too, so I stayed away." She let out a choked sob, then continued, "Sarah helped me to understand that I have nothing to fear. I promise I will come to visit you often from now on, dear Joanne."

Rebecca smiled and wiped her eyes with her handkerchief. "I know you do not understand me, sugar, but I think your spirit does. Please forgive me for neglecting you. I love you so much, and God loves you. He will make you well and whole one day. Just think what a great and glorious day that will be when we can talk with each other." She bent to kiss Joanne on the cheek. "Good night now, sweet sister. I shall come to see you tomorrow. Sleep well."

The next day, Rebecca was true to her word and visited her sister in the morning. They had a lovely time together, doing things Joanne enjoyed the most. Rebecca brushed Joanne's hair, took her on a walk in the garden, and splashed a little water on her face at the creek. Then they drank milk and ate oatmeal raisin cookies before retiring for a nap. It was a grand reunion. Rebecca promised herself that she would prioritize time with Joanne from this point forward.

Chapter 27

Unbeknownst to Rebecca, Mrs. Stuart was watching her daughters from the atrium windows. As she saw her girls frolicking about and enjoying each other, her mother's heart was full to overflowing with joy. She put her hand on the window, as if caressing her girls. Mrs. Stuart whispered thanks to God for answering her fervent prayers.

She anticipated the joy her husband would also feel when she told him about this monumental moment. Mrs. Stuart was impatient for him to get home, but she understood his many absences. Their railroad business was very demanding. Sometimes she accompanied him to work, but mostly she stayed home. She had an estate to run and a family who needed her attention.

She was so blessed to be at home this day to see the miracle of her two daughters happy together at long last.

Chapter 28

Sarah and Samuel had an outing in the town of Stone Mountain. They had a very special errand to do at the jewelers.

Right there in the store, Samuel held Sarah's eyes and slipped a gold wedding band onto her finger.

The jewelry store owner said, "This is the best part of my job, to see the expression of young love and hope for your future together."

They smiled at him, and then Sarah put the matching gold ring on Samuel's finger. He looked at it and said, "I am very happy with the choice we made to each wear plain gold wedding bands."

They were both ready to say, "I do!" The wedding rings fit perfectly, and so did their personalities. Samuel paid the man, who bid them good wishes for a happy life; then he wrapped up the rings in a small parcel tied with a white satin ribbon. It was always the jeweler's custom to hand the parcel to the lady.

The loving couple went on to accomplish a few other errands in town. All the while, Sarah repeatedly touched the little package in her soft reticule, which held their wedding bands. She felt exceedingly blissful. Her new life was a perfect fit.

I shall always miss my family, but I know they would be happy for me.

Unfortunately, Blanche Tarte was coming out of the General Store as they were attempting to enter. Blanche stood there, blocking the doorway, with disdain in her narrowed eyes. She looked ready to do battle, but thankfully all she did was murmur a grunt and rush away from them as fast as she could. Sarah and Samuel exchanged a look of great relief that the encounter with that wretched woman had passed without incident.

Sarah requested that Samuel take the open carriage drawn by one horse and drive it himself so they could be alone. Sarah wanted nothing to interfere with this particular moment. They enjoyed the ride back home and talked, laughed, and kissed as they desired. It was late afternoon as they approached the manor. The sun was turning a deep yellow orange, making all green growth and colorful flowers even more vivid. The breeze remained a constant gentle caress, and the humidity was low. It was a perfect day in every way.

Chapter 29

Coming around the bend in their carriage, they both instantly knew something was wrong. Servants were scattering and rushing all around the lawn and surrounding areas. Samuel stopped the carriage, stood erect with reins in hand, and called to his man, "Joe, what has happened?"

Coming rapidly toward them, the middle-aged Joe caught his breath for a moment before stating, "Miss Joanne is missing, sir!"

Sarah gasped. Stunned, Samuel asked, "How can this be? Where is Nanny?"

"Sir, Nanny was found unconscious on the floor, and Miss Joanne is gone."

"When did this occur?"

"Not a half hour past, sir."

"Fetch the doctor for Nanny and tell me what has been done to locate my sister." Samuel resumed his seat in the carriage. Sarah remained quiet, taking it all in as best she could.

"Yes, sir! Everyone available has been on alert, searching the grounds and the house. There are no signs of her yet, sir," Joe said as he walked toward the doctor's cabin.

Samuel abruptly sat and whistled to the horse, then slapped the reins. The carriage horse made a quick start and took them to the manor house. He handed the horse and carriage off to the groom, who awaited further instruction. Samuel helped Sarah down from the carriage, and they rushed inside the front door.

Samuel called, "Mother! Father!" His voice boomed throughout the house, and in just seconds, Mrs. Stuart appeared at the head of the stairway. She was very distraught and held a crumpled handkerchief to her swollen eyes.

She and her son met on the stairs and embraced as he inquired, "What news?" Sarah noticed how her beloved took command and got right to the heart of the matter with few words. No wonder he was a great general.

Mrs. Stuart replied in an anguished tone, "Nothing yet, no news at all. Everyone is looking for Joanne throughout the house and grounds. Your father is also out and about looking for her. I stayed here in case she appears. She may be disoriented and cannot find her way back to her rooms. I hope that is all that has happened. Oh, my baby, my baby girl! What is to become of her? She has never before been alone. Never." She burst into fresh tears as she cried against her son's shoulder.

"Mother, we shall find her. She cannot have gone far. Rest yourself now. We shall find her," he repeated with firm conviction as he patted her back for comfort.

He looked at Sarah with all the strain and grief of a lost loved one reflected on his face. He stated resolutely, "We must find Joanne."

Sarah touched his forearm with a squeeze and smiled encouragingly. "I will help you. We shall find her together, sweetheart."

The three of them stood in a little circle and held hands as Samuel led them in prayer.

Bessie rushed into the room and said, "Mrs. Stuart, I have an idea. Remember how much Miss Joanne likes to go on an outing?"

Blotting her swollen eyes once again, Mrs. Stuart looked at Bessie blankly for a moment, then said, "Well … yes. Yes, she has, hasn't she?" With realization dawning on her face, Mrs. Stuart continued, "Joanne has been out several times to Magnolia Creek. She always liked to take off her socks and shoes and go wading in the cool water. You don't think she could have gone there all by herself, do you?"

Bessie replied with confidence, "Yes, ma'am, I do think that it is possible. She has her limits, but from what I've seen of her lately, she communicates and expresses some of her likes and dislikes quite well. She may be more capable than we realize, ma'am. I think Miss Joanne may have become frightened when Nanny collapsed. She probably wandered off to the place that brought her happiness and fun. I wouldn't be a bit surprised if that is where she is right now, at Magnolia Creek. Why, she is probably having the time of her life splashing in the water."

Grabbing her son's arm, Mrs. Stuart said anxiously, "Son, do you think Joanne could make it there by herself?"

Samuel thought for a moment and nodded. "Yes, I do believe she could. I'll go to the creek right now and see."

"Oh, dear, merciful God, please let her be there unharmed!" Mrs. Stuart prayed aloud.

"Bessie, please stay with Mother."

"Yes, sir." As she turned to Mrs. Stuart, Bessie squeezed out a cool cloth over the washstand, then placed it over Mrs. Stuart's swollen eyes.

Samuel and Sarah rushed back out of the house and into the waiting buggy. The groom had stood by, anticipating that the carriage would soon be needed again. They traveled the quarter mile to Magnolia Creek in record time, disembarked, and ran through the wooded area on the well-worn path. Sarah could smell the freshness of the water and hear its movement before actually seeing it. The air was noticeably cooler in the shade. All at once, they stopped dead in their tracks. As they caught their breath, their eyes beheld the object of their quest.

There in the cold, shallow water, soaked clear through, was Joanne. She was splashing the water up into the air. Her shoes and socks were off, sitting on the bank near her. Samuel looked at Sarah with great relief, squeezed her hand, and breathed a whispered prayer of thanks.

Joanne came easily to Samuel, and he put his coat around her shoulders. With the fun and excitement over, Joanne must have realized she was cold, and she started shivering. She cuddled close to her brother for warmth. Sarah retrieved her socks and shoes while Samuel carried his younger sister to the carriage. The three of them sat close together to keep Joanne warm, and the ride back to the manor was quick but not so fast as to scare Joanne. She always loved carriage rides, and she was smiling. Samuel drove home with one hand on the reins and one arm around his precious sister. Sarah quietly sang a lullaby and held Joanne's cold hands to warm them. She also put Joanne's socks and shoes on her feet.

Great rejoicing filled the air as all family and servants cheered their homecoming. The bell of their family chapel repeatedly rang, announcing to all the search parties that Joanne was safely home.

Samuel said, "Bessie, we owe you a debt of gratitude. Thank you for your wisdom."

Bessie smiled, "We are all thankful that Miss Joanne is safe, sir. I will get a hot bath ready for her as fast as possible." With that, Bessie slipped out of the room.

Mrs. Stuart attended to her daughter personally. She washed Joanne in the hot bath, dressed her into her nightclothes, fed chicken soup and biscuits to her, and then tucked her into bed. She was warm and snug with her favorite quilt, which her mother had made for her out of her colorful baby clothes. It was soft and worn with age and use, but it was kept mended. It was Joanne's favorite snuggle blanket.

Mrs. Stuart asked Bessie to bring her toiletries and nightclothes to her. She wasn't about to leave Joanne's side this night.

Samuel and Sarah asked the doctor about Nanny. He said that at Nanny's age, fainting spells weren't unusual. The doctor suggested that they train a younger servant to take care of Joanne. Samuel had already discussed an idea with Sarah upon their approach to the doctor's cabin there on the estate. The doctor was the Stuarts' family doctor, and he attended everyone who lived on the Stuart plantation.

Samuel explained, "Nanny has been the caregiver for Joanne since her birth, and there is no way I would separate them."

Sarah smiled at her fiancé and saw his tender heart in action once again. Samuel continued, "I will have a younger servant assigned to assist Nanny and be on hand in the event that she has another fainting spell." This decision settled the issue.

They went into the sickroom at the doctor's cabin to visit Nanny. "Sir, I am so sorry! Is Miss Joanne found yet?" She tried to get up, but Sarah comforted her, and Samuel waved her words away in the air.

He said, "Nanny, you couldn't help fainting. Joanne is fine. She took a little jaunt all by herself to play in Magnolia Creek. We found her having fun, so no harm is done. I will have an assistant servant assigned to you, though, to help you with Joanne. You will always be Joanne's nanny for as long as you live. You are a member of our family, you know, so no fretting yourself. You just take care and rest. The doctor will send you back to your room when he thinks you have recovered sufficiently."

He smiled and held Nanny's hand as he spoke. He felt the tension leave the older woman's body, and he was glad Nanny could now relax and recover. "Mother is staying with Joanne for now. She will help train the new assistant." He glanced at Sarah, and they exchanged a knowing smile. Facing Nanny again, he said quietly, "You may like to know that we have chosen Bessie to be your assistant."

Delight filled Nanny's eyes, "My daughter will help me with Joanne, sir? How wonderful! But what about Mistress Rebecca and Mistress Sarah? They need Bessie as their lady's maid."

Sarah responded, smiling, "We can work it all out, Nanny. We both feel that Bessie is the best choice to help you with Joanne. You just rest now. All will be well."

CHAPTER 30

"Sarah! Really! You are going to pinch your cheeks off if you do that one more time," an exasperated Mrs. Stuart exclaimed while she gently but firmly pulled Sarah's hands away from her face. "Your face is full of color, and any more brought on by your continual pinching will cause you to look like you have hives, my dear."

Sarah looked uncertainly at herself in the mirror, not wanting to be pale for her wedding day. Without taking her eyes off her reflection, she replied, "Are you sure? I don't want to be pallid."

Rolling her eyes heavenward, Mrs. Stuart replied, "I am certain that you are not pallid, Sarah. In fact, I have never been so sure of anything in my entire life. Now stop worrying and let us get your veil into place. You do not want to be late for your wedding, now do you?"

"Here it is, Mama," offered Rebecca as she and Bessie picked up the long wedding veil from the stand across the room.

Gasping, Sarah exclaimed, "Oh, it is gorgeous! It looks like it is floating all on its own."

They all smiled and looked at the long, white veil, fluffed and flowing. It was the most exquisite—and by all likelihood—the most expensive veil ever seen. The crown was full of glistening seed pearls and a delicate whisper of light lace. Best of all, it was the veil the Stuart ladies had worn for three generations. Rebecca would be next. Mrs. Stuart lovingly placed the veil onto Sarah's shiny, dark, auburn hair, as if she were crowning a reigning queen. Sarah imagined trumpet fanfare.

Mrs. Stuart said, "I remember when my dear mother placed it on my head so many years ago."

Rebecca and Bessie spread out the length of the train, then stood up. The four women were speechless as they stared at Sarah's reflection. They exhaled in delight as they beheld the stunning bride before them. All at once, as if on cue, Mrs. Stuart, Rebecca, and Bessie placed their hands over their mouths and shed joyful tears. Sarah radiantly smiled and turned from the mirror to face her new family. She hugged each woman individually.

Mrs. Stuart lovingly chided the others in an attempt to gain self-control. "No! No! Don't get tears on your silk dresses. It will stain them. Oh my, oh my!" she stated as she reached for her lace handkerchief and blotted the corners of her eyes. "Whatever have I done to deserve two such special daughters? I thank the good Lord!"

They all embraced again and laughed joyously. Bessie put the finishing touches on Sarah's upswept chignon, then said, "Miss Sarah, Mr. Samuel will be mighty surprised when your hair comes down so fast." They had planned her hairstyle to be held up by only one pin. They smiled at each other with the joy of the surprise awaiting her soon-to-be husband. "He won't have to get distracted tonight by removing so many hairpins." They all giggled.

During their movements, the feminine sounds of rustling silks and satins whispered in their ears. Sarah was especially aware of them. She was memorizing every detail about her long-awaited wedding day.

I only wish my family could be here too.

She felt like a resplendent princess in her beautiful bridal attire. The Stuarts had spared no expense for the wedding of their only son and had encouraged Sarah to select the gown of her dreams. So she happily and gratefully complied. Honoring her in-laws, she included the opinions of Mrs. Stuart and Rebecca as she chose her bridal gown. Sarah hoped all her requirements to meet in the future could be such a natural blessing. Her gown would be the talk of the decade, and many imitations would appear in one form or another for years to come. The bridal dress felt perfect in white lace, seed pearls, satin, and silk. It was fitted at the waist, scalloped at the collarbone, and had puffed sleeves that pulled tight at the elbow to the wrist and tapered to the hands in a point. The full skirt swayed and swished just like every little girl dreamed of having for her bridal gown. Her train was a white royal robe, spreading nobility and distinction within its reach as she walked. Her veil was nearly as long as her train, and it required several attendants' assistance in getting her prepared to begin her wedding procession. The ladies could easily see Sarah's face through the thin lace veil. Her glowing, colorful pinched cheeks were noticeable. Thanks to Mrs. Stuart, they hadn't become blotchy.

Suddenly remembering their first meeting, Sarah said to Rebecca, "When you introduced yourself to me that first day in the carriage, I wished that I had four names like you. Well, now I shall have my four names—Sarah Louise Gordon Stuart!"

Rebecca smiled and teased her a little bit as she adjusted her veil. "Yes! How nice for you. However, when I marry, I will have *five* names. There won't be any way for you to catch up with me then."

"Well ... then you simply can never marry." They laughed and hugged and enjoyed their sisterly bond so very much.

"Are you ready, my dears?" Mrs. Stuart inquired.

As they descended the staircase, it was the last time Miss Sarah Louise Gordon would make her entrance. From now on she would be Mrs. Samuel Benjamin Stuart.

Sarah slowly approached the sunny lawn where she had chosen to be married. She had carefully walked the area a few weeks ago to make sure this was the very spot where she had last seen her brother and his family before her time travel. Somehow by being married in this location, she felt a connection with her family, whom she had left behind in the future. A tear escaped her eye as she thought of them.

I am getting married, Colin and Tess and Ann, Shelby, and Scottie! I miss you all so much, and I wish you were here.

The area looked beautiful now with flowers and arch, a wedding canopy, and a white linen bridal carpet. Hundreds of wedding guests obscured the view of the lawn. The weather was perfect, exactly what Sarah had desired—cool and sunny with a light breeze and thankfully low humidity.

Mr. Stuart approached Sarah with the dignity bred into him through generations of Stuarts. He looked like Sean Connery in his full Scottish regalia. He smiled lovingly at her and patted her gloved hand, placed gently in the crook of his arm. She looked up with a tender expression, gratefully thanking her nearly new father-in-law. They had a rapport that needed no words. They took their positions and waited.

Sarah looked up at the magnificent sky and thought, *I hope Father and Mother are looking down from heaven at my happiness.*

The arrival of an unexpected wedding party attendant interrupted the moment. The beautiful, beaming Joanne Stuart joined them, escorted by her nanny. The crowd murmured since no one could discern her retardation at this moment. Few people had actually seen Joanne before, and they were all amazed at her appearance. She looked like a young woman in love with bright eyes and a gentle smile. She was dressed exactly like her sister, Rebecca, in pale lavender and cream lace, satin, and silk with matching hats and formal gloves. Beautiful miniature white rosebuds adorned their curled hair. Their gowns were of a similar design as the bride's, much less majestic yet quite impressive. They each carried an elegant arrangement of colorful roses in a teardrop shape, mixed with baby's breath and green leaves, and trailing purple and white satin ribbons. The bridal bouquet cascaded with white roses and a few purple thistles for accent color.

Joanne's nanny stood aside as she handed her over to her sister. Rebecca held her sister's hand, and they situated themselves to walk down the aisle together.

Pauline Hendricks, their dear family friend and neighbor, was seated near them. Rebecca said to her in a hushed tone, "I am so thrilled to have this sweet moment with our cherished Joanne." She nodded her loving approval and smiled as she gazed at these precious sisters, whom she loved as if they were her own daughters.

Suddenly, glorious bagpipe music from the Highland Regiment struck up and filled the air for the wedding procession to begin. The pipes and drums played most beautifully for this blessed moment, and Sarah briefly recalled the life-changing DVD she had seen not too long ago, back in the future, of these pipers and drummers. She marveled that here she was, living in this era, about to be married to a Confederate general, and the bagpipe band was playing in person for her wedding.

Rebecca, the maid of honor, cried and smiled as she walked down the aisle with Joanne. Sarah could tell from the distance that Rebecca was overwhelmed with love for her sister. Joanne behaved unexpectedly well and smiled, as if enjoying herself very much indeed.

I am so thankful that God has granted grace to Joanne to be part of our wedding.

Sarah gasped as she saw her groom at the altar in his full Scottish regalia. He was wearing a kilt of the Royal Stuart tartan. Its predominantly red plaid consisted of navy, yellow, and white weave, which boldly and proudly stated his royal ancestry. His navy Prince Charlie jacket set off the sterling clan crest badge pinned on his fly plaid at his shoulder. Samuel's balmoral cap had a single feather. A tasseled dress sword hung from his left side, while his great-grandfather's leather sporran hung from his waist in the front. His jeweled sgian-dubh (skeen doo) knife was positioned in his knee-high hose, held up by his flashes garter; his highly polished black leather gilly brogues on his feet completed his outfit.

And this impressive man is about to become my husband! She never took her eyes off Samuel.

Her father-in-law escorted her toward her groom to the tempo of the bagpipes and drums playing her current favorite pipe tune, "Bonnie Blue Flag." Sarah's choice honored her new family and new life in the Confederacy. The "Bonnie Blue Flag" was the Confederates' tune with lyrics written by Ulster-Scot Harry McCarthy in 1861. It was about the Southern rights they all believed in and had fought for unto victory. It was a perfect choice. Showing their approval, the guests stood, smiled, and clapped as their new national anthem played for the couple's wedding processional. As she approached her groom, Sarah thought, *I know I was destined to be the wife of this valiant man.*

Samuel held out his hand to his stunning bride, and his father placed Sarah's hand into his son's. God's hands were holding them both as their marriage covenant began.

The minister wore his long, black robe and stole. He read the traditional wedding vows, and the bride and groom repeated their parts while standing under the flower- and ivy-adorned arch.

Sarah handed her wedding bouquet to Rebecca; then she grasped Samuel's proffered hands.

"I, Samuel, take thee, Sarah, as my lawful wedded wife; to have and to hold, from this day forward, for better for worse, for richer, for poorer, in sickness and in health, forsaking all others, as long as we both shall live." Samuel placed the wedding ring on his beloved's finger as he pledged his troth.

Sarah repeated her vows in a clear voice. "I, Sarah, take thee, Samuel, as my lawful wedded husband; to have and to hold, from this day forward, for better, for worse, for richer, for poorer, in sickness and in health, forsaking all others, as long as we both shall live." She slid his gold wedding band on his ring finger and spoke her pledge of love and commitment.

His hands are so strong but so gentle.

The minister smiled and said to Samuel, "You may kiss your bride."

Sarah held her breath as Samuel slowly and intimately lifted her veil to reveal her face. He placed it ever so gently behind her head and took a moment to look at her. Sarah's stomach lurched as she anticipated his lips on hers for the first time as man and wife.

Why are you taking so long? Kiss me already!

Finally, after what seemed like minutes but was in reality only seconds, Sarah's new husband touched her cheek with his index finger and moved it gently down to her chin.

I think I am going to die of joy. I can't breathe.

Sarah held Samuel's penetrating gaze and watched him slowly tilt his head slightly to the right and move toward her in painfully slow motion.

I am your wife, my darling! Please claim me now!

The moment of the couple's wedding kiss could have been recorded in history as the most reverent and cherished kiss of all time. The audience chuckled their approval and applauded.

Sarah could smell the faint aroma of her husband's spicy Italian cologne. She didn't even know that her eyes had shut during the kiss until she reopened them to see her beloved husband's face so close to hers. Reluctantly, their lips parted to conclude the wedding ceremony.

Whew! Wow! I want more kisses like that!

Samuel held Sarah's hand as they turned toward their family and friends.

Rebecca handed the wedding bouquet back to Sarah.

In his deep baritone voice, the minister announced, "May I introduce to you for the first time General and Mrs. Samuel Benjamin Stuart." People were on their feet with cheers and whistles of celebration and spirited applause. Smiles, hugs, and good wishes filled the air.

Almost as thickly as the colorful confetti at a Macy's Thanksgiving Day parade.

The progression of the receiving line took some time to dwindle. Then everyone enjoyed the chamber music and dance floor for several waltzes and the Scottish country dances. The weather was a gift from God; not a drop of rain came this day, and a steady, gentle breeze caressed them all.

As they waltzed, Sarah said, "Samuel, the only way I could be happier is if my parents, Colin, Tess, and the children and Lexi could have been here with us."

Samuel said, "Take comfort that they live in your heart, my dear, in the love you all share. Nothing can stop love … not even time travel or death."

Sarah nodded in agreement and felt consoled by his confidence in what she felt too. She squeezed his hand in a thankful gesture and smiled.

Celebration and social duty concluded, the bridal couple proceeded to their waiting bridal carriage. It was decked out with white bows, lace, flowers, and streaming white satin ribbons. The couple waved goodbye to everyone as the horses slowly trotted out of the wedding reception area.

This was the making of a fairy tale, riding off alone into the sunset in a horse-drawn carriage on her wedding day, just like Princess Diana.

The couple enjoyed a meandering scenic ride around their plantation. The reds, golds, and burnt-orange colors of the autumn leaves were at full peak as if in celebration too. The lake waters sparkled in the late afternoon sun and hosted a family of swans leaving ripples behind them as they glided across the expanse. Five little cygnets followed closely behind.

Sarah decided then and there to name it Swan Lake. She could hear her favorite classical cello solo piece, "The Swan," in her mind as they rode near the lake. Everything was perfect. Now that she was relaxing, she realized that her cheeks hurt from smiling for so many hours. They murmured together about the details of the wedding and just enjoyed each other's company.

After this interlude of transition, Samuel and Sarah slipped away into the vacant manor house from the rear entrance. The family and house servants had decided to visit nearby cousins and friends for a few days so the honeymoon couple could have their start alone.

The only house servants on the premises were Bessie, James, and the cook. They stayed well apart in the servants' quarters to await being summoned by their master and mistress. Sarah had told them yesterday not to expect to be called on very often, though. Sarah had seen the three of them smile and respectfully bow their heads when they reacted to her statement.

Sarah remembered thinking, *Oops, maybe that was too direct for these folks. I have to learn to be more discreet in what I say in this time period so I don't embarrass people. I am so glad that Joanne and Nanny's quarters are far enough away to ensure our honeymoon privacy, but I won't say that out loud.*

The newly married couple stood silently before Samuel's master chamber entrance. Sarah had waited impatiently for this particular moment. She turned to her new husband and said, "I have never seen the inside of your apartment. I am thrilled that my first encounter of it is as your wife."

Swiftly, Samuel scooped up his laughing bride and carried her over the threshold. The large room was very much like Samuel's study, and Sarah instantly liked the ambiance. The small crackling fire gave off a warm orange glow, just right for cozy effect and slight warmth. Sarah closed her eyes for a moment to inhale the masculine fragrances of burning wood and leather.

Samuel placed his beautiful bride back on her feet and closed and locked the door. He lovingly looked down at her and gently took her hand. He said in a deep voice, "Sarah, my precious wife, let us dedicate our lives and our love officially at this moment to our Lord Jesus and to God's service for all of our days."

"I like that idea very much."

Kneeling down to pray side by side and hand in hand, Sarah's wedding gown fluffed all around her. Samuel prayed, "Dear Lord, we come before you boldly because we can, as Your servants. We ask that You will bless our union, make us fruitful, and use us as Your instruments for Your service all the days of our lives."

Sarah interjected, "Yes, Jehovah God. I thank You for the blessing of such an excellent man to be my husband. I pray that I will always purpose to be a Proverbs 31 wife."

Together they said, "In the name of our Lord and Savior, Jesus Christ. Amen."

Then they rose together.

Samuel and Sarah stood quietly facing one another. For a moment, they just enjoyed the silence. After all the splendid noise of their wedding celebration during the afternoon, the quiet was welcomed and helped them to relax. Sarah felt shy but not afraid of this admirable man she had come to love with all her heart. She thought of how unique and special the Lord's plan, described in Genesis 2:24, was for marriage, when a husband and wife "shall be one flesh." However, since surely nothing else could be remotely like it, Sarah had no idea what to expect. She did feel a little nervous, and apparently this anxiety showed on her face and in her demeanor.

"Sarah, look at me please," Samuel requested softly as he gently raised her chin. She hadn't even realized that she had been staring at the floor. She looked up at him and felt her heart pound and her breath catch. He was looking at her in a way he had reserved for this very moment, in a way that was private and dedicated to her alone. She felt instantly united in spirit to her new husband during that intimate gaze and was prepared to be his wife in all ways.

Samuel placed his warm, strong hands gently on her shoulders and said tenderly, "I love you, Mrs. Stuart, my wife, my beloved. Shall I summon Bessie to assist you in changing?"

Thankful for his thoughtfulness, Sarah said, "Yes, please." Samuel smiled and then disappeared out their chamber door.

Bessie came to her mistress and quietly began to unbutton the many pearl buttons of Sarah's wedding gown. She worked in silence and allowed Sarah time to gather her thoughts. They exchanged smiles a few times, then Bessie went to hang up the wedding dress. While she was gone, Sarah freshened herself with the water and scented soap in the washstand. She was just finished drying herself off when Bessie returned with the beautiful wedding night dressing gown she had helped to sew. It was soft linen with many pleats, European lace, and satin ribbons. Bessie slipped it over Sarah's head, and they both were pleased with the results. Sarah looked gorgeous.

Bessie squeezed her mistress's hands and quietly said with a smile, "Trust in the Lord." Then she silently slipped from the room.

Sarah stared at her reflection in the full-length mirror. She thought about Bessie's statement to trust in the Lord. Sarah nodded to herself in the mirror and said aloud, "Yes, trusting in the Lord Jesus is how I live my life, and here I am, trusting Him on my wedding night. Thank You, dear Jesus!"

A few minutes later Samuel entered their chamber and paused as he looked at his beautiful wife. "You take my breath away."

He walked over to her and put his hand out, much like he had when he asked her to dance. Sarah placed her hand on his, and Samuel led her toward their marriage bed. The entire room had the heady aroma of gardenia. Petals were scattered on the floor, creating a path to their precious world, about to be discovered as man and wife. As Samuel lowered his head to kiss his bride, she raised her mouth and closed her eyes. With the placing of their wedding bands on their fingers and by the covenant they two had made together with God, there was no longer any need for restraint. Their kiss deepened in blissful delight until Sarah felt she could remain standing no more. Their journey together as husband and wife began.

Sometime later, with marital bliss spent, they lay lost in private thoughts. They looked at each other, smiled widely, and then laughed with the delight both were feeling for the first time. Sarah exclaimed, "I am so blessed to be your wife!" And she snuggled closer.

Samuel traced the outline of her jaw, then caressed her full lips with the tip of his finger. He whispered, "You are my beautiful dove!" They fell asleep in each other's arms, the happiest either of them had ever been in their entire lives. They relished tender moments, cherished each other, and loved as God designed with respect and awe.

The candlelight now flickered and cast light and shadow on them. Sarah said, "I have always dreamed of my knight in shining armor being strong and courageous and of noble character—one who would take care of me, protect me, and provide for me until his dying breath."

"And you had to settle for me instead poor, dear lady," said an amused Samuel as he moved Sarah's hair off her face.

Sarah poked him in the arm and said, "You, my dear Samuel, are far better than even my wildest imagination. You are everything I just said and so much more. It is a delightful feeling to know that you love me and have pledged yourself to me alone for all your life. It is the most secure feeling to know that I'll always have you by my side, for better or worse, and that you'll take care of me and provide for me. I trust you, Samuel, to lead us in God's path always."

With evening upon them, the candles and the fire had burned low. Samuel wrapped into his robe, lit the oil lamp, and placed another log on the fire. As he stirred the coals with an iron poker, Sarah admired his muscular form. Everything about him permeated her senses.

Samuel entered into a connecting room and returned quickly with the refreshment tray he had ordered earlier in the day. A tempting bridal repast awaited the hungry bride and groom. Displayed on a large sterling silver tray were colorful fruits, cheeses, bread, butter, jam, pastries, and her favorite, buttered popcorn. Accompanying this small feast was cool, fresh spring water and some sweet tea in crystal glasses.

Sarah said, "Oh, my darling! You think of everything. Thank you!"

The next morning, Sarah slowly came awake. As her eyes blinked open halfway, she was aware of the sunlight being much brighter than usual. In her groggy state, Sarah wondered why Bessie had let her sleep so long. Then she thought, startled, *I'm married!* Her eyes were wide open now, and she was very much awake.

She didn't move a muscle but instead lay quietly for a few moments, listening to her new husband's deep breathing. She could tell he was still sound asleep, so she carefully turned over to see him. Sarah admired her husband's firm chin and his rugged but gentlemanly looks. His hair was a mess, and she grinned. *I think I did that.* She took a deep breath and remembered the incredible evening they had enjoyed last night when they began their marriage.

Sarah tried to slip out of the sheets without waking her beloved to use her chamber pot. She stood, slightly light headed and wobbly at first. Sarah rejoiced that she was a thoroughly loved new wife. She went to her new dressing room, used her chamber pot, washed her mouth out with crushed mint water to freshen her breath, and then slipped back into bed. Rejoining him in the cozy sheets, Sarah saw Samuel's eyes open. He smiled broadly, put his arms around his sweet wife, and pulled her into a loving embrace. Samuel buried his face in her cascading hair. He said into her hair to mask his morning breath, "Good morning, Mrs. Stuart. How did you sleep?"

She hugged him back, snuggled even closer, and replied, "Very well, sir, I thank you." Giggling shyly, she added, "And I was quite happy before I went to sleep too."

Samuel smiled, saying, "What an incredible night we had!" He felt her cheek and neck, then commented, "You are so soft." He kissed her forehead and reluctantly rose to visit his chamber pot in his separate dressing room; then he freshened his breath. He raked his hands through his hair in an attempt to tame it.

As he returned to bed, Sarah suddenly remembered, "Oh, I have a wedding gift for you, sweetheart."

Samuel replied, "What more could you possibly give to me?" He smiled the most dazzling smile she had ever seen, a smile of total contentment, adoration, and esteem.

Crossing the room with her white robe trailing, she retrieved a small wrapped gift from the dresser drawer.

Samuel said, "I like watching your every move. Do you realize that your long hair is in total disarray? I like the look on you."

Sarah flipped her hair behind her shoulders and commented, "You should see *your* hair too. Now, here, my love." She presented the gift to him.

He said, "I didn't notice that in my drawer earlier."

Grinning at her husband, Sarah said, "It wasn't there when you were dressing for our wedding. I asked your valet to put it in here after you left for our ceremony. Go on, open it, please." She sat on the bed on her knees, bouncing slightly like an excited young girl.

Samuel propped himself up on one elbow and slipped the gift wrapping off. He looked at her questioningly and raised his eyebrows.

"This is my most favorite chocolate candy bar in the whole world. It was in my knapsack. I always carry some. You never know when the craving will strike, to be sure. Here, open it up and try some, my darling."

But she didn't wait. Sarah tore open the top half of a large Hershey bar, broke off a section, and popped it into Samuel's mouth. He raised his eyebrows in surprise, and his eyes widened as he chewed. The delighted groom rolled the melting chocolate all over his tongue. He said, "Most delicious! Here, I shall share some with you." The taste of chocolate still in his mouth, he kissed her and said, "Absolutely delicious … and so is the chocolate!" They licked their lips and laughed and loved.

No one saw them for days except for necessary servants when summoned; their marital bliss was fully realized, cherished, respected, and remembered during their long life's journey together.

Chapter 31

Sarah entered the music room and picked up her violin. She tuned up, as usual, then began playing a tune she had floating around in her mind. It was a lovely sound full of happiness. She decided to write it down and save the composition before it left her. She decided to call it "New Life" in honor of her marriage. She couldn't wait to play it for Samuel.

The reality of life finally beckoned them at the end of their honeymoon. A lingering parting kiss kept Samuel's lips and memory vivid as he rode away on horseback to Atlanta.

As he left, he told Sarah, "I know that I am the most blessed of men. I give thanks to God over and over for you, my beautiful new wife." Her last parting vision was of her beloved waving goodbye as he rode off to duty. Waving goodbye became their family tradition.

Sarah began the tasks of being the lady of the house. She was most respectful and kind to her mother-in-law and made sure she had as much of the planning to do as she wanted.

Sarah loved the fact that families lived together in this time period. This created such a unity of family spirit and offered respect for everyone's privacy. *Mrs. Stuart has taught me so many things about running the estate. What a compliment she gave to me to say that I am a quick study and that her son made a very wise choice in marrying me.*

A few mornings after their parting, Sarah was in the music room, playing a beautiful Scottish slow air, "Shingly Beach," on her fiddle. Her heart longed for her absent husband, and she expressed her yearning through her violin strings and style of playing. At the end of the tune, Sarah opened her eyes and realized Bessie was standing there with a note in her hand.

"Oh, Mrs. Stuart, your playing is so beautiful it brings tears to my eyes. I didn't want to interrupt you. Here is a message for you that just arrived."

Instinctively, Sarah knew the note was from her beloved, and she rushed to open it. Reading his now-familiar handwriting, Sarah grinned.

Samuel requested her presence at his Atlanta office on the following day at four o'clock in the afternoon for the meeting they had previously discussed and planned. He said for her to pack for an overnight stay.

"Bessie, I need you to help me bathe and wash my hair so I will be fresh and ready to go in the morning. You'll need to pack for both of us too."

"How exciting, ma'am! I will enjoy seeing my friends there too."

"Yes, I am sure that you will."

The next day Sarah entered the capitol building in Atlanta with courage and confidence in each step. The entrance hall felt cool from the brick and stone construction. She was excited to see the incredible General Jackson, General Lee, and President Davis again, but mostly she felt thrilled to see her beloved husband. Bessie did her best with Sarah's hair, and she felt quite presentable and ready.

When Samuel sent word for her to join him, he indicated it was time to discuss the facts of the future with these particular leaders. Sarah knew this moment was the time God wanted her to share her knowledge of the future with these intrepid men. During her husband's absence, which had felt more like two weeks than just a few days, Sarah had prayed diligently in anticipation.

Escorted by the butler, she approached the president's office door and unnecessarily dusted the front of her burgundy brushed cotton skirt. She pulled down on the edges of her matching waist-fitted jacket, adjusted her hat, pulled her gloves to a tighter fit, and took a deep breath. She was anxious to look her best. Sarah nodded; then the two armed guards standing on either side of the presidential office opened the doors.

"Madam Stuart," the butler announced. Sarah quickly surveyed the room upon her entrance. The mahogany-paneled walls glowed with the light of the brass lamps affixed every few feet in between high leaded-glass windows. Two large fireplaces burned brightly on the side walls, and in the center of the room was President Davis's stately desk. To one side was a long cherry wooden table, polished to a mirror image. Every inch of wood in this grand room was highly polished and dust free.

In front of the desk were four large leather chairs, obviously well used during meetings. The men had been standing, immersed in working on the structure of the government of the new Confederate States of America. As Sarah entered, they looked up and came to attention, then bowed as Sarah curtsied.

Samuel smiled and took full strides toward his wife. He greeted her with a longer kiss than was politely expected in public society. The other men chuckled at this young, enthusiastic groom. Slightly embarrassed at his display of affection, he stepped away from his wife but held her gloved hand and cleared his throat. Sarah enjoyed the delight her husband expressed upon seeing her. It matched her own. She smiled lovingly at Samuel and thought again of how amazed she was that this excellent man was now her husband.

She turned and greeted President Davis with a deep curtsy, then General Lee and General Jackson individually to show her respect and admiration.

To General Jackson, Sarah said with a twinkle in her eye, "Sir, I imagine you thought me quite strange when I first bumped into you so abruptly at the manor and babbled about how authentic you and your clothing looked."

General Jackson held Sarah's gloved hand and bowed over it for a long moment. Straight and tall once again, General Jackson said, "Mrs. Stuart, I had the great pleasure and honor to be the first person you saw upon your arrival. I shall always be thankful for that privilege. Knowing that God sent you here to assist us to win the War of Northern Aggression puts me forever in your debt," he said genuinely, and he bowed deeply once again. The other gentlemen added their words of agreement.

"It is I who feel blessed to have been the one chosen for this miraculous mission," Sarah replied sincerely.

President Davis said, "Mrs. Stuart, would you care for refreshment?" He indicated the sideboard display of hot tea and cakes. Sarah noted the elegant silver tea service and recalled the one her grandmother had given to her that looked very similar.

Removing her soft leather gloves, Sarah said, "Yes, thank you, sir."

She sat at the indicated place for her, and a servant appeared quickly and began to serve the refreshments—the lady first, of course.

As all the gentlemen sat down, Sarah removed her feathered hat. She wore this hat, in particular, to honor her beloved husband since he had recently given it to her. In fact, she created her entire outfit based on the rich dark maroon of the hat. Placing it next to her on the table, with her husband on her other side, Sarah opened her matching drawstring purse. She removed a piece of vellum, unfolded it, and cleared her throat. She took a few sips of tea, and then after the servant left the room, Sarah addressed the gentlemen.

"With your permission, I would like to share with you the condition of the future when I left it. I hope that you can and will make decisions now to prevent the corruptness and disobedience to God that prevailed in 2018 when I left it." She looked meaningfully at her captive audience and saw she had their full attention. "I come to share these facts and opinions with you only after much prayer. I feel that God wants me to tell you the things I am about to reveal so that you can implement wording in the Confederate States of America Constitution to prevent the horrible moral decline and disrespect in society and politics I saw before I left in 2018. Samuel and I have fully discussed these points at home. May I suggest that you take notes, for what I am about to tell you will need some study." Quill pens and full inkwells were already on the table, along with the necessary paper.

Samuel affirmed with a nod. "This has been a matter of great concern to Sarah. We have both prayed diligently about her revelation to you and feel it is the right thing to do."

General Lee said, "Whatever it may be, you have my word as an officer in the Confederate States of America and as a Southern gentleman to do my utmost to have God obeyed now and in the future."

All of the men said, "Amen."

President Davis looked directly at Sarah, nodded, and said, "Mrs. Stuart, please proceed."

Sarah took a deep breath and looked at her list. "I hardly know where to begin. I mean, I don't know in what order of priority you would consider this information, so I'll just begin and leave it in your capable hands to discern." She went on, "There are many good things about the future. We have the highest quality of medical care ever, with many lives saved. Most people in America have countless luxuries. There is considerable freedom, compared to other countries. However, the amendment about having church and state being separate is greatly distorted. Laws made by the federal government directly disobey God's Word. By leaving God out of politics, the government passes many laws in direct conflict with God's laws."

The men began murmuring between themselves and wrote more notes. Sarah went into detail about the widespread immorality, loss of integrity, disrespect, political manipulation, rejection of decency, and some specific laws passed as legal in the US government that were in direct violation of God's Word. As Sarah elaborated each point, these formidable men appeared greatly distressed.

Flushed and with a passionate voice, she finished, "Gentlemen, I implore you to create the Confederate States of America Constitution in such a way as to never allow these evils to prevail in the lives of the Confederates. With noble integrity, perhaps the Confederates can be a good witness and influence the United States of America. As time goes on, they will see how well the Confederate States of America thrives with God's hand on them because of their obedience to Him. I hope and pray both nations will love and serve God."

With a stress-relieving sigh, Sarah slowly folded her vellum, replaced it into her purse, and quickly pulled its strings taut as if capturing the evil inside. She rested her hands on her lap and waited. She heard only the ticking of the pendulum clock and the scribbling of the scraping pens on papers as the minutes passed.

"May I interrupt you, please?" Sarah inquired. She had thought of something important.

The men all stopped writing and looked at her immediately.

"A man named John Wilkes Booth was a Confederate spy," Sarah stated directly.

General Lee said, "I know of the man."

"Well, what you don't know is that on April 14, 1865, Booth assassinated President Lincoln at Ford Theater in Washington, DC, while the president was watching a play. With history altering now, most likely this man will not attempt to assassinate President Lincoln, but please make sure he cannot do this. It is the only right thing to do to save Mr. Lincoln's life."

President Davis glanced at General Lee and said with confidence to Sarah, "We will see to your request. Mr. Booth will be stopped."

"Thank you, sir," Sarah replied with relief.

The men went back to writing. So focused they were that no one commented on the chiming of the clock every quarter hour. Sarah hadn't been dismissed, so she stayed in case they had more questions for her, which they did.

Sipping her fourth cup of tea, Sarah said, "Please excuse me, gentlemen." She needed a place to refresh herself, and she was sure Bessie could direct her. All the men stood instantly as gentlemen always do for a lady when she gets up.

With serious faces, they nodded at her. Sarah told them she would be in the antechamber until they called on her for anything else they may need to discuss with her. She curtsied in response to their bows and then exited quietly. These men had much to talk over in private.

Sarah found Bessie waiting for her. "Bessie, I am sure that you can guess what I need to do." They chuckled and went about their business, then sat in the hall to wait.

Sarah awoke with a start when her husband gently touched her arm. She didn't realize she had fallen asleep in a comfortable chair near the warm fireplace in the hall while waiting to be summoned.

Bessie sat quietly in the corner, watching her mistress. She may have dozed a bit too. It was obviously hours later because the evening was upon them, casting shadows where brightness had been earlier. Sarah had no idea how long she had slept, but she felt rested.

Samuel said, "Darling, please join us again, will you?" He smiled his charming smile, and she quickly arose. He gently held her hand as he escorted her into the office.

More candles and lanterns gave brilliance to the room, and Sarah noticed many more writings scattered on the long table. President Davis began, "Mrs. Stuart, you have given to us more information than we can process at this time because much of what you said has created many questions for us. For example, you referred to the fifty states. Just before the War of Northern Aggression, there were thirty-four states, eleven of which seceded for our cause of states' rights." He paused.

"We have all agreed, however, to stay on task and not get distracted by our plethora of questions. We have no right to know about the future in detail. Our purpose now is to create the Confederate States of America constitution in such a way that our nation will always honor God. Please pray for us as we embark on this enormous task and know full well that we shall with confidence do as you have asked of us. We shall base our constitution on God's holy Word, from the King James Bible and the Geneva Bible. As we all know, God's Word will not return void. God charges us never to change His Word. We are on the right path." He smiled broadly, then continued.

"Allow me to introduce to you my first three cabinet members: my secretary of state, Robert E. Lee; my secretary of war, Thomas Jackson; and my secretary of the treasury, Samuel Stuart." She smiled and curtsied deeply in respect for each man.

She said, "I am thrilled that you shall use the Bible as the format for the constitution. It has every answer for every situation. There could not be a better constitution than one with direct quotes of God's Holy Word Remember King Solomon's words in Ecclesiastes 12:13: 'Let us hear the conclusion of the whole matter: Fear God, and keep His commandments; for this is the whole duty of man.' May I be so bold as to suggest that you consider abolishing slavery in the way Mr. Stuart Sr. has done by instantly making his slaves indentured servants upon purchase? Only now it could be considered payment for their passage instead of a purchase. All other indentured servants come and serve for seven years for their passage. A plan such as this could give the plantation owners and the servants seven years to adapt to our new era and for our economy to adjust. Godspeed, gentlemen."

She curtsied once again as the president and the new cabinet members bowed. Sarah felt the enormity and significance of this moment and relived it many times in her memories.

Her husband escorted her out of the room, kissed her briefly on her cheek, and left her in the care of Bessie. "I do not know how long I will be tonight, my dear wife. Please settle into our accommodations here in our private chamber. Bessie may enjoy the company of her friends belowstairs after she sees to your needs. Please do not wait up for me. I will join you when I can." He kissed her again and went back to the official meeting; the door closed quietly behind him with the click of the latch. The guards had changed, and the new ones remained at attention.

Much later, Sarah woke up a little as Samuel slipped into bed next to her. She stirred slightly, put her hand on his chest, and whispered, "Good night, secretary of the treasury of the Confederate States of America. I love you."

He kissed her briefly and replied, "I love you, Mrs. Stuart, my dear heart."

Exhausted from the day, they both slept deeply and peacefully.

Chapter 32

The unexpected package was delivered earlier in the day while retired US Army colonel Joseph Scott Jenkins, now gentleman farmer in Philadelphia, Pennsylvania, was outside, overseeing the work in his fields. He worked hard, right along with his people.

Joseph came into the empty house to wash up. Drying his hands on the linen tea towel, he noticed the parcel lying on the kitchen table. He was surprised to see it was from Mr. Samuel Stuart, secretary of the treasury of the Confederate States of America. It had been two years since the war ended, and they hadn't communicated since then. Curious to discover what lay beneath the hemp and brown wrapper, Joseph sat down at the head of the well-worn kitchen table. The wooden chair joints creaked with his weight.

As he opened the package, he found a personal letter from Samuel Stuart and another wrapped parcel. Looking at the letter first, he felt confounded by what he read. With raised eyebrows and a frown, he thought for a few minutes and contemplated the extraordinary contents. Joseph Jenkins was thankful for the unusual silence of the empty house. His family was off to town so he could try, without interruption, to grasp the message imparted to him.

He placed the letter on the table and picked up the wrapped parcel from inside the box. In neatly written handwriting, the owner's name and instructions were explicit. "Deliver to Lexi Carolyn Jenkins, address included on the back. Open on the morning of Thanksgiving Day in the year of our Lord 2017."

Joseph Jenkins stared at the parcel, then got up and took the package and the letter to his office to read again. Samuel Stuart wrote,

> Dear Joseph,
>
> It is with great pleasure that I recall our time together in my study. I trust our Lord has blessed you and yours

greatly these past two years. I have a rather unusual request for you and your family. It is one you will have to undertake with great faith. My lady wife, Sarah, whom you will recall was the one to find you in our woods, is the one who requires your assistance. Her request is as follows: The enclosed parcel is to be handed down throughout the generations of the Jenkins family, unopened, until Thanksgiving Day, in the year of our Lord 2017. It is then to be given to Miss Lexi Carolyn Jenkins of 555 Skukyll River Road, Apartment 10A, Philadelphia, Pennsylvania 19999 USA, by 9:00 a.m.

I understand completely how inexplicable this request seems to be. However, I can only emphasize that the timely delivery of this mysterious parcel is a matter of life or death. My lady wife and I ask this of you, Joseph, knowing full well that we can and do trust you to carry out these instructions exactly. Please see that all your descendants honor your step of faith in complying with this request and deliver the package as instructed. Thank you for your honor and faithfulness. I remain your brother in the Lord Jesus Christ,

Samuel Stuart.

Joseph Jenkins pondered this implausible request. He considered the fact that on October 3, 1863, President Abraham Lincoln had proclaimed a National Day of Thanksgiving in honor of God to be celebrated on the last Thursday in November each year. President Jefferson Davis had joined in support of this proclamation, which unified the North and South for the first time after the war. It was a good-faith measure on both sides. Healing began.

He wondered how this relatively new national holiday of Thanksgiving related to the package delivery in the future year of 2017. It made no sense. He would have dismissed it had the request come from a lesser man. Joseph knew Samuel Stuart to be a man of good character and integrity, and his wife in essence had saved his life.

Just then, his thoughts were interrupted, and he instantly smiled when he heard his beloved family burst through the door. Their pleasant, youthful voices were heartwarming and always brought delight to him. As he rose to greet his loved ones, he knew in his heart what he would do with this strange request from the Stuarts. He would pledge his commitment to fulfill it. He would charge his progeny to fulfill this responsibility with the honor, integrity, and excellence of the Jenkins family name.

CHAPTER 33

2017

Lexi Carolyn Jenkins sat alone in the living room of her fashionable Philadelphia apartment. She had turned on the *Macy's Thanksgiving Day Parade* but wasn't interested in it. Her interests in life were clouded with the burden of guilt. How could she have done it?

She felt the bleak emptiness, results of her gnawing sin. It had been an intense shock to see the name of her abortion doctor, Dr. Gosseck, in the laptop screen news article. After over forty years of slaughtering children in the womb, the evil man had finally been reported and arrested. Every time a news item spoke of him, it brought back Lexi's painful reality. Jailed for three life sentences without parole—at least that was some accountability. Lexi said aloud to herself, "The tormentor of my worst nightmare. I will never forget his face. How could I have allowed the abortion?"

Lexi had other personal issues as well, including deep depression at times. The doctor had prescribed medication for her depression, but she didn't think it helped and often didn't take it. Lexi reached the point of no return in her current thinking. She felt so depressed, but she didn't think of taking her medication. Instead, she thought of ending her life.

Filled with despair, she wanted to die. She felt that she didn't deserve to live. She began planning ways to take her own life. She could go to the train station and simply walk in front of an oncoming train, drop off a waterfall, or take an overdose of sleeping pills.

Fearful, her common sense held her back for the moment, but she was determined. Her inner battle revealed to her that she didn't have the strength to live or die, so she sat, staring blankly at the parade on the television, thinking that a person could take only so much. Why could all this inner pain never end?

She was so full of regret that she had allowed her tiny baby to be taken from her womb. Reliving the day, she recalled the attending nurse trying to comfort her as she lay on the cot, crying silently as she waited for the abortion doctor. The nurse told her that her little seven-week-old baby was just tissue and that there wasn't any reason to cry. She tried to believe her, but she didn't. Fear and helplessness gripped Lexi as she lay still on the operating table for the procedure. She went through with the abortion only because her sorry boyfriend, Alvin, wouldn't marry her and wanted her to get rid of the baby. What choice did she have? Today, the pain felt so acutely fresh because it was the dreaded anniversary month of her abortion. The guilt ate at her.

I could have said no. Why didn't I refuse? Oh, my poor little baby! I don't deserve to live.

The ringing doorbell startled Lexi out of her morbid thoughts. She looked unkempt and disheveled, but she didn't care. As she opened the door, she gripped her bathrobe more tightly around her. A cold wind swirled and brought dry, floating leaves into her apartment. A well-dressed, middle-aged man with an old-looking wrapped package stood on her doorstep.

The stranger took off his hat and said in a firm voice, "Are you Miss Lexi Carolyn Jenkins?" Another gust of cold wind assaulted them.

Wearily, she replied, "Yes, I am Lexi." Secretly, she wished she wasn't the woman he'd sought.

He thrust the package toward her, smiled broadly, and said, "This is for you, Miss Jenkins. It has come a long way to be delivered to you. I am most pleased to have the privilege to hand it to you personally."

Frowning, she silently took the package from him.

"I am your fourth cousin on your father's side. I know we have never met before, but we are related. My name is Jonathan Scott Jenkins. This package has been handed down through the generations of our family line since 1865. Our progenitor grandfather, Joseph Scott Jenkins, originated the command that this parcel be handed to you on Thanksgiving Day 2017 by nine a.m." He presented his digital watch to verify it was indeed nine o'clock exactly. Then he smiled triumphantly, relishing the honor to be the one in the family line to complete the command.

"Is this a joke?" Lexi asked. Not able to stay focused, she was distracted by his perfect white teeth when he grinned. Lexi thought they were probably dentures. No one that age could have such straight, pearly teeth.

"No, Miss Jenkins, this is not a joke. Far from it." He reached into his breast pocket, pulled out an envelope, and handed it to her. He explained, "This is the original copy of the command from our direct-line grandfather, Joseph Scott Jenkins, and a letter from a Samuel Stuart requesting our great-great-great-grandfather's compliance. As you will see, it says that it is a matter of life or death. Perhaps you will know what to do once you open the parcel. My card is also in the envelope. Please call me if I may be of any further assistance. We are, after all, distant cousins."

He offered a broader smile and a slight bow for emphasis. He stood straight, replaced his hat, then turned and walked away with a jaunt in his step.

Feeling bewildered at the mention of a life-or-death situation, Lexi only nodded mutely in reply. She watched this stranger, who claimed to be her distant cousin, walk down her sidewalk, get into his sporty blue Miata, and drive away. She glanced at his card and shot up an eyebrow, now entirely intrigued.

A lawyer?

As she closed and locked the door, she scraped her cold fingers through her loose, shoulder-length blond hair. She sat down and tucked one leg under her, as was her usual fashion. She read the letters first, then unwrapped the mysterious package. It felt like oilskin wrapping, and it had turned yellow with age. Inside was a beautiful brown leather Bible with her full name engraved on the front in gold lettering.

What in the world?

The first page revealed a message to her from her dearest friend in the world, Sarah. It read,

October 10th, 1865

Dearest Lexi,

> I know this will be hard for you to believe, but you must trust that what I am about to tell you is absolutely true. I have been your best friend for a long time. God

used me to go back in time for a mission to 1863. I
left home on the twenty-fourth of April 2018. Since I
haven't gone back in time yet, according to the date you
are reading this, we are best friends now. And no, this
isn't a joke. (I knew you'd ask that!) I know that you
are contemplating suicide, but you MUST NOT do it!

Lexi began to shudder. *How could Sarah know my suicidal thoughts? What does she mean that she went back in time? I just saw her the other day. What in the world is going on?*
She began reading again.

> Lexi, tell Jesus how sorry you are about the abortion and receive His forgiveness.

Lexi jerked as if a huge jolt of electricity had shocked her and threw the letter on the floor.
Sarah doesn't know about my abortion. What on earth?
She picked up the letter, then continued reading.

> Forgive yourself and others and go forward with your life, my dear friend. When you share your burdens with Jesus, He takes them from you. You don't have to carry them anymore, dear Lexi. Life will change, and you will have joy and purpose, I promise. I would have tried to get this message to you before you had to agree with your horrible boyfriend, Alvin, to have the abortion, but I didn't know what date it happened. You never told me. I wish I could have saved you that pain, dear heart, and helped you save your baby's life; but understand that God forgives you. He has a special plan for your baby in heaven, and you will see him. I say "him" because God revealed to me in my mind and spirit that your baby is a son, and his name is Maranatha. Isn't that way cool? He is alive in heaven, waiting to spend all eternity with

you when you get there. I speak the truth. But it will be God's timing when you go to heaven, not your own decision, my friend.

We all have regrets, dear Lexi, and we wish we could take back things we have said or done. It is vital that we forgive ourselves and move forward. Perhaps you could have a new ministry to help teenagers to choose to keep their babies or to give them up for adoption. That would be an amazing purpose for you.

I also have a special request for you. My parents will die in a car crash on December tenth, 2017. I appeal to you with all of my heart for you to prevent them from getting into any vehicle on that day. Thank you, my beloved friend. I know that you will do your best to save them and love them as a daughter after I am gone. Don't tell me anything about this because when you read this, I will not have traveled back in time yet. I can't know anything about it, so you are sworn to secrecy. You can keep a secret, I am confident. You always have.

I miss you all so very much, but I am happy. I am married to a wonderful Southern man named Samuel Stuart. He was a general in the War between the States. He is an amazing person, Lexi, and we are expecting a baby. Please be happy for me. Don't grieve for me when I am gone. We'll all be together again in heaven one day. I love you eternally! Your best friend forever,

Sarah

P.S. Are you impressed that I figured out who your great-great-great-grandfather was? I thought you might be. He is the one we briefly researched when we were looking for our ancestral roots … remember? Research him more, Lexi. He's a wonderful man. God used me to save his life during the war. True. And my husband had the pleasure of sharing Jesus with your grandfather, and he was saved right in my husband's study. We live in Stone Mountain, Georgia. Look us up in the history books. I know this all sounds impossible, but remember, with our God, *all* things are possible. Even time travel. He created time, for heaven's sakes, so of course He can use time for His glory and purpose. You have so much to live for, my dearest friend. See you in heaven one day. I love you forever! Your best friend, Sarah.

Lexi sat back, stunned, trying to take in her friend's words. So many thoughts flew through her mind, and she wasn't able to grasp any of them. How did Sarah know she was considering killing herself? *Sarah will travel back in time next year and marry and have a baby? Impossible! What does she mean that her parents died in a car crash on December 10th of this year? And ... is it true that Jesus could forgive me entirely and remove my burden of guilt?*

She reflected more on the past. Yes, pressured and forced by Alvin, he gave her no choice but to go through with the abortion. The lowlife even made her pay for it with her own money because he didn't have any.

I just felt that I couldn't be an unwed mother. Little did I know that the guilt of the abortion would far exceed the shame of being an unwed mother.

Questions kept flying through her mind. All thoughts of suicide left her, just as Sarah had planned.

Suddenly, with dedication of purpose, Lexi rose and rushed to the bathroom to shower and get ready. Her blood coursed swiftly through her as the adrenaline she'd experienced charged her energy level. It was difficult to believe that only a short time ago she had been a person ready and willing to die. Now she had purpose, and that purpose was to seek out Sarah and get to the bottom of this strange circumstance. It just had to be a joke. There was no way all this could be true.

She dressed in a lovely long-sleeved brown velour dress with matching suede boots. Her fair hair fluffed just below her shoulders from the blow-drying. She applied her usual minimal makeup and gold jewelry, and she wrapped her black woolen cape around her. As she stopped at the foyer mirror to position her matching hat and put on her black leather gloves, she paused to stare at her reflection.

Just a while ago, Lexi couldn't have imagined ever looking this good. She had washed away her depression with the hot shower and was feeling so much better. She decided to take her medication. Perhaps it helped, after all. She felt common sense restored to her. She placed her stylish hat on her head and grabbed the letters, Bible, and car keys, then headed out into the cold November day.

Lexi wrapped her warm cape tightly around her as she lowered herself into her forest-green Audi. As the engine roared into the cold wind, she shivered and prayed the heater would work quickly. The beige leather seats were very cold, even with the seat heater turned to the high position. Scarcely time to get warm, Lexi drove the short distance to Sarah's parents' house. She waited impatiently at the front door after knocking, and Sarah finally greeted her with delighted surprise.

"Lexi, I thought you weren't coming today."

"Well, I changed my mind. Okay?"

"Of course it is okay. Come in, come in! It is so wonderful to see you for Thanksgiving."

The pleasant aroma of a roasting turkey with cornbread stuffing, sage, onion, and bacon filled the air.

Sarah helped her friend remove her cape, hat, and gloves; and she hung them for her in the hall closet. Sarah admired Lexi's ensemble. "Wow! I haven't seen you look this good in weeks. You look beautiful!" Eyeing her friend suspiciously, Sarah asked, "Have you met somebody new?"

"Don't be ridiculous, Sarah. Can't I get dressed properly for Thanksgiving without causing speculation?" Lexi replied testily, wondering when Sarah would confess or inquire about her prank with the package delivery this morning.

Sarah smiled and said, "Yes, of course, you can. I know you are a private person, and I respect that about you. Come on in. Dad and Mom will be so pleased that you decided to join us after all."

Sarah's parents, Fred and Louise Gordon, greeted Lexi with their usual warm embrace and expressed their pleasure that she had come for the family Thanksgiving dinner. Louise promptly set another place setting at their holiday table in Lexi's usual spot next to Sarah.

"It just wouldn't have been the same without you this year, Lexi. You are part of the family, for sure, dear," said Louise sincerely, patting Lexi's hand. Fred agreed wholeheartedly and gave Lexi a fatherly hug. He smelled like Old Spice and wood smoke, and he wore his favorite forest-green cardigan sweater.

They all sat in the cozy den, enjoying the wood fire snapping and crackling as Fred kept feeding it logs. He loved a full, blazing fire. The football game preliminary was on the television, but the volume was low so they could chat about this and that. It was a sweet family time, and Lexi felt like she was part of them.

They ate some delicious hot hors d'oeuvres of spinach and artichoke dip, chips, pepperoni with cheese and crackers, and the ever-present popcorn with butter, salt, and Parmesan cheese. Sarah often said God had made popcorn just for her because she loved it so very much.

The girls excused themselves and went up to Sarah's bedroom on the third floor. The room was decorated in the style of the Biltmore Estate with rich golds and deep pinks; even portraits of Edith Vanderbilt, their family, and the famous waltz oil painting in a gilded frame were in the room. Her canopy bed was the replica of Edith Vanderbilt's in black and gold.

Lexi threw herself across the gorgeous bed as she usually did and lay on her stomach, head propped up on her elbows and hands. She began, "Sarah, are you up to any mischief?"

Sarah frowned as she hung up her clean laundry. "Mischief? Me?" she inquired innocently.

Noting the look on Sarah's face, Lexi said, "No, seriously, are you?"

Sarah shrugged as she buttoned the top button of her lace blouse on the hanger. "Nothing out of the ordinary. Why?"

Lexi replied with a question, "Well ... do you believe in time travel?"

Sarah burst out laughing, "Oh! You do come up with the craziest ideas sometimes, Lexi. Of course, I don't believe in time travel." She squinted and looked pointedly at Lexi. "What are you up to?"

Noting that her best friend's response was true and heartfelt, Lexi paused before answering. She rolled over onto her back and studied the canopy. "Oh, nothing. Nothing at all." Lexi continued, "Sarah, is it all right if I go to church with you and your folks tonight?"

"Church! Oh, Lexi!" Sarah was across the room and gripped her friend's hands in a second flat. "I've been daily praying that you would want to come to church with us, and now you do." Sarah had tears threatening to spill over from her joy due to her friend's request.

Smiling, Lexi said, "Well, I guess it's about time I start going to church. You certainly have asked me enough times, and I'm sorry I've never gone before." Lexi thought of the dark shadow cast over her and had always felt she was unworthy to step foot into God's house. With the miracle she'd experienced this morning, she felt ready to go and seek God's forgiveness for all her sins.

"Leave the past in the past. You're coming tonight, and that's all that matters!" They embraced, sisters in heart.

Later that night, after their delicious Thanksgiving feast, they all went to church. Sitting side by side in the church pew, Sarah noticed Lexi's Bible on her lap. She whispered, "Is your Bible a family heirloom? It looks ancient."

Lexi whispered back, "Yes, it is. A distant cousin of mine delivered it to me this very morning, in fact, and said it was from my great-great-great-grandfather, Joseph Scott Jenkins—you know, the one we researched."

Impressed, Sarah raised her eyebrows in response, then turned her attention back to the sermon. The pastor was preaching about the love of God, and Sarah silently prayed for her friend to understand the conveyed message.

Lexi decided to spend the night with Sarah. Alone in Sarah's room, Lexi put all questions of the morning behind her, except for one. "Sarah, can Jesus free people from guilt and shame?"

"Oh, yes! Yes, He can, and He does. When we confess our sins, God will forgive and forget."

"He forgets? How can God forget anything?" Lexi asked.

"Well, I am not sure, but that is what the Bible says. He casts our sins as far away as the east is from the west and remembers them no more. The key to everything is Jesus. If anyone believes in Jesus as God's Son, and they accept Jesus as their Savior, they receive forgiveness for their sins. It is called being 'born again.' Total forgiveness replaces guilt and shame. Jesus died on the cross for the sins of us all. He sacrificed His sinless life as payment for every sin for those who believe in Him. Only those of us who love Him and receive Him as personal Savior will be going to heaven."

With a most serious look on her face, Lexi said, "I want to ask Jesus to be my Savior. How do I do it?"

Smiling, Sarah replied, "Just by praying and asking." She reached over and lovingly took her friend's hands. "God sees your heart, Lexi. He knows you truly want Him to make you born again, and He will save you. Just pray what is in your mind, and I'll pray with you."

They held hands, and Lexi began with her eyes tightly closed and her heart wide open. "Dear God, I'm not sure how to do this exactly. I did a terrible, horrible thing in my past." She burst out sobbing. Lexi would never reveal her secret to anyone. She continued, pressing harder on Sarah's warm hands, "You already know everything about me, God, so you know what I've done. Please, let Jesus be my Savior. Please, make me born again, God. I beg you! I cannot go on with this terrible burden of my guilt. I am so, so sorry for what I did. You know I didn't want to do it. Please forgive me. Please ask my baby to forgive me too."

Lexi prayed and sobbed throughout the prayer. Sarah respected her friend's privacy and wouldn't mention the child revealed in her confession.

So this is what has been tormenting my dear Lexi all this time.

She put her arms around her cherished friend to comfort her.

Sarah let Lexi cry and sob out her anguish. Tears streamed down Sarah's face, and she said, "Oh, Lexi, Lexi, I am sorry for the pain you have experienced. God has forgiven you, and He has forgotten. You must forgive yourself. When you do, healing will begin, and you will be set free from the chains of your guilt. You can forgive yourself, because Jesus said that if you don't forgive everyone everything, then He won't forgive you. That includes forgiving yourself too, dear Lexi."

Finally, Lexi gained control, blew her nose, and looked up with her tear-stained face. She took a deep breath, and her whole body seemed to relax at once. She looked amazed and said with astonishment, "Sarah, I feel relieved. I feel peace." She closed her eyes and said in a whisper, "Thank You, dear God, thank You, Jesus, forever!"

Sarah got up and swiftly brought back a cold, damp washcloth for Lexi's eyes. Lexi pressed it onto her face and was quiet for some time. Then she drank some of the ice water Sarah had gotten for her.

Lexi reached for her Bible, which had been given to her that morning, and said to Sarah, "This Bible belonged to my great-great-great-grandfather, Colonel Joseph Scott Jenkins, who fought on the side of the Union during the Civil War. He sent it to me through the generations. Someone gave it to him." Lexi waited for Sarah's reaction.

"Oh, what a family treasure for you to have! How wonderful for you to possess it. May I see the inscription?" Sarah inquired, reaching for it.

Lexi pulled it back close to her breast and held it tightly. She gently refused Sarah's request. She must not see the inscription. Sarah misunderstood Lexi's refusal as her need for privacy. She didn't take any offense.

At that moment, Lexi realized the truth of the mystery of the morning. She knew, without a doubt, that Sarah wasn't playing a joke on her. Lexi knew God had saved her life this morning and had saved her soul this evening. God used her beloved friend as His instrument. At that moment, she purposed to dedicate herself to His service all the rest of her life.

One of the hardest things I will have to do will be to let my friend go back in time. We have just a little over five months to spend together before God calls her to the journey of her lifetime. Every moment with Sarah will be precious. I shall cherish the blessing of having the foreknowledge of Sarah's upcoming time travel so I can prepare myself. Wow! Sarah will be so happy and so amazed when she goes back in time.

Chapter 34

Lexi decided to go on a cruise a few days before Sarah's departure date. They made cherished memories together over the last five months. However, now Lexi knew that if she stayed with Sarah any longer, there would be a risk in showing the depth of emotion welling up inside her. She thought of how much she would miss her dear Sarah. Of course, Lexi knew she and Sarah would be together again in heaven for all eternity. Somehow at the moment, though, that knowledge didn't fill the void she knew would remain for the duration of her earthly life. Sarah was her dearest and most beloved friend ever. Sarah had saved her from suicide, and in return, Lexi was able to save Sarah's parents' lives.

What a surprising day that had been! Lexi stopped packing for the cruise and stretched out on her bed. She recounted the events of that unusual day when she had prevented Mr. and Mrs. Gordon from getting into their car on December tenth.

God provided the way. I slipped on ice on the Gordon's driveway, broke my ankle, and had to go to the hospital by ambulance that morning. I made Sarah and Mr. and Mrs. Gordon promise to stay home and not get into any vehicle that day. They must have thought I was crazy, but thankfully they listened and are safe.

Suddenly, her cat, Blackie, jumped into her suitcase and knocked it onto the floor. The noise brought Lexi out of her daydream of remembering that miraculous day in December. She shook her head slightly to regain her thoughts on getting ready for her cruise.

She shooed her cat away and resumed packing. The Bahamas would be lovely this time of year, so she got out her favorite summer clothing to take, along with a few light sweaters.

Lexi thanked God once again for using her to save the Gordons' lives and for the wonderful time she had cherished with Sarah over the past few months. She knew she just couldn't manage to be with her friend any longer at this point. It was just too difficult to think of saying goodbye for the rest of their lives here on earth. It was especially hard since Lexi knew Sarah would be time-traveling soon, but Sarah didn't even know it. *It seems like God prepares one person for an event before He prepares another.* Lexi wondered a thousand times how it would all happen. She would probably never know for sure.

Her packing finished, she took a few minutes to sit down and read the King James Bible her beloved Grandfather Jenkins had passed down through the generations to her. As she picked it up from her night table and sat down on her nearby Windsor chair, she turned to Psalm 91. Lexi read it aloud to herself, feeling strengthened by the reminder that God cared so very much about her. She loved the beautiful, archaic language of the 1611 King James Bible. It was so flowing and descriptive, and it always uplifted her spirit as she read it daily.

Lexi thought of the other translations available to people now and had been shocked to recently learn that there existed over four hundred copyrighted translations of the Holy Bible. How can man copyright God's Word? She concluded that people changed God's Word to suit themselves and their particular denominations and copyrighted it for financial profit. Somewhat of an intellectual, she had spent hours comparing verses of the most popular translations of the day. As a new student of the Bible, she was passionate to learn all she could. Lexi determined that in general, people didn't understand that the basis of the King James translation came from the original Greek text of the New Testament, the textus receptus, which had been in existence since the time of Jesus Christ. She was committed to using only the King James Bible because it was the actual English translation from this original Greek text. There were reportedly other texts at the time that weren't the correct ones, and from those sprang all the other translations. She wanted to fill herself with the purity of God's Word and not be confused by man's interpretations. It would be her mission to help others know God's truth as well.

She learned about the significance of God's warning when she read in Revelation 22:18–19, "For I testify unto every man that heareth the words of the prophecy of this book, If any man shall add unto these things, God shall add unto him the plagues that are written in this book: And if any man shall take away from the words of the book of this prophecy, God shall take away his part out of the book of life, and out of the holy city, and from the things which are written in this book."

The consequences were unthinkable. Who would want their name taken away out of God's Book of Life?

Finished with her time of reading God's Word for the moment, Lexi packed her Bible into her suitcase and zipped it up. She took it to the foyer door in readiness to go. Lexi recalled how she'd had to talk her way through not inviting Sarah on this cruise. Sarah had seemed upset and even angry that Lexi would go without her. But when Lexi told her she wanted some time alone to start writing her memoirs, Sarah thought it was a great idea. Sarah said that she, too, would start a journal of her life while her friend was gone. Lexi was indeed going to start writing down an outline of the main points of her life to develop later into stories. She also had other more critical research she planned to do.

Sarah agreed to drive Lexi to the Philadelphia airport to see her off. The traffic was as terrible as ever, but they enjoyed talking and listening to their favorite Beach Boys songs. They sang along and laughed as they pretended to be singing into microphones. Lexi glanced at Sarah and struggled to put the time travel out of her mind so she wouldn't start to cry.

Standing at the airline entrance gate, with the crowds pressing in and the loudspeaker announcements confusing everyone, Sarah and Lexi said goodbye. Lexi didn't even try to hide her tears at this point. She claimed that she hated goodbyes and always cried. She told Sarah how much she would miss her. She just didn't have any idea of how long their parting would be.

Sarah thought it a little odd to see her friend's flowing tears. "Lexi, I will pick you up when you get back in a few days, for heaven's sake. Don't cry! Have a great time, and when you return, I will read all of your pages you write in your memoirs, and you can read all of what I have written in my journal, okay? Hey! Send me one of those corny conch shell postcards, please. I know you will get back before the postcard arrives, but I want it all the same."

Lexi tried to smile in response. They embraced again, then Lexi turned and walked away. She looked back one more time, dabbing her eyes with a tissue. Sarah was waving and smiling. Lexi waved back and had to grin when she said aloud, "Boy, oh, boy! Are you ever about to go on an incredible journey! Oh, how I shall miss you!"

Lexi threw a kiss to her friend, smiled, and took a deep breath. She turned and disappeared down the tunnel entrance to her waiting jet and into her new life season without Sarah. It would be difficult, but she knew God would fill her and give her new purposes and friends along her new path. No one would ever be like Sarah, though.

When Sarah got home from the airport, she announced to her parents, "I've made a decision. I'm going to visit Colin, Rebecca, and the kids. They will be spending a few days at Stone Mountain Park in their new RV, and I want to do the tours there with them. It will be fun." She had already called and set up the event with her sister-in-law, Tess. She instantly found an acceptable flight online, booked it, paid for it with her credit card, and printed out her tickets.

Her dad said, "I just can't get used to the speed of online dealings."

Sarah assured them that she would be safe flying to Atlanta and visiting her brother and family. Her dear mother was always concerned about flying. She wouldn't fly because she was sure that whatever plane she boarded would blow up or crash.

Her hasty decision to leave to visit her brother somewhat surprised her parents, but they understood. They knew how hurt Sarah had been at first that Lexi hadn't wanted her to go with her on the cruise. With a shared glance, they decided to support her decision for this spur-of-the-moment trip.

"Please give them our love and tell them we are looking forward to seeing them this summer when they come up for their annual visit."

Sarah kissed both of her parents. "Bye, Mom and Dad! I love you!" Full of energy and joy, she bounded up the stairs as she used to do when she was a young teenager.

Lexi thinks she has something on me with her vacation. Well, I'm going on a trip too. It may not be as far south as the Bahamas, but Stone Mountain has beautiful spring weather, and I will get to see my big brother and family. That will pass the time with Lexi away on her cruise and quench the tiny bit of envy I am feeling.

Chapter 35

Mr. and Mrs. Gordon were at the Philadelphia airport terminal to greet Lexi when she arrived home. It was the early evening of the twenty-fourth of April. Lexi had planned this cruise for this exact return date. She expected that Mr. and Mrs. Gordon would pick her up since this was the day for Sarah's time travel. With one look at their faces, Lexi knew it had happened. She embraced them both.

"Lexi, Sarah is missing!" Louise Gordon exclaimed and collapsed into tears.

Fred Gordon continued, "She went to her brother's for a spontaneous visit after you left on your cruise. Colin called us a few hours ago and said she has disappeared. He requested that we pray for him to find her." He just managed to get the words out without breaking down into sobs.

"Don't worry! I know where she is," Lexi replied confidently with a bright smile.

The Gordons stared at her in shock. Their mouths flew open with silent words shouting for an explanation.

Smiling, Lexi placed her hands into the crooks of both of their arms and started to lead them toward the baggage claim area. She said, "Come on, let's get my suitcase and go home. Then I'll tell you the whole story. You have nothing to worry about, I assure you. I have some wonderful news to share with you."

She grinned as she thought about her library research before her trip. She had several history books in her suitcase, marked with tabs to quickly show them photos and information about their beloved daughter, Sarah, and her life in 1863 and beyond. She had spent her entire cruise reading these books and bookmarking them. She could share every detail with these dear people, who were like her parents, and now they would be family for the rest of their days together.

Chapter 36

1865

"Samuel!" cried Sarah frantically. She listened anxiously as he closed his Bible and quickly arrived at her dressing room. Concern creased his brow.

Sarah rushed toward him. She flung herself into his arms, trembling, and tried to gain control of her emotions.

In earnest, Samuel queried, "Darling, what alarms you?"

"Oh, Samuel! I'm … I'm … spotting! I know I shouldn't say such personal things to you, but … our baby," Sarah managed to get out before she broke into sobbing tears.

He held her carefully, comforting her in his soothing, deep voice and caressing her silky, loose, long hair. He gave her time to control herself, then guided them to the edge of their bed and sat down. He gave his handkerchief to his wife and said, "You can say anything you like to me of a personal nature, Sarah. Now, can you tell me, do you think something is wrong with the baby?"

She cried into his handkerchief and nodded in horrified assent.

Samuel remained calm and had Sarah breathe deep, cleansing breaths. Then he assisted her to lie down. He pulled the soft white coverlet up over her, kissed her briefly, and said quietly, "I shall go get the doctor, sweetheart. Just rest now, and I will send Rebecca and Bessie here to be with you."

Sarah reluctantly let go of her beloved husband's hand, then breathed deeply again. She knew she had to calm down. Sarah nodded and attempted a little smile as her husband left the room. She was alone for only a few minutes when Rebecca rushed through the door.

Sarah cried, "Oh, Rebecca! Help me! I'm cramping! Oh, my baby! Oh, dear God! My baby!"

Rebecca swiftly knelt by her bedside and tenderly but firmly grasped Sarah's cold hand. "Oh, Sarah! What happened?"

Sniffing and choking on her sobs, she managed, "I don't know! I was changing into my nightgown and used the chamber pot. I noticed that I was spotting blood, and now I'm cramping! Oh, Rebecca! We've waited a whole year! Now, to think of losing our precious baby. I cannot bear it!"

Rebecca's heart broke for her, and tears spilled from her eyes. "I am so very sorry, sweet Sarah!"

"I want this baby so much, and I can't do anything to keep my child in my womb. The cramps are getting worse. I can't stand it! I want my baby!" Sarah cried in anguish.

As Rebecca stood up and lifted the quilt, she discovered that Sarah's nightgown was drenched in blood. It had a sobering effect on her, and Rebecca spoke with calm authority. She was very much like her mother—calm and matter of fact in a crisis. Her fear for Sarah's life took precedence over her grief of the miscarrying baby.

"Sarah, we'll talk about the baby later. Listen to me. You are bleeding a great deal. We must get your bleeding stopped. Fight for your life, Sarah. Think of Samuel. He couldn't bear to lose the both of you!" In an attempt to slow the bleeding, she began to press towels around Sarah and under her to lift her hips slightly.

Just then, the door flew open, and Samuel and their family doctor rushed in. Samuel's face turned ashen when he saw the amount of blood on Sarah's nightgown and sheets. He kissed her forehead and murmured comforting words of love, all the while praying aloud for his wife's life.

Rebecca stated matter-of-factly, "Doctor, she has lost the baby. Please, you must stop the bleeding immediately!" Now that the doctor was here, she allowed herself to cry openly.

Instructions and servants flew around the room. It was the longest night of the Stuarts' lives. The doctor handed some ergot tea to Bessie to brew for her mistress. Samuel gave repeated sips of the tea to Sarah. The ergot tea had proved to stop the hemorrhaging. Rebecca stayed by Sarah's side, talking to her and putting cold cloths on her forehead. They kept her from the state of unconsciousness that was trying to claim her because the doctor had given strict orders not to let her sleep. The doctor worked expertly, and in a few hours he had the bleeding stopped. However, Sarah was pale and weak. She wouldn't respond to voices, and she finally slipped into a deep state of unconsciousness. Attempts to awaken her received no response.

Samuel felt like an old man in his overwhelming grief. It appeared that his wife's life was slipping away. He went to the family chapel, collapsed alone on the floor, and wept openly. He cried out to God as he pleaded for his wife's life. He didn't know how long he was in there in prayer, but suddenly, in the midst of his deep anguish, he felt a peace wash over him.

The servants washed Sarah and changed her bedclothes and nightgown while the master was out of the room. Bessie suggested that they all sing "Amazing Grace" while they worked. Everyone knew how much music meant to Sarah. They sang quietly and beautifully in harmony.

The singing brought Sarah back to consciousness. When Samuel returned, she seemed to be resting comfortably, but her breathing was shallow.

"Oh my beloved! You are awake!" The sound of her husband's voice revived her more fully.

Sarah reached for his hand. "My darling. I am so sorry about our precious baby." She began to cry.

Samuel said, "Our baby is in heaven, and we will be reunited one day. I am so thankful that you are still with me. I love you so."

Sarah replied weakly, "I love you. I need many fluids to recover. Please bring water, tea, and broth." It took all of her strength to say these things. She was totally exhausted.

With helpful hands holding her head up, she forced herself to drink.

Samuel held her hand and spoke tender words to her of their future together. He pleaded with her to keep fighting for her life. She felt a little strength returning to her body. Samuel tenderly placed his head on the pillow next to his wife and smelled her damp hair and kissed her cheek. He whispered, "Thank You, dear Jehovah God, in Jesus's name!"

Chapter 37

Sitting in her favorite garden spot with the soothing sound of the small waterfall, Samuel felt it was time to speak of their child.

"My darling," Samuel said as he sat near to her and took her hand. She smiled up at him as she shaded her eyes from the sunshine with her other hand.

Samuel said as gently as possible, "Sweetheart, the doctor said that even though our baby was quite small, he could tell he was a boy."

Fresh tears spilled from Sarah's eyes as she said, "Oh, honey! A boy? Why didn't you tell me before? Did you see him?"

"Yes. Yes, I did see him. He was quite small, but his little arms and legs were formed. He was just about two inches, Sarah."

Samuel held his beloved wife as they both cried anew for their little son and for what could have been had he lived.

"You were so near death yourself. I knew that you needed to have all of your strength to regain your health. That is why I have waited these weeks to tell you. I buried him in our family cemetery. When you are strong enough, I will take you there to visit his grave. I named him Colin Gordon Stuart to honor your side of the family too."

Clutching at her husband, Sarah cried, "Oh, Samuel! My arms feel so empty. I ache to hold our son. Our son! I have been trying so hard to recover from my miscarriage, but I feel more sad than I can even say."

Sarah tried to recover, but the sparkle in her eyes was gone. Nothing would lift her spirits again until she knew she had another little life growing within her. Blowing her nose on her handkerchief, Sarah said, "Thank you for telling me that our baby was a boy and that you named him after my brother and added my maiden name for his middle name. Somehow this helps my heart a great deal, my love. I do want to visit his grave when I am stronger."

"Of course. You just let me know when you feel ready, and I will take you there."

Now when I think of my baby, he has a name, and I can imagine his life with us had he lived. What a glorious day it will be when we meet him in heaven!

Her sweet husband was kind and patient with her and always encouraging. He sat with her in their garden when the weather was beautiful, and they talked for long hours about their future as a family.

I feel like I am beginning to regain my strength now. I can't believe it has taken several months. I must really have been near death.

Samuel shared with her much of what he was doing in the new government. She was quite interested and gave her opinion on issues about how much a stable, godly government was necessary to ensure a people who loved and served God. These discussions often turned lively, and Sarah came to herself once again.

I hope for another baby now that it has been a half year since the miscarriage. I feel healed and healthy.

After a physical examination, their doctor gave the young couple permission to try again for a child.

Sarah said, "I am so happy. May God grant us a healthy baby and a safe delivery."

Life settled into a routine of Samuel and Mr. Stuart being away to Atlanta to work quite often and of Sarah and Mrs. Stuart running Stone Hill Manor.

My life as Samuel's wife is everything I ever hoped for and more.

Samuel supported her in every way, and she pursued activities that were important to her. One mission near and dear to her heart was helping the servants' children learn to read and write. Sarah regularly held classes for them in the barn. Any of the adult servants who wanted to join them were invited to learn as well.

Sarah began plans to build a schoolhouse on their plantation, and Samuel was impressed with her undertaking.

"You have such passions in life," Samuel said. "I enjoy seeing you in action. Once you get an idea, there is no stopping my lady." He beamed with pride for his amazing wife.

Sarah had another idea too. She faithfully kept a daily diary and wrote stories about her life with Samuel. *Somehow, Colin and Tess and the kids may read these at some point in the future.* She wrote as if they would read it, and in this written form of sharing, Sarah felt connected with them. Her longing for them eased as she wrote.

Sarah also began teaching violin lessons to many students of all ages, and a music room was part of her schoolhouse plan. She purchased several sizes of violins, and her students shared them for practice times.

She decided that school classes would be held during the hottest part of the day so parents and children could get their education as well as some relief from the heat. Sarah planned on Bessie as her assistant teacher. The only textbook they would need was the Holy Bible. Bessie was quite skilled in reading it, understanding it, and teaching it.

The elder Mrs. Stuart wasn't accustomed to a lady being so involved in these kinds of activities, but she had no objections. For her, life continued much as it always had been, with her in charge of most of the day-to-day running of Stone Hill Manor while Sarah was otherwise engaged. It was an agreeable situation, in which both women felt valued and purposeful. As the mother-in-law and daughter-in-law relationships went, theirs was functional and nearly as perfect as possible. They shared a mutual respect and love for each other. Sarah considered writing a small booklet on the subject since their plan worked out so well. She made a mental note to do just that. *Maybe I can help others by our example.* She knew of several mothers-in-law and daughters-in-law who had deep problems, usually rooted in jealousy, selfishness, and unforgiving spirits. *There is so much joy to be had, and there is no sense in suffering needlessly.*

Sarah started to work on her booklet in the evenings. Her theme focused on developing loving relationships between women who were related by marriage. Her premise was that there didn't have to be a forced closeness, just simple respect, and kindness toward each other.

People are kind and courteous to strangers; can they not be so toward their family?

Writing this booklet became an evening passion for Sarah. She worked on it after the family had finished their gathering in the music room after supper. They sang and played beautiful pieces of their favorite music together. The expression of music was lovely for them all to share. They always looked forward to that time together in the early evenings.

Being a night owl, Sarah had quiet time after the family went to bed. It was a valuable opportunity for her to write late at night. Samuel stayed up with her and did work of his own too. He surprised her with her own desk in his study. They enjoyed writing and discussing ideas as they worked. Time passed quickly and with joyful purpose in these endeavors.

Life is good!

Chapter 38

One morning Sarah ran to the wash basin to be sick. After the wave of nausea passed, she broke into the broadest grin her face could allow.

I am with child again. Praise be to God!

She freshened her mouth, then called for Bessie to dress her quickly. Bessie had stayed very close to Sarah during her recovery from the miscarriage. Another very skilled servant assisted Nanny with Joanne when Bessie needed to attend to Sarah.

Seeing that huge smile back on her mistress's face, Bessie guessed her news. Without being asked, Bessie said, "I believe Mr. Samuel is in his office right now." Sarah grinned at her in response.

So you have guessed my secret, have you?

Sarah rushed through the house and burst through the door of Samuel's study. He had put his Bible back on the shelf and turned to head to the dining room for morning coffee and breakfast. As was her usual way, Sarah collided with her husband in her rush.

"Oh, my darling! I have the most wonderful news! I am with child!" She embraced her beloved husband with all the energy and joy she felt.

Returning her embrace with matching enthusiasm, Samuel swung her around and said, "Praise God! Praise God! I was just this moment reading Psalm 128 and praying for you to be like a fruitful vine, Sarah. God does work quickly, doesn't He?" They laughed joyously and spent their morning full of hope and plans.

Sarah's pregnancy was uneventful this time. She was confident that she would have a healthy delivery. She did gain too much weight—fifty pounds, in fact—but no one minded.

When she fussed about her weight gain, Samuel said, "You are the most beautiful creation that God has ever made. I shall spend much of my time telling you so and reassuring you, my darling." Sarah hugged him as closely as she could with her huge belly.

The night she went into labor, she felt unable to sleep. Finally, after tossing and turning, she got out of bed and went to have some weak tea.

While drinking it in the parlor, she felt the first pain. It wasn't much, but she realized the anticipated moment had finally arrived.

Soon I will be holding our precious baby and nursing! She felt ecstatic. She didn't want to awaken Samuel yet, so she stayed in their study and picked up a book to read. *I can't concentrate. I have read this same paragraph five times.*

Sarah was amazed that the pains were so light, yet regular, at five minutes apart. Finally, she went to awaken her beloved to include him in her excitement.

Gently touching his shoulder and face, Sarah said in a soft voice, "Samuel. It is time to wake up."

He replied, "Hmm? What is it?"

"Our baby is coming, sweetheart."

Samuel jolted out of his sleepiness and was up in a flash. "What? When? What can I do? I will go get the doctor!"

"No sense in waking Doc up now, honey. I feel confident that I can give birth just fine with the aid of the Nanny." Nanny had been the assisting midwife for years on the estate.

"I am amazed at your courage and confidence, my lady, but all the same, I am going to go get the doctor," Samuel replied firmly. Sarah knew that tone. There would be no arguing with him. He got dressed as fast as possible, kissed his wife, and flew out the door.

Sarah called after him with a chuckle, "Okay, I will be waiting for you in the study."

Bessie had heard the conversation between Mr. and Mrs. Stuart, so she joined Sarah in the study. "I will get some hot tea and toast and eggs for you, Miss Sarah. You need to keep up your strength for the long day ahead."

"Yes, thank you, Bessie. And you had better awaken Rebecca. She would be devastated if I didn't include her."

"Yes, ma'am," Bessie said before she left the room.

Samuel and the doctor arrived in a rush. After just a few questions, the doctor said, "Well, it may take a while. You are at the beginning of the birth pains. I will be here with you for the entire process, of course."

"Thank you, Doc." Sarah fondly called him that nickname. "Why don't you go to the kitchen to get some breakfast? Samuel will get you when we need you."

"Yes, ma'am, I believe that I shall get something to eat. We have plenty of time, I think."

Truer words were never spoken. Nothing much happened for a long time, except Sarah became increasingly irritated about how long the labor was taking. She even grew exasperated when the doctor wanted to check her progress, seemingly too frequently in her opinion.

To pass the time, Rebecca read to her as they sat in the study, even though she knew Sarah wasn't listening. Samuel pretended to be hard at work on some papers at his desk. When he glanced up at Sarah, she glared at him.

"Stop looking at me, please!" Sarah said testily. He looked away quickly.

Rebecca interjected, "Sarah, let's go take a stroll outside. Maybe a change of atmosphere will help."

"Help? What do you mean, help? I don't need any help!" Sarah exclaimed, but she noticed the glances between Rebecca and Samuel.

What do they know anyhow? I am the one having this baby, for heaven's sake!

But she did get up and go outside with Rebecca, more to get away from her husband's stares. Sarah didn't stay long at any one place. She had to keep moving. After a few hours of being outside, she said to Rebecca, "I think it is time for that blasted doctor to check me again." They went to Sarah's bed so she could lie on her back for the examination.

Standing ready, the doctor checked her and announced, "Mrs. Stuart, I can see your baby's head crowning!"

Rebecca and Bessie shrieked with delight and clapped their hands. Sarah glared at them and breathed deeply and rapidly, feeling the full pain of transition. *I am so irritated that they are acting so gleeful. I may just throw the contents of my water pitcher at both of them and drench them. Don't they realize how painful this feels?* Then Sarah let out a yell to prove what she was thinking.

"I will go get the master. He is in the chapel," Bessie said, holding her skirt as she began to run toward the door. "Mr. Stuart can't miss witnessing his child being born."

Samuel and Bessie entered the bedroom just one minute before the baby appeared. "Doctor, is all well?" Samuel asked in a nervous voice.

"Yes, indeed! You are about to have your baby, sir!"

Oh! He is about to have his baby, is he? Then why doesn't he get over here and push?

As Sarah had prearranged when she hadn't been irritated with him and everyone else in the world, she wanted her husband with her when their baby was born. It was certainly unusual for this period of time, but it was an exciting moment she wanted Samuel to share with her. He held his wife's hand as the doctor said, "One more push, Mrs. Stuart, and we shall have a baby!" Sarah gripped Samuel's hand with surprising strength as she prepared for this last push.

Drenched in sweat and determined with all her might, Sarah gave a yell and pushed as hard as she could. Her face was beet red.

I feel like a watermelon is ripping through my body! Will I survive this?

When the precious gift of their baby daughter made her first cry in the world, twenty-four hours had passed since Sarah felt the early pains.

Instantly, all pain forgotten, Sarah cried tears of joy and said, "It's a baby! It's a baby!" She looked up at her beloved husband, who kept kissing her and saying repeatedly, "Praise God!"

Exhausted but thrilled to have her new little daughter cling to her breast to nurse, Sarah began to relax. Bessie's mother, Nanny, was right there to help the baby get latched on without delay.

"Look at her!" Sarah exclaimed. "She latched right onto my breast like she knew what she was doing. Oh, you smart little girl."

"Yes, ma'am. She is a smart little one, for sure," Nanny replied.

Most of the people in their station of life had a wet nurse employed, but Sarah would have none of that. She emphatically insisted on nursing her baby, and seeing her determination, the family had all agreed.

Samuel said, "I am so proud of you for deciding to nurse our baby. It is as precious as can be to see you feeding our baby daughter."

The baby made adorable little noises and stuck her tiny forefinger up near her mouth as she nursed.

Everyone chuckled in joy at the sound of her eagerness to drink her mother's milk.

Distracted by the nursing process, the couple barely noticed how efficiently and quickly the doctor, Bessie, Nanny, and Rebecca had Sarah and her bed tidied up. They all excused themselves from the room.

On her way out the door, Rebecca asked, "Shall I go get Mother and Father now?"

Samuel and Sarah replied, "Oh, yes! Of course." Rebecca went on her way to locate the new grandparents.

When they returned, Mrs. Stuart Sr. rushed to kiss Sarah, Samuel, and then her new little granddaughter. "Oh, she is so precious!"

From the doorway, Mr. Stuart Sr. stayed in place. He wasn't comfortable being in a birthing and nursing room, but he smiled all the same. Of course, being modest, Sarah had a little blanket over her breast so it wasn't exposed to anyone's view. Just their beautiful daughter's tiny, perfect face could be seen.

Mr. Stuart cleared his throat and asked, "What is the name of my granddaughter?"

Samuel and Sarah looked at each other. In their silent communication, they agreed, "We thought that you and mother may like to choose her first name."

Honored by this respect given, Mrs. Stuart said with a smile, "Then I say we shall call her Jennifer after my mother-in-law." Mrs. Stuart looked at her husband and saw he was pleased.

"That will be a lovely way to honor my mother's memory, my dear. Thank you for your thoughtfulness," Mr. Stuart said.

Samuel announced, "Jennifer Ann Stuart shall be her full name."

Sarah added, "Yes, *Ann* is for her middle name because I have a favorite niece named Ann." She continued in a soft voice, "Hello, little Jennifer Ann Stuart. Welcome to our family." Sarah kissed her daughter on the top of her forehead right near her hairline. The baby's hair was a deep, dark auburn and about a half inch long all over her head.

Bessie and Nanny were standing just outside the servant's entrance in case they were needed again. Sarah could hear their conversation.

Bessie asked her mother, "Remember when my son was born, Mama? What a happy day that was for us."

"Indeed it was, dear Bessie," Nanny replied. Her face showed her pain at missing her grandson.

"We won't give up praying for them to come home, Mama." They smiled at each other, trusting that God would bring their family back together someday. Bessie went on, "General Stuart mentioned to me a few days ago that he has had a lead on their whereabouts. He said that he will do all he can to find them and bring them home to Stone Hill Manor."

Nanny replied, "Then it is as good as done. We know that General Stuart is a man of his word."

Bessie nodded in return. "Oh, yes, he is. Oh, Mama! When they get home, what a day of reunion that will be! General Stuart said that we may have that nice cabin near the stables for our little family's home. He is getting it all ready for us. Isn't that so generous of him?"

Nanny said, "Yes! How wonderful!"

Bessie replied, "Yes, I know. And General Stuart said that I may have a week off my duties to get reacquainted with them, and he is even going to assign a servant girl to us for that week to bring our meals to us. I am so happy and excited. They will be home soon, Mama. Very soon. I just know it!"

The two women embraced and cried tears of joy. "God is blessing us all in so many ways." They looked heavenward and said in unison, "Thank You, Jesus!"

Sarah whispered in agreement, "Thank You, Jesus!"

Chapter 39

"Come to me, precious one," Mrs. Stuart, the elder, said as she picked up her little granddaughter.

She was so thrilled by the hustle and bustle the baby caused once again in her home. The entire atmosphere of the manor transformed with the sweet gift of Jennifer Ann.

Mrs. Stuart spent much time with the baby. One day she took her to see her Aunt Joanne. Joanne petted her hair, then seemed to have little interest in such a small baby.

Having adjusted to the new baby over the months, everyone rejoiced when Sarah announced she was with child once again. Jennifer Ann was only nine months old when the next baby's life began in Sarah's womb.

I am going to burst from the joy of my blessed life. Another baby! Thank You, dear God!

Their doctor came one afternoon to give the expectant mother a checkup. He took care of the health needs of the entire family and the estate residents, so he was quite a busy man, but he was always available immediately to the Stuarts.

He explained, "Mrs. Stuart, I am going to use a new instrument called a stethoscope to listen to your heartbeat and your baby's heartbeat. It was invented early this century, and it just recently became available for purchase. Don't be concerned. It won't hurt or give you any discomfort." He put the earpieces into his ears.

Well, it may be a new instrument to you, Doc, but I've had one at my doctor's appointments all my life.

The doctor first listened to Sarah's heartbeat. Then he put it on her abdomen and moved it to several different places. When finished, he smiled at Sarah but said nothing.

The doctor packed up his instrument bag, clicked the latch shut, then turned to Samuel and asked to see him in his office for a moment. Sarah wondered why but gave the matter no further thought. *Men in this century often want some male time together to discuss things out of earshot of the ladies.* Mostly, Sarah was okay with not hearing what they had to say, but at times she was a bit curious.

Today wasn't one of those times when she was interested in what the men had to say to each other privately. She was so happy. She straightened out her clothing, put her hand on her abdomen, and smiled at the thought of her new baby growing there.

Sarah went to play her violin for Jennifer Ann in the music room. It was the coolest part of the house. She was playing her favorite childhood tunes for her daughter, who perked up when she heard her mother's violin music. Sarah had already ordered a one-sixteenth-size violin for her precious daughter to begin to learn to play when she was ready, probably at about two or three years old.

It will be so fun to teach her to play with me—and the next children we have too. We may end up with the Stuart String Quartet.

Smiling at the thought, Sarah looked up as Samuel joined them. She could tell immediately from the look on his face that something concerned him.

"Honey, what is it?" Sarah inquired.

"My darling," he began with a heavy sigh, "I know you would want to know the truth immediately, so I must tell you what the doctor told me in my office, sweetheart."

Alarmed by his pale face, Sarah put her violin and bow on the settee and asked again, "Samuel, what is it?" She instinctively picked up her daughter and held her very tightly to her chest.

Samuel put his arms around his wife and daughter, and he said quietly, "I am so sorry, my darling, but the doctor said there is no heartbeat from our baby in your womb." He put his hand lovingly on her abdomen and said in a choked voice, "The baby is dead, Sarah."

Sarah pulled away from him, clutched Jennifer Ann even more tightly, and cried, "No! No! How could our baby be dead? He must be wrong! Yes, that's it. He has made a mistake." Sarah willed it to be so. Her eyes were full and round with fear, and her voice trembled. She smelled Jennifer Ann's hair and breathed in the freshness of her baby girl's skin for comfort.

As gently as possible, Samuel said kindly but firmly, "I wish it to be so, my precious wife. However, the doctor said that most likely within two weeks, you will miscarry. This one may be harder on you than the last one because you are four months along now. The doctor suspected it, and that is why he asked me to order the stethoscope so he could be sure. Apparently, something went wrong inside, Sarah. There isn't anything that you did wrong. You couldn't have done anything to prevent this, my love. Sometimes these things just happen."

Bessie had been standing at the entrance of the music room, as Samuel had asked her to do. She had heard everything.

"Bessie, please see to Jennifer Ann."

She swiftly took the child from Sarah's arms, who then collapsed into the warm embrace of her beloved husband. They cried together for the life of their child, and Sarah prayed that God would have mercy and let their baby live.

"Maybe the stethoscope isn't working properly," Sarah tried to reason.

Samuel knew it was too late, but he allowed his sweet wife to work through this death as she needed. She finally grasped the reality that their baby was dead, and she sobbed into her husband's chest. The familiar smell and feel of him comforted her.

Finally, Sarah calmed herself and requested Samuel's handkerchief to wipe her eyes, then her nose. She looked at him so sadly and asked, "Why?"

He replied tenderly, "It is not for us to question why, Sarah. There is only one way we can face this. We must get our strength from our Lord, and remember, our baby's life began in your womb. Then God took him or her to heaven without living on this earth. Sin never touched our little one, my darling. For that we may be thankful. God has a special place for our baby in heaven, and we shall be with our child for all eternity when we get there."

They prayed together again, and then Sarah said, "We are so blessed to have one healthy child." She tried to focus on the blessings and not on the loss of her baby, but it was difficult. Grief has its season, and one must get through it.

Ten days later, Sarah was sitting in the music room and reading.

It was the Sabbath, their day of rest, and the family had experienced heartfelt worship at the morning service at their chapel. Sarah brought her violin to church and played four verses of "Amazing Grace." The congregation was in tears, sensing the depth of her heart flowing into the music. Word had spread quickly, and everyone knew and prayed for the Stuarts.

The pastor went home with another family for dinner after church this Sunday so that the Stuarts could be alone. Jennifer Ann was fast sleep for her afternoon nap, and so were the senior Stuarts. Rebecca was visiting Joanne. Sarah and Samuel were by themselves in the music room. It was Sarah's favorite place to sit and relax, and Samuel enjoyed it as well. The ornate tray ceiling with gilded gold, the floral paintings with matching gilded gold frames, and the various instruments and music stands around the room were a pleasant and comforting sight. Gatherings of neighboring musicians often filled the room with gorgeous music.

Today, though, there was no gathering. Sarah had kept the hope in her heart that the doctor was wrong about the baby being dead, but she knew now he was correct.

The dreaded cramping began, and Sarah grabbed her abdomen and exclaimed, "Oh, Samuel! It is happening! I am cramping!" She broke down in tears.

He swept her into his arms and carried her to their bed. Preparations had been made for this unwelcome event.

Bessie and her mother were near at hand. They had refused to take a day off until their mistress was out of danger. "Miss Sarah, we are here. We are here for you. We are going to help you," they comforted her over and over.

Samuel sent for the doctor, and he joined them quickly. He, too, had been prepared for this moment.

Samuel kissed Sarah, then said, "I am going to the chapel to pray. Please send for me when you need me."

The doctor almost lost Sarah during this miscarriage because she hemorrhaged severely. Bessie and Nanny kept a steady stream of clean towels and hot water for the doctor to use.

Finally, the baby emerged. The doctor tenderly handed the tiny body of the baby boy to Bessie. She cleaned him, then wrapped him in a linen and lace handkerchief that had belonged to great-grandmother Stuart.

Sarah weakly said, "I want to hold him."

Bessie tenderly gave the handkerchief and the miniature baby to his mother.

Crying with great grief, Sarah opened the handkerchief to see him. She kept him in the palm of her warm hand and memorized him as she held him for a long time. She touched him with the point of her right index finger. At only four months old, he was perfectly formed, with tiny arms, legs, a body, and a head. His eyes were dark buds under his perfect flesh. She saw every little vertebra of his spine.

With her tears washing over him, she raised him to her mouth, kissed him goodbye, and wrapped him tenderly in the family heirloom handkerchief.

"Bessie, please go get my husband."

When Samuel entered the room, he rushed to kiss his wife. She said with a choked voice, "Look, my darling. Look at our tiny son." She passed him to Samuel. The baby looked even tinier in Samuel's large hands. Tears streamed down his face uninhibited.

"Let's name him Jeremiah Scott Stuart," he said.

Sarah agreed and had a last look at him before they covered him and said goodbye.

Samuel then placed him in the tiny coffin he had carved with his own hands and went to bury him in their family cemetery. Sarah was too weak to join him. She remained in bed, heartbroken over her child's death.

The doctor knew the placenta was still in her womb, causing the hemorrhaging. There was a steady flow of blood streaming from her body, which was how many women died in childbirth. Fortunately for the Stuarts, their doctor knew to feel for a bit of the placenta in the birth canal when he examined her again. He was sure there was a small piece protruding. Attended by Bessie and Nanny, he took a chance to remove it with a special clamp he had previously used in these cases.

He pulled gently but firmly and steadily on the placenta. Sweat poured down the doctor's forehead, and Nanny blotted it for him.

I feel like I am watching a TV show, like this isn't really happening to me.

Thankfully, the placenta came out slowly and in one piece. Sarah felt it leave her body. She described the feeling later as if a dish towel had been removed from inside her. It was the strangest sensation, but she felt instantly better.

With the placenta gone, it gave the blood vessels a chance to heal. It was a miracle that they were finally able to get her bleeding stopped. She was pale from loss of blood, but she kept drinking fluids, consistently one sip at a time, and she began to revive. Sarah knew how important fluids were to replace the blood loss, so she used what little energy she had to keep drinking water, tea, and broth. She was determined to live for her husband and Jennifer Ann.

When Samuel returned from the cemetery, his tearstained face matched hers. One in their grief, they bid farewell in prayer to their beloved son, holding hands and mixing their tears as their foreheads touched.

Sarah said, "Oh Samuel, do you think we will ever have another baby?"

"I hope that we do, my darling, but God will decide the size of our family. We shall trust in Him." Samuel got on the bed and snuggled with his wife. They fell asleep, exhausted, in each other's arms.

Bessie stayed posted close by in the hallway in case they needed anything. She prayed aloud, "Dear Jesus, please help this family in their time of need as only You can." Those were the last words Sarah heard before she fell asleep.

Chapter 40

Sarah swung her small daughter up into the air, relishing her laughter. When she brought her down again, Jennifer Ann snuggled her head into her mother's neck.

"I wuv you, Mommy," she said.

Sarah closed her eyes, breathing deeply. "I love you too," she said. She put Jennifer Ann down. *There is no good in overdoing it,* she thought, moving toward the living room.

"Aunt Rebecca is coming." Sarah peeked out the window. *It's hard to believe it's been several months since ...* She shook her head. No time to think about that now.

Sweet Rebecca and Luke Carnegie arrived home from their elopement and honeymoon abroad. Being sensitive to her brother and Sarah's grief, they had decided not to plan a marriage or celebration at home. It turned out to be an enjoyable and romantic endeavor for them to elope and tour Europe. Rebecca spent hours telling details of all their adventures. They were the picture of a young, happy couple in love.

Sarah explained to Samuel just how financially successful Andrew Carnegie would become. He would indeed become one of the wealthiest men in the world. Sarah said that Andrew Carnegie believed in the "Gospel of Wealth," which meant that wealthy people were morally obligated to give their money back to others in society.

The Carnegie name will give Luke and Rebecca many philanthropic opportunities in the near future. The commitment to helping others was a family trait of these Scottish Americans.

Samuel was quite impressed and most happy for his sister's good fortune in love and security. No one would suspect from their humble demeanor that they may be of the Carnegie family and would never want for anything.

Their family dinner was excellent, but Samuel noticed that Sarah hardly ate a thing. He whispered to her where she sat on his left, "Sweetheart, do you feel ill?"

She whispered back, "Oh, not exactly ill. The smell of the steak made my stomach queasy tonight. I don't want to hurt cook's feelings, so I am not going to say anything about it. Did you find it acceptable?"

"It was delicious to me. I do hope that you are not getting sick."

Sarah drank some water and said, "No, I think I am fine. Thank you for your concern." *I am fine, but my stomach isn't! Ugh! This aversion to the smell of cooked meat is worse than morning sickness.*

After supper, the whole family gathered and enjoyed a lively evening of music and song.

"This has been great fun, Rebecca. No wonder you speak of these family evenings with such joy." Luke said.

"Yes, my love. And we will have similar evenings as our family grows." She blushed and glanced at Sarah, who was smiling at her, understanding the newness of married life.

Samuel said, "Indeed, indeed!" He put his arms around his precious sister and enjoyed her company very much.

"Luke, it is good to get to know you better, and we look forward to many more times together."

The men shook hands and showed their delight in being brothers-in-law.

Their visit went by all too quickly. Before they knew it, it was time for the newlyweds to leave.

Standing on their front porch, Sarah tearfully waved goodbye to the bride and groom as they departed for their new home in Atlanta. Sarah turned to her husband as she blotted her eyes and said, "Oh, Samuel, I shall miss her so. She is my dearest friend and sister. I shall always remember her faith and belief in me when I first arrived here. May our Lord bless them all of their lives."

"Yes, my dearest! They seem to be meant for each other, just like we are, my love." Samuel kept his arm around his lady wife and smiled as if he were still a new groom.

Before they turned back to the entrance of the manor, Sarah said brightly, "Darling, I have been waiting for just the right moment alone with you to tell you some good news." She placed her hand on her abdomen and smiled. "Sweetheart, God has blessed us with a new little life!"

Samuel picked her up and twirled her around. They were both laughing as he said, "So that is why you didn't like the smell of the meat."

"How astute of you, dear sir, to figure that out so quickly." They kissed a long, tender kiss to celebrate their joy.

Chapter 41

Seven months later at full term, lively Courtney Tess was born into the happy Stuart family—however, not without a great cost.

During labor, Sarah pushed so hard and long that she became delirious.

Something is terribly wrong!

A blood clot emerged, and Sarah, in her weakened state, panicked. She thought the baby was coming out in pieces, and she was frantic.

Attempting to calm Sarah proved ineffective. She kept crying out over and over, "The baby! The baby!" She was petrified that she had pushed so hard that she had harmed her baby. The doctor had to give her a dose of laudanum to quiet her.

She finally cooperated by lying back, and the doctor examined her. Even with the laudanum, she was writhing in pain. He realized the baby's head was lodged in Sarah's pelvic bone. He knew he needed another pair of skilled hands to assist him to release the baby. He sent for Nanny, who'd delivered and assisted on most of the servants' babies.

The doctor told Nanny, "I am going to have to give a stronger dose of opium to Mrs. Stuart. She is going to have to be completely still while we do what we must."

As soon as Sarah was completely unconscious in her drugged state, the doctor and Nanny worked together and successfully turned the baby's head enough.

"Now, Nanny, push on her abdomen in the way that she would bear down if she were awake." Nanny did this repeatedly, and not long after, the first cries of the new little girl graced the room.

"Bessie, go get General Stuart." The doctor always called him "General."

When Samuel entered the room, he was scared that his wife had died. She was so still and ashen. "Is she … gone?" His words stuck in his throat.

"No, sir! She is still with us, but she has had a very hard time indeed. You have a new daughter." But Samuel knelt by the bed and stroked Sarah's sweaty hair back from her forehead. He murmured loving words, even though she couldn't hear him at the moment.

In a few minutes, Samuel stood and walked over to Bessie, who held his new little daughter. He took her in his arms and kissed her tiny flushed face. "Your birth wasn't easy on you either, was it, little one? Your mother and I love you. Your name is Courtney Tess." Even with his concern for his wife, he couldn't help but smile at his new little girl.

It was another miracle that both mother and child had survived. Bessie and Nanny took turns helping Courtney Tess to nurse when she was hungry. It took weeks for Sarah to recover physically from this traumatic birth, but she was a survivor.

During her recovery, Sarah confided in her husband, "I never knew so many things could go wrong during pregnancy and delivery. I thought a woman just got married and had children. It is a wonder any of us live through the birthing process. I am going to have something to say to Eve when I see her in heaven."

She remembered these words when just a few months later, she had her third miscarriage. Sarah hadn't even known she was pregnant until the dreaded cramping started. She watched for the evidence, and she was able to see the little start of the baby that had formed for just a few weeks. Since it was very early during the pregnancy, no one could tell the sex of the baby.

This time there was no issue with bleeding, but the doctor recommended to this couple that they have no more children. The various difficulties Sarah experienced could be life threatening if she kept getting pregnant. Samuel and Sarah accepted their doctor's advice.

Chapter 42

Sarah sat alone in the music room one afternoon, reflecting on her children. She opened her journal and relived special moments she had written about her girls.

As they grew, Jennifer Ann was the most verbal and mischievous of the three. She recalled when the family was entertaining Pastor Ross one Sunday afternoon. Jennifer Ann held his attention with her stories and tales, then ended their conversation, telling the pastor she didn't have any more to say because her "mouth had run out of words."

During the same visit, little Courtney Tess asked Pastor Ross to tell her the part of Psalm 23 that said, "My cup got run over." Then, when finished eating her meal, Courtney Tess announced, "Thanks for enjoying me!"

Pastor Ross enjoyed the little girls so much, particularly so because he had no children of his own.

Once, Jennifer Ann stared into Pastor Ross's eyes and noticed red lines. She said, "Your eyes are cracking!" Then she was so full of her Sunday dinner that she put her fork down and said, "No more food will get on my fork!" Jennifer Ann showed her interest in her French lessons by announcing at one meal, *"Je m'appelle eat!"* The adults chuckled because the translation meant "My name is eat."

Prompted by her journal entry, Sarah's mind vividly recalled the time when Courtney Tess came shrieking into the parlor, exclaiming, "I have tree blood on my hands!" Bessie had quickly cleaned her up with turpentine and explained that it was tree sap, not tree blood.

These sweet sisters kept the family and the pastor laughing at most Sunday meals with their adorable little ways.

Sarah turned another page and read about the time when Courtney Tess climbed up into her mother's lap, hugged, kissed her, and said, "Mama, I like you, and I love you." She remained close and stared at Sarah's face. Studying Sarah's eyebrows, she said, "Mama, your umbrellas look pretty." Sarah laughed and hugged her little daughter as close as could be.

Smiling to herself, Sarah reread about one morning; while enjoying a few minutes of snuggling with her firstborn, she heard Jennifer Ann say, "Let's get up now."

Sleepily, Sarah asked, without opening her eyes, "What do you want to get up for, darling?"

Jennifer Ann answered matter-of-factly, "I do it every morning."

Sarah chuckled and closed her journal as if on cue.

Just then a slamming door and the sound of the girls shrieking, fighting over a favorite doll, brought Sarah out of her reflections. She got up from her chair to be a referee once again. "These girls!" Sarah said with a smile and a shake of her head, loving every second of the chaos. She must teach them to close doors quietly, not to mention hundreds of other social graces.

A heartwarming memory of her mother teaching her to be a lady came to mind. Sarah remembered her teenage rebellion when she accused her mother of being "too much Emily Post." Now Sarah was so thankful for the gentility and good manners she had learned from her beloved mother. She mused that Emily Post was born in 1872, so it would be a while before Emily published her book on etiquette.

Sarah was prepared for the monumental task to teach her tomboy daughters proper social graces, no matter what it took. She had every confidence that she could do it. She marched toward the sounds of the girls arguing, knowing full well she would have this opportunity and many more to turn difficult situations into learning experiences.

Chapter 43

"Rebecca! Luke! My grandsons!" Mr. Stuart Sr. met them with excitement on the porch as they arrived for a long-awaited visit. "It has been months since you came home!"

"Oh, Papa! You know we come as often as we can. I have missed you." Rebecca rushed into her father's outstretched arms and lingered longer than usual. It always felt so good to her to be in her father's loving embrace.

"Sir, how are you?" Luke said as he shook hands with his father-in-law.

"Just fine. Just fine. Where are my grandsons?"

The boys snuck up on their grandfather and grabbed his legs.

"Whoa!" he said. "Where did you come from, you plucky, little squirts?"

The boys laughed, thrilled that they had surprised their beloved grandfather. Brian and Franklin reached into his pants pockets first thing to retrieve their pieces of candy. Grandfather always had pieces of candy for them hidden in his pockets.

"Hey, how do you know those are yours?"

They laughed again as they popped the candy into their mouths, then hugged their grandfather properly and said in unison, "You always have candy for us, Grandpa!"

"Indeed I do! Indeed I do! Now, which one of you is Franklin, and which one is Brian?" Identical twins, they were very difficult to tell apart.

Pointing at each other, the boys teased, "He's Brian! He's Franklin!"

Rebecca chided them slightly and said, "Now you two! Don't tease your grandfather. Be honest about who you are." She was the only one who could easily tell them apart. They took advantage of that fact and had fun with everyone else who tried to identify them.

Rebecca and Luke Carnegie visited often before they had the twin boys, Franklin and Brian. As is usually the case, children tended to change lives and availability for travel, so their visits to Stone Hill

Manor became less frequent. They did, however, manage always to get together for holidays and special occasions. The family visited them all they could in Atlanta too.

"Well, praise God that you are all here at the manor for Thanksgiving for a whole week together! We have many family memories to create."

Sarah, Samuel, Courtney Tess, Jennifer Ann, and Mrs. Stuart heard the commotion and joined them on the porch. "You are here! You are finally here!"

After hugging everyone properly, the children ran around, playing. They needed less supervision now since they were a bit older, but certain servants were always nearby, keeping an eye on them. The cousins loved to get together.

"Isn't it a pleasure to see our children playing so well together?" Sarah asked.

"Yes, and I am very happy that we get some time to visit too, now that they are more independent!" Rebecca responded.

The adults enjoyed their hot tea while they chatted.

Watching and listening to them, Mr. Stuart was overcome with love for his family and told them so. "I am so proud of all of you!" he said.

"And we are of you, Papa. You are the most excellent of men," Rebecca said, and everyone else agreed. Mr. Stuart had always been such a rock of strength for them, and they loved and respected him highly.

As Mrs. Stuart put her china cup and saucer down, she got up and kissed the top of her husband's head. "We are so thankful for you, Pete! You are our rock." His wife had nicknamed him "Peter the Rock" because of his steadfastness. She often called him "Pete."

"Here, here!" Samuel and the others chimed in with the compliment. They toasted him with their raised teacups.

"Awe, go on, now!" A humble man, Mr. Stuart never liked full attention. "I love you all, and I want you to know how happy I am that we are all together again. These are my happiest days. I am a very blessed man."

Bessie entered the room at just the right time. It was two o'clock sharp, which was the family's traditional time to serve holiday dinners. "It is my pleasure to announce that your Thanksgiving meal is ready in the dining hall, sir." Bessie always addressed Mr. Stuart as her sign of respect to him.

"Wonderful! Wonderful! Let's go, family!" Mr. Stuart always had the habit of repeating his words.

The children had already been rounded up, hands washed, hair combed, and clothes changed. The family always dressed for dinner as a rule. They thought it was polite to each other to be at their best for dinner, especially even more so at Thanksgiving. Wearing their finery, they all strolled to the dining hall, murmuring their individual conversations as they walked.

Mr. Stuart thought, *I have been blessed with such a fine family. Thank You, dear Lord!*

When the bountiful meal was over, Mr. Stuart wiped his mouth with his linen napkin and said as he patted his stomach, "My compliments to the cook! That was the best Thanksgiving meal we have ever eaten." They all smiled because Mr. Stuart always said the same thing every year.

He pulled on the gold chain to look at his pocket watch. It easily came out of his vest pocket. Checking the time, Mr. Stuart clicked the watch cover closed and excused himself from his family. "Well, it is time for me to take our Joanne on her Thanksgiving Day outing into the garden for our walk."

He turned back at the door before he exited and said to his wife, "My dear, would you like to join us this year for our walk?"

Mrs. Stuart actually blushed at the honor of being included in this special outing. It was a traditional time set aside for just Pete and Joanne. "I shall be delighted to join you. Thank you for asking me." They walked together to Joanne's quarters.

Joanne was always filled with glee when she saw her father. Anyone could tell she loved him dearly, and he loved her. Joanne also went easily to her mother, but the obvious bond Joanne had with her father was unsurpassed.

"Hello, Posie. Happy Thanksgiving, sweetheart." Mr. Stuart tenderly took Joanne's hand and kissed it, and Mrs. Stuart took her other one. Nanny had Joanne all ready for her outing, so off the trio went to their beautiful garden. Joanne seemed thrilled to be with her parents and to be outside in the brisk autumn air as they strolled. Her father kept patting her hand since he had it in the crook of his arm, and her mother kept kissing her on the cheek. It was a special, tender moment for these loving parents.

The day after Thanksgiving, Joanne was especially happy when her father took her to their small rowboat to go fishing on their pond. She had developed an interest in fishing that was very unusual because of her minimal capabilities. Unable to concentrate on most anything else, Joanne seemed to have full attentiveness when it came to fishing.

With great enthusiasm, Joanne boarded the familiar rowboat with her beloved father. "Sit down, Posie! Don't rock the boat so much!" Mr. Stuart always talked to Joanne as if she could understand him.

The two set off alone, and the boat glided on the lake as Mr. Stuart positioned the oars and rowed slowly.

The cook had prepared a picnic basket with leftovers from Thanksgiving and delicious sweet tea. They usually stayed out on the pond for several hours, then reluctantly came ashore.

The air was a bit cool on this particular autumn day and could even be considered nippy. The wind was blowing the colorful autumn leaves all around, swirling them into enchanting patterns that floated in the air and landed in the boat and on the water.

A flock of Canadian geese in V formation added excitement to the excursion as the birds flew overhead, honking to each other. Mr. Stuart put his hand up to shade his eyes from the bright sun, and he tilted his head back to see the birds. Never one to hunt birds, he found great joy in watching God's creations fly by so quickly and in such perfect form.

"Look at the birds, Joanne." Not understanding what he meant, Joanne kept her fingers trailing in the water. She laughed and made happy sounds as she created ripples in the cold water. The lapping water was an easy, pleasant sound.

"Here we go! This is our best fishing spot, remember, Posie?" He hooked a worm on the fishing pole and threw the hook out as far as possible. Joanne's fingertips kept playing with the water.

After catching a few little fish, Mr. Stuart concentrated on pulling in what felt to be a huge catch. "Oh boy! We have ourselves a big one now."

Consequently, with his attention diverted to the catch, he wasn't prepared for Joanne's quick movements when she stood and reached for the cookie tin in the open picnic hamper on the other side of the little rowboat. Before he realized it, Joanne lost her balance and fell into the water with a splash.

She panicked and flailed with super strength but started to sink fast. Her father threw his fishing pole down, quickly took his jacket off, and dove into the water beside his beloved daughter to rescue her.

She was so frightened and out of control that she grabbed him and tried to climb up onto his shoulders and head.

"No, Posie! Be still! I will get you, but you must be still! Don't grab my head." Mr. Stuart's commands weren't comprehended. Joanne kept grabbing his head as a drowning victim grabs onto a life preserver.

Her grip felt superhuman to Mr. Stuart. Instead of getting the stability needed, she kept dunking her father, and he would sink. It took all his strength to come up for air each time he could.

"Posie! No!" he screamed. Then he would unfortunately be pushed back underwater by his precious one, who was trying to keep her head out of the water. Joanne hated to have her head underwater, and it frightened her. It was impossible to calm Joanne in her panicked state.

Mr. Stuart soon became exhausted with the struggle. His beloved daughter's strength was more than he could handle. After countless times of dunking and bobbing in her frenzy, Joanne caused them both to drown. They sank together, as bonded in death as they had been in life. Mr. Stuart held onto her hand in his last attempt to comfort her as their final breath left their bodies.

The little rowboat drifted, carrying now only the picnic hamper, one oar, and the small fish they had caught. Mr. Stuart and Joanne could no longer hear the steady lapping of water against the wooden rowboat.

Chapter 44

Back at the manor, Mrs. Stuart knew it was about time for her husband and her "silent angel" daughter to return, so she put her light woolen shawl around her shoulders, added a hat and gloves, and strolled down to the dock to greet them, as she usually did.

"Pete! Pete, I am here. Where are you two?" She waited a bit for his answer.

"Pete, where are you?" she said in a singsong voice.

Maybe they got off the boat to eat.

She began walking around. The leaves beneath her feet crunched slightly as she walked.

Feeling the chill in the air, she pulled her shawl around her more closely as she searched for her husband and daughter.

She then noticed the empty rowboat floating freely. "Pete! Answer me, please!" She called repeatedly, but there was no answer. She stopped to study the rowboat and put her hand above her squinted eyes to aid in her view.

Surely they aren't lying down and taking a nap in that little boat.

"Pete! Wake up! I am here! It is time to go home!"

She glanced away from the rowboat and saw an oar floating some distance away. She knew her husband always secured the oars.

Horrified with dreadful realization, she screamed and screamed, paralyzed with fear that they had drowned. Her arms stretched forth as if summoning them to her, and her shawl fell to the ground.

Samuel and Luke had been shooting game nearby and heard the piercing screams. They ran to Mrs. Stuart as fast as they could and saw her in her terrified state.

"Mother! What is it?" Samuel inquired with great concern. He picked up her shawl and put it around her shoulders.

All Mrs. Stuart could do was scream and point to the boat.

It didn't take half a second to comprehend the situation. The two men instantly stripped down to their underclothes, ran the length of the dock, and dove into the chilly pond water. The shock of the cold water left the men quickly as they focused on their lifesaving task. The suspended water droplets from their splashes caught the sunlight.

Trusting in the strength of the young men, Mrs. Stuart quieted herself. *Surely they will find them. Dear Lord, please let them find them and rescue them.*

She watched in the distance as the figures of her son and son-in-law dove underwater time and again in hopes of saving their loved ones. She could hear their gasps for breath each time they came up for air.

Time seemed to stand still. In what seemed like hours but was only minutes, the men finally found their father and sister. They were able to secure the boat and oars, and drag the bodies up and onto the craft. Solemnly, they rowed back to shore.

In shock, Mrs. Stuart stared blankly at her dead husband and daughter. She was as numb and paralyzed as if she had turned into stone. Unable to move, she couldn't speak, cry, or do anything but stare at their lifeless bodies.

Chapter 45

Out of breath and heartbroken, Samuel tried to comfort his mother. He put his wet arm around her and said in choked emotion, "Mother, God will help us through this. It is a terrible shock, but God will help us."

Mrs. Stuart stood stone still and acted like she didn't hear her son.

Samuel quickly slipped on his shirt and pants. He murmured gentle, peaceful words to help calm her as he led her back to the house. "Mother, we are going back home now. Let me help you."

She seemed detached from reality as Samuel led her back to the manor. As soon as they reached the foyer, she looked up at her son as if she didn't know him. Her blank stare greatly concerned him.

"Mother?" Then she collapsed.

"Sarah! Rebecca! Come quickly!" Samuel shouted in his commanding voice.

The two young women appeared and asked in unison, "What is it, Samuel?"

They were shocked at the scene before them. Seeing the state of Samuel's clothing and their mother on the floor, they knew something terrible had occurred.

"Tend to Mother. There has been a tragic accident with Father and Joanne." Samuel rushed back outside.

Samuel had to round up help. Luke had stayed behind with the deceased to await assistance. He dressed as he waited and prayed for the family. It would be a terrible shock for them all.

With the help of some servants, they placed Mrs. Stuart on her bed. "Mama, we are here with you. We are taking care of you, Mama. Just rest now." Rebecca covered her with a warm blanket. Mrs. Stuart never responded. She just kept staring, uncomprehending.

Bessie entered the room with a cup of hot tea. She handed it to Sarah.

"Mother, here now. Take a few sips of this hot tea. It will help you."

Sarah put the tea cup to her mother-in-law's lips, but Mrs. Stuart didn't move a muscle.

Sarah looked at Rebecca, and they both knew their dear mother was in shock.

"Bessie, please stay with Mrs. Stuart and try to slip a little bit of tea into her mouth every now and again. We are going to go find Samuel and Luke, and find out what has happened." They left the room, shaken.

Samuel had returned to Luke with several men to assist them. He left a message with the butler for Sarah and Rebecca to come alone to the pond. Samuel explicitly said to trust their mother and children to the care of the servants, which they did.

Instinctively, Sarah and Rebecca held hands and walked silently on the pathway to the pond. Knowing the state of their mother, they could expect only the worst and tried to prepare themselves for it. They walked as quickly as they could.

By the time they arrived, Samuel and Luke had both Mr. Stuart and Joanne lying on their backs in the fading green grass. Samuel and Luke had folded their father's and sister's hands upon their abdomens and also straightened their clothing. The bodies of their loved ones looked as if they were napping in the afternoon sun, drying off after a frolic in the water, which Joanne liked so much.

Sarah and Rebecca took a moment to absorb the dreadful scene before them; then they rushed to kneel next to their cherished father and sister. They didn't even realize they had both groaned the guttural moan of profound grief. Sobs escaped from their hearts, and their breaths felt shallow as they held the hands of their loved ones for the last time. Sarah held Rebecca's trembling hand as she gently arranged Joanne's hair.

It was bewildering to see the lifeless forms of their loved ones' bodies. Their spirits were no longer there, and they looked like mannequins in a wax museum.

When the ladies looked up at Samuel and Luke, Sarah said, "You dove into the water and tried to save them."

"Yes. But we were too late. We were hunting nearby and heard

Mother's screams. Mother saw us bring their bodies to shore," Samuel replied.

"If only your mother hadn't seen this day," Luke empathized.

The servants began to assist in moving the bodies. Sarah and Rebecca slowly followed them.

Samuel said, "The morticians will come soon to prepare the remains for the viewing and service."

Rebecca said, "It all feels like a horrible nightmare."

"Yes, it does," Sarah replied sadly.

The men went in a different direction when they got to the house to wait for the mortician.

The ladies went directly to Mrs. Stuart. She stayed in bed and was never the same again. The doctor examined her daily and said she had succumbed to apoplexy due to the shock. It was just too much for her to bear. He instructed the family to keep her as comfortable as possible.

Mrs. Stuart couldn't swallow any of the food and drink offered to her, and she couldn't speak. Her eyelid and mouth on her right side sagged, and her right arm and leg were unusually bent.

Sarah thought, *No doubt, my dear mother-in-law had massive brain damage from a stroke.*

Rebecca and Sarah took shifts between doing child care and sitting by their mother. Bessie and Nanny never left Mrs. Stuart's side. In less than two weeks of mere existence, the formidable Mrs. Stuart gently passed away in her sleep.

Just a little over two weeks apart, the funerals were exceptionally hard on the younger Stuarts. Walking slowly away from the family cemetery and back toward the manor, Samuel confided in his wife, "I had known that eventually I would be the heir to the manor, but it is such a shock that it happened so fast. Both parents and Joanne gone within two weeks of each other!" Samuel ran his fingers through his hair. This characteristic of her husband was now very familiar to her.

Sarah hooked her hand into his elbow and said, "I know, my darling. We are all in a state of shock. It is going to take some time for us to heal." They walked on in silence for a little while, and then Sarah continued, "You know, you have essentially been running the business of the estate for years and doing an excellent job. I believe in you to continue well."

Samuel patted his wife's hand. "Thank you for your encouragement, my dear. It is going to take some adjustment to go on now without my parents."

"Yes, it will. I understand exactly how you feel. God is near. He will help us all," Sarah stated.

It was a slow adjustment for the entire family. There was a solemn hush about the manor. Servants, children, and everyone on the estate felt the drastic change in the atmosphere. A new normal would set in as time went on, yet profound grief was their companion for some time.

Sarah announced at supper one evening, "There is to be a new baby in our family."

"Is Rebecca expecting again?" Samuel inquired as he wiped his mouth with his linen napkin.

"No. It is *our* baby." Sarah grinned, and the children were overjoyed.

Samuel stood and said, "Sarah, you have had so many difficulties in childbirth. Forgive me, but I have cause for concern, not joy, at this news. Excuse me." He turned to leave the dining room, but Sarah stopped him.

"I assure you that I feel strong and optimistic about this pregnancy. I am quite certain in my heart that this birth will be just fine. Don't you see? Being pregnant again against all the odds is like a message from God for us. He is saying that life continues and will continue forever in and through Him." She put her arms around his waist, and he turned and hugged her and smiled in spite of his fears. The children all gathered, and they joined the family's group hug.

The happy anticipation of another child helped the family to recover from their losses of Mr. and Mrs. Stuart and their precious Joanne. They were at a point in their grief that they were comforted by the fact that they would all be reunited in heaven one day with their loved ones who had gone. The joy of expectation of the new baby grew as the little new life developed within Sarah.

The next morning, Sarah sat at her ornate desk to write a letter to

Rebecca. She wrote, "I have fantastic news to share. I am going to have a baby!" She knew Rebecca and Luke would be thrilled for them.

At the expected time, the Lord blessed Sarah with her easiest, fastest, and least complicated pregnancy and delivery of all when she produced a healthy baby boy. They named him Samuel Henry Stuart, and everyone was thrilled with him, most of all his parents. He had a winning personality right from the start. Henry's intelligent dark-blue eyes and brilliant smile captured the admiration of family and friends alike. In this child was the hope of the Stuart line and the promise of all future generations. Samuel and Sarah dedicated their son to the Lord and prayed that God would use him in a mighty way all the days of his life. More than anything, they wanted all three of their children to spend their lives loving and serving God and keeping His commandments.

Samuel said, "I love you, my precious wife." He kissed the top of Sarah's head, then bent to kiss his nursing son.

"I wonder what will happen next, Samuel? We certainly have a full to overflowing life, don't we?"

"Indeed we do. Let's take one day at a time, and God will reveal His will to us, as He always has."

Looking into each other's eyes, they quoted aloud together Proverbs 3:5-6, "Trus in the Lord with all thine heart, and lean not unto thine own understanding. In all thy ways acknowledge Him, and He will direct thy paths. Amen."

Chapter 46

2028

Folding Ann's clean sheets together, Tess listened in dreaded disbelief at what her daughter was telling her.

Nineteen-year-old Ann Gordon pleaded, "Mama, I have to go. It is 2028, and Aunt Sarah just has to know about the success of her efforts. I've been thinking and praying about this for a long time, Mama, and I feel that this is what God wants me to do. If time elapses the same in our parallel existence, it is 1873 where Aunt Sarah is now. It has been ten years since Aunt Sarah time traveled, and I just know just know I can be of help to her and others there. Please, Mama, let me go."

"Ann, I understand your feelings, honey, honestly I do. But I can't let you even try. What if you really do go? We may never see you again. I couldn't endure it, my precious daughter," Tess said with emotion and hugged her only daughter. She tried all the while not to let the tears spill, but her eyes were welling up. She blinked rapidly but to no avail. Both women cried as they embraced, thinking of life without each other.

Tess knew in her heart that her precious daughter would be going back in time to Sarah, but she just couldn't bring herself to face the fact yet. The Lord had been preparing her over the last few months. But oh, how could she ever give her consent to Ann?

She struggled with the thought of how short life seemed; all those years of her young children requiring so much of her time, energy, and patience now felt like just fleeting moments. Her daughter was on the brink of leaving her forever.

How did we get to this point so quickly? How did it happen so very fast?
They sat on Ann's bed.

Ann reached for two tissues on her bedroom night table and handed one to her mother. They made a scraping sound on the tissue box opening as she pulled them out quickly. They both wiped their eyes, blew their noses, and then chuckled at their diverting sounds.

Sitting next to each other on the bed, Ann lovingly took her mother's hands in hers. "Mama," she said softly and looked at her mother directly in the eyes, showing all of her love. "Mama, I love you and will miss you, Daddy, and the boys so very much, but I just know I have to go. Let me explain why." Ann launched into her deep feeling of being called of the Lord to go, and the time was now. She felt an urgency, in fact.

Taking a deep, cleansing breath of resignation, Tess replied, "Well, if you're positively certain it is the Lord's will for you to go, Ann, then I give my consent to you. Jesus will give me the strength to get through our parting. We've all had His strength in dealing with losing Sarah, haven't we?"

She smiled and asked for another tissue, then blew her nose again. They didn't bother to use a trash can at the moment, and the bed was becoming littered with used, balled-up tissues they had collected over the past half hour. It looked like a growing supply of snowballs ready for a snowball fight.

"Mama, you know we didn't lose Aunt Sarah. It's as if she has gone to the mission field without furlough. Remember, we always said that, and God gave us all the grace to have peace, even in the midst of our grief of missing her. Remember how good God was to us when Aunt Sarah first turned up missing? It was only a few hours before we found her message carved out on Stone Mountain next to the pirate's carving. Remember, Mama?"

Ann pressed her for encouragement. "God is good, and you and Daddy have always taught me to have great faith. I do have great faith, and I am going to use it for His glory. I don't know what He wants of me in the year 1873, but I'm willing and able to be at His service."

"I know, I know, my daughter. You are living out my vow to God to love and serve Him all of your days, but I didn't realize the sacrifices I would have to make for you to do so." Tess felt convicted as soon as those words were out of her mouth. She knew the sacrifices Jesus had given of His life, death, and resurrection for her. Anything short of that had to be fulfilled by people when God asked it of them—and done with a willing and obedient heart.

"As you've told me many times, God will give you the grace you need when you need it, and that is something we can always count on," Ann said emphatically, then continued. "I love you, Mama, and Daddy and Shelby and Scottie. It is almost inconceivable to think of life without you near me. But I know that I must go. God has given this strong feeling to me, and it just won't let me rest until I obey."

"But how will I know how you are doing? A few words carved into Stone Mountain like Aunt Sarah did won't carry me through the rest of my life without you, my precious one."

Tess wiped fresh tears from her eyes, blew her nose, and retrieved a new box of tissues from the hallway closet. There were so many used tissues now piled on the bed that they looked like a foundation for an igloo. It would take only a moment to swoop them all into a trash bag, but that was the least of her worries.

"Well, I've been giving that some thought, and here's my plan. First, I'll let you know that I arrived safely by placing my carved message in Stone Mountain next to Aunt Sarah's message. Then check the public library for old books. I'll probably write several volumes over the years ahead for you all to read and know about our lives. I will include many details. You know how detailed I am."

She smiled, then continued, "I will write it as a fiction novel, but it will be the facts of what has happened with Aunt Sarah and me." She stated this triumphantly as if she had already accomplished it.

Her mother stared at her, wide eyed. "You have given this matter a lot of thought. What if no one will publish your novels?"

A little irritated by this question, Ann straightened her back and stated, "Mother! My books not published? Come on! God gave me the ability to write, and I am going to do it. Believe in my ability now like you always have, please. It will all work out so beautifully. I know that I won't be able to hear from you and Daddy and the boys. However, I know Jesus will take care of you all, and who knows, maybe God will send us all back when we complete our mission. I mean, back to the future—which is the present right now. Oh dear! I wonder how Aunt Sarah deals with this time travel thing." They both burst out laughing at what would seem to any rational person to be a reason to get to a good therapist.

Blowing her nose yet again and grabbing yet another tissue, Tess said, "All right, Honey Bunny," she said, using her childhood name for her precious daughter, "you have my blessing. I will admit to you that God has been working in my heart for a while now too, so your request isn't exactly a surprise."

"Seriously?" Ann asked with wide eyes.

"Yes. True. Now, to convince your father."

They hugged again, and their eyes began to dry. Their decisions were made. With resolve, they started to move forward. First, it was time to get that trash bag, swipe away the pile of tissues, and then have a talk with Colin. They took a moment to wash their faces with cold water too, and pat them dry. Not much could change their tearstained eyes, but that was okay.

They went bravely hand in hand to Colin's office and knocked softly on his door.

"Enter." He always said that, and mother and daughter smiled at his expected reply.

As they went inside, they found him sitting at his desk, reading his newspaper. His feet were propped up on the desk. His reading glasses were below his eyes, and he looked up at them above the rims. Then he lowered the paper. This familiar sight, along with the crinkle of the newspaper whenever her father gave her his full attention, was a picture in her mind Ann savored and memorized. She could smell the dampness of the newsprint too, because it was a rainy day. Even the plastic sleeve couldn't keep the newspaper completely dry when thrown into their yard. She recorded it all in her mind to take with her into her future.

He grinned, then joked, "I know my girls well enough to know that when you both come into my office hand in hand, it is about to cost me something."

They looked at each other, then sat in the two leather chairs in front of his desk and told him everything. He listened without much comment while his wife and daughter advised him of their plan.

After they finished, there was a long silence. Colin got up and held his hands out to them. "Let's pray together." They made a little circle as they all stood and held hands. Colin asked God to give him the same peace by the morning that his girls felt. He kissed them on their cheeks and said he would let them know tomorrow whether he would give his blessing.

Ann memorized what each of them wore. Her mother was in black slacks, black flat sandals because her feet were always hot, and her favorite purple blouse with tiny sparkly diamond jewels all over it. It was three-quarter sleeved and styled to be loose and flowing. She had on a silver necklace and earrings, and her shoulder-length salt-and-pepper hair was swept up into a clip on the back of her head. Her mother's fingernails had had a French manicure. She always purposed to look her best, even when casual.

Her dad was wearing a navy-blue long-sleeved golf shirt, embroidered with their country club insignia, khaki pants, and a maroon leather belt, black socks, and shined penny loafers. Dad was always a classic gentleman. Ann had on her favorite, pretty multicolored flowered dress and matching shoes she loved. As they stood there, Ann noted the ticking of their grandfather clock. How many times had she heard it chime over the years? She could smell a hint of her dad's Old Spice aftershave and her mother's favorite Chanel No. 5 perfume. Ann had chosen to wear that same perfume today as well. Sights, sounds, and smells were all mentally filed to relive whenever she wanted to think of this moment during her journey of life ahead.

Chapter 47

For Tess, it was the longest night of her life. Feeling restless, she finally got up at about two o'clock in the morning and wandered to her daughter's room. She stood in the doorway and watched her baby girl, now a young woman, sleep peacefully. The nightlight in the hallway cast just enough light for her to make out her precious daughter's features. She watched her for a long, long time, remembering so much. Then she crawled into bed beside her, put her arm around her as she used to do when Ann was little, and fell fast asleep in their last mother-daughter snuggle.

Dawn arrived, accompanied by Colin's peace. The whole family began preparing Ann for her mission trip, as they thought of it. Colin suggested that she carry a leather knapsack full of essentials needed for the year 1873. Many antibiotics for adults and children, along with instructions, were first on the list, among other medicines. Included was a War of Aggression history book, showing the altered history, and letters from Colin and Tess, as well as other items each member of the family deemed necessary. Of course, they included a gift of Sarah's favorite chocolate.

Ann slipped a letter into the knapsack from their family friend, Lexi Jenkins, and one from her grandparents, Nana and Grandpa Gordon. She had visited these loved ones last week and had advised them of her plans, even before asking for her parents' blessing. They had composed letters to Sarah at that time for her to deliver and had said their goodbyes to Ann then. Colin's mother gave their family Bible to give to Sarah. Ann reverently placed it on top. Just as she was about to fasten the pack, her brothers rushed in with their letters for their Aunt Sarah. They gave a quick hug to Ann too, and she messed up their hair as she used to do when they were little.

Two days later, Ann was ready. She had prepared well over the past weeks for this moment. Her family waited for her at their SUV in the driveway. She dressed in an appropriate dress in peach and cream with a matching hat and linen gloves. Her long hair was in an upsweep, and the bulging leather knapsack was in tow. The reality of the situation struck their hearts as they remembered so vividly the moment when Sarah had joined them in their van in 2018, dressed similarly. It had been just hours before her departure back in time, as it was now, for their Ann.

The family drove slowly to the area that had once been the Antebellum Plantation, where they had last seen Sarah. It was a beautiful private manor now on the historic registry. The grounds were perfectly landscaped and looked the same as they had ten years ago. The place was open to the public for guided tours on certain days. No one had much to say, since all their hearts were heavy in anticipation of the parting soon to take place. No one questioned whether it was going to happen.

Shelby and Scottie held their sister's hands and asked, for the thousandth time that day, "Are you sure you want to go through with this, Ann?"

Scottie, being so tenderhearted, allowed his free-flowing tears as he looked adoringly at his older sister. "How come you have to go, Ann?"

Ann hugged Scottie close to her and replied patiently, "I don't know why I have to go. I just know I have to."

"If you don't know why, then why do you have to go?" Scottie broke down in tears and clung to his sister.

"It is difficult to explain. When you get older, God will give you ideas and feelings so that you will know, beyond a doubt, what you have to do. That is how He works."

Shelby didn't allow himself the luxury of tears, but the threatening knot in his throat altered his voice when he did manage to speak. "Ann, we may never see you again," he said simply.

"Oh, my sweet brothers, yes. We will see each other again." She held tightly to each of their hands and said, "We have God's promises to cherish, and we shall look forward to our reunion in eternity." She smiled, but her tears streamed down her face too. "You know as well as I do what the Bible says. When Jesus comes back for us, we will all be together again forever with Him."

"But how do we get through all the years of this life without you until we do meet again in heaven?" Scottie embraced his sister harder and smelled her sweet perfume and the familiar smell of her hair.

"Here," she said. "Let me give you a lock of my hair to keep with you." She reached into her knapsack for her Swiss Army knife and cut off some long curls, not only for Scottie but for every member of the family. As they all held these precious gifts in their hands, everyone in the vehicle cried.

"This is the hardest choice of my life, my dear family, but I know, as painful as it is and as sacrificial as it is for us all, I must do this. I know it is God's will for me to go. I don't know why or for what purpose yet, but I just know that I must go. The dreadful part is leaving all of you."

Shelby spoke up. "Obeying God is not always easy, is it? Sometimes it is the hardest thing we have to do." Then he brightened noticeably and said, "But what blessings we have when we do obey. Our family is earning a crown or two in heaven for this one, eh, sis?" He smiled a smile Ann held captured forever. She felt sure her Shelby would become a preacher for his life's work. She suspected that her very tenderhearted youngest brother would be a physician, like their dad, because he liked to help people.

When Colin stopped the SUV, he said, "I'll be right back." He got out and walked away.

Tess sat in the front seat without speaking or moving. She couldn't do either. They all waited in silence.

Colin returned in a few minutes and said that the owners of the manor, the Stuarts, permitted them to visit the grounds. It was a day closed to the public, but they said the Gordons were free to stroll around by themselves. There was no charge for their admittance.

They drove over to the same stable area where they had assembled with Sarah that last time. Everyone got out. The sunrays split through the clouds like beams of light from heaven guiding their path.

Tess grasped her daughter's hands, and the two stood still to gaze into each other's tearful eyes. Tess said, "Every mother should have a daughter like you. You have been one of the greatest joys of my life. I am so very proud of you, Ann Sarah Gordon. I love you forever!" She broke into choked sobs and clung to her only daughter. Colin stood nearby, snapping pictures with his digital camera.

"Oh, Mama, whatever am I going to do without you? I almost want to change my mind now!" Ann cried.

Hearing her daughter's need for encouragement strengthened Tess. She gently pulled apart from their embrace. She looked straight into her daughter's beautiful eyes and said with more emotional control, "Darling," she began, then smoothed back a piece of Ann's hair from her face, "God will never give us more than we can handle. And you won't be without me. Our love keeps us close and always will. We have a bond that cannot break. Space and time will separate us for a while, but you know we believe we shall meet again in heaven. All will be well, Honey Bunny. I love you forever!" And she smiled and gently caressed her daughter's cheek, then kissed her.

Colin cleared his throat and said, "Let's tighten up into a Gordon group selfie, and I'll take the photo since I have the longest arms." Their faces beamed their love for one another as Colin snapped several photos.

Colin then said, "Let us pray." Holding hands, as they always did for family prayers, Colin lifted his face heavenward and said the prayer in a strong voice. The warmth of the sunrays and their father's familiar voice made them feel comforted. All the family joined them in the "amen." They broke the circle with a squeeze of their hands, as usual.

Colin said, "Well, this is it, my daughter. Come, give a big hug to me, and then we'll see about your trip to your Aunt Sarah and your mission there with her."

As father and daughter embraced, no more tears were spilling. Love and grace bound them in their purpose.

Colin lifted his daughter's chin and said, "I love you, little one." He smiled and said, "You are so like your mother." Then he kissed her cheek for the last time.

Colin didn't know it, but Tess was snapping photos of his goodbye with his cherished daughter.

Smiling back, Ann said, "Daddy, I love you too, so very much. I will be fine. Now, don't forget to look at the library next year for my first book. It will be especially for you all. I will get to work on it right away."

"I won't forget, my sweet Ann," Colin said. He reluctantly released his daughter from their embrace and into her life without them.

Her brothers took their silent turns to say goodbye to their beloved sister and to hold her close one last time. They all put on brave smiles. Colin kept his camera snapping dozens of photos of these final moments with Ann, and so did Tess with her cell phone camera.

Lightening the moment, Ann gathered her leather knapsack, made a full twirl, and said, "These old-fashioned dresses are so much fun to wear. I hope it's the right style for the time when I get there. I love it, don't you? Does my hat look like it is at the right angle? Fashion was important then, you know," she said, adjusting her hat.

Her mother smiled and replied, "I am sure it will be just right. Give your Aunt Sarah our love, please."

"Of course, Mama."

Colin stated, "Well, this is the general area where we last saw your Aunt Sarah. Since we have no idea what to look for, let's split up and check around for something unusual."

"Right! Okay!" they answered.

Everyone headed off in different directions. The boys headed for the stables and blacksmith area. Colin and Tess headed toward the restrooms in the detached carriage house. They'd used these facilities ten years ago while Sarah went to look around on her own just before she disappeared. Ann headed for the slave cabin. It had been restored correctly in the historical style of the original brick, mortar, and wood.

Something caught Tess's eye in the lawn, and she said, "Wait a minute, Colin. I think I've found something." She pointed to a brass buckle that had apparently been lying there for many years, just barely sticking out of the earth in the lawn. After a bit of digging with a small rock and stick, Tess unearthed the remains of an old leather knapsack. They heard a sound of metal scrape against metal as she pulled it from the soil.

On one side of the sack, which had stayed buried and was better preserved, was a circular piece of black metal. Colin knelt and gasped as he immediately recognized what it was.

"Tess! This is Sarah's clan crest badge our father gave to her on her sixteenth birthday. Look! It is sterling silver, and that's why it is all black with age." Rubbing the dirt from the grooves and etchings, Colin said as he handed it to Tess, "Read the back, Tess. Engraved on the lower half of the circle, it says, 'Sarah Louise Gordon. Love, Dad.'"

Tess held the circle at an angle toward the ray of sunlight that seemed to keep guiding them. She, too, gasped. "Oh, Colin! It is! It truly is Sarah's!"

Wide eyed, Tess looked up at her sweet husband as he said, "Sarah probably buried it here because she knew this was the area of the restroom where she left us that day. She knew we'd come back and find it, Tess. Oh, what a wonderful sign! All is well, my dear. All is well."

Colin called to his children, "Ann, Shelby, Scottie! Come! Quickly!"

In seconds, the boys were there, breathing hard from the quick sprint. "What Dad? What's happened?"

Colin held out the crest badge and said, "Look! It is your Aunt Sarah's. And here are the remains of her knapsack. She buried them here for us to find. I am sure of it."

"Wow! Really? Awesome!" their sons answered in unison as they reached to touch it.

Tess straightened and said, "Let's go show this to your sister. She must not have heard your father call."

In their excitement, they all wanted to hold on to the precious treasure as they walked.

"Ann, come look at this!" Scottie called as they approached the brick slave quarters she had gone to investigate. They walked through the open door and looked around. With one glance they saw that the room was empty.

"Well, she's not in here. Let's look in the backyard."

After looking here and there for a few minutes, Tess abruptly stopped dead still. She grabbed her husband's arm and whispered, "She's gone."

Chapter 48

Colin took a deep breath, expelled it, and said matter-of-factly, "Let's go to the library and get Ann's book."

He led the procession quickly with a protesting Scottie behind him running to keep up. "But Dad, Ann just left us a few minutes ago. She hasn't had time to write and publish a book in a few minutes."

Colin turned to face his youngest son. They stopped walking as he put his right hand on his son's shoulder. Looking straight into his son's eyes, Colin smiled brightly and said confidently, "Scottie, your sister may have just left us, but that was over a hundred years ago for her."

Scottie looked amazed and said his favorite expression. "Cool beans!"

Everyone walked swiftly to the SUV. They piled into the vehicle and couldn't get to the library fast enough to suit them. Thankfully, there was little traffic. They reached their destination and had a difficult time keeping their chuckles of joy quiet enough for a library as they rushed through it to the old-book section. Colin's index finger touched and traced the book spines in the G section until he suddenly stopped. Everyone held his or her breath.

Colin's eyes grew wide when he saw his beloved daughter's name on not only one book but four. Reverently, he removed the four thick books and handed one to each family member. It was difficult to share their excitement, tears, and smiles in hushed tones. Right there in the aisle of the public library, they hugged Ann's books to their chests as if hugging her. What treasures!

Shelby looked at the dedication page in his book. He exclaimed as emphatically but quietly as he could in a library, "Look! Ann put what I said to her!" He pointed and read her words aloud in a stage whisper. "This book is dedicated to my hilarious brother Shelby, who said, 'If your book is any good, I may buy a copy!' He grinned as he looked up at his family.

Colin whispered, "Thanks be to our merciful God! Let's go read, family." They proceeded to check out the four old books.

Tess determined the chronological order of the books and began reading the first one aloud to them as they drove home. They were overjoyed to have these precious written words of their beloved Ann and couldn't wait to read all about her life, Sarah's life, and their missions.

Chapter 49

1873

Ann stood just inside the entrance of the restored slave cabin with her knapsack hooked over her right shoulder. It took only a few seconds for her eyes to adjust. She felt a bit awkward to have walked in on a family apparently deep in prayer. They didn't seem to notice her, but how could they with their backs to the entrance? Out of respect for their intercession with God, Ann stood still. She saw the man kneeling next to his wife, and on the other side of her, their two young daughters were next to their mother. She wondered about them all being in old-fashioned clothing.

The kneeling woman began crying loudly and praying in great earnest. Ann knew she should exit, but she felt mesmerized by the scene and couldn't move. Grief clung to the air like dense humidity. Ann found it difficult to breathe.

Clutching her infant son to her breast, the suffering woman pleaded, "Oh, God! Please, God! Hear my prayer and answer it right away! Our son, our only beautiful baby son that You gave to us, is going to die soon if You don't answer immediately. His fever is climbing, and he can't nurse anymore. Please, God! Please take us all through time to the future, to the year 2018, or to whenever You want, Lord. Just take us somewhere in time that we may get the medicine we need for our little Henry." Her body bent in sobs as she moved.

As Ann heard the woman's voice, she was stunned and astonished. Then she fully comprehended the scene before her. Her Aunt Sarah had headed toward the stables and the slave cabin just before she disappeared in 2018. Incredulously, Ann asked in awe, "Aunt Sarah?"

Slowly turning, as if it were her last movement here on the earth, Sarah looked back toward the interrupting voice of the young woman. She gasped and struggled to her feet with her husband's assistance. She kept her baby close to her chest and stared hard at the young woman.

"You look so much like Tess Gordon." Sarah wiped tears from her eyes with the back of her hand to see more clearly. "Are … you … Ann?"

Ann rushed forward to her beloved auntie and embraced her and the baby in one swoop. Through the blanket and her clothing, Ann could feel the child's severely elevated temperature and was instantly afraid for him. All explanations and introductions would have to wait. The baby needed medication.

Ann immediately knelt on the floor and flipped back the top of her knapsack. She said with confidence and clarity, "I have antibiotics." She shook the bottle of liquid infant penicillin, squeezed the correct dosage into the dropper, then gave it to Sarah.

Relief flooded Sarah so quickly that she swayed and almost collapsed. Her beloved Samuel had a firm grip on her and assisted her to sit next to this unexpected niece. The family remained silent as the moments unfolded before their eyes.

"Just squeeze this into the back of his throat, Aunt Sarah, and pinch his nose closed for just a wee moment. He'll swallow it. I'll also give you some infant's ibuprofen and acetaminophen. Alternate between the two every three hours to get the temperature down. It should come down very quickly." Ann smiled an encouraging smile and lovingly patted her aunt's shoulder.

With a trembling hand, Sarah took the thin, cotton baby blanket off her precious son's face to reveal the most beautiful baby boy ever to behold. He was perfectly formed and handsome yet almost lifeless. His skin looked stark white except for the fever flush. His dark auburn hair was full and slick from sweat. The sight of the precious sick baby, her first cousin, won Ann's heart instantly. She reached out to touch his forehead lightly, and she murmured soothing words to him.

Sarah gently worked the dropper into little Henry's mouth and squeezed the life-saving liquid medicine into his small body. She didn't even have to pinch his nose. He swallowed instantly.

Sarah then smiled at Ann, looked up toward heaven, and said with tears of joy, "Oh! Thank You, dear Lord Jesus! Thank You for saving our precious son and for bringing my beloved Ann to us! Thank You! Thank You!" She broke into sobs of sheer relief.

Samuel handed his handkerchief to his wife and comforted her with his firm, assuring hand on her shoulder. He had been standing at her side the whole time.

Sarah composed herself and looked at her beloved husband and daughters, saying in introduction, "This is my niece, Miss Ann Gordon, my brother Colin's daughter. I haven't seen her since the day God sent me here to be with you. Ann was just nine years old then."

Speaking out in her forthright way, Jennifer Ann said emphatically, "Well, she is not nine years old anymore, Mama."

"No, daughter, no, she is not," replied Samuel Stuart in his rich voice.

Looking at the newcomer, he said, "I am married to your Aunt Sarah; therefore, I am your Uncle Samuel. It is a pleasure to meet you, Ann." Ever the gentleman, even in his distraught state over his only son's illness, Samuel bowed gallantly.

Ann giggled, stood up, and curtsied. "I'm so pleased to meet you as well, Uncle Samuel, and my cousins." She smiled at the children.

The baby stirred a little, and all eyes watched him for a few moments. There was no change in his condition yet, so the conversation resumed.

"Mama named me after you. I am Jennifer Ann Stuart." And she curtsied.

"And I am Courtney Tess. Mama named me after your mama."

"What smart girls you are and how sweet of your mother to name you after my mother and me." Ann hugged them, then hugged her Aunt Sarah. It had been so long.

Sarah confessed, "I never dreamed my prayer would be answered in the form of you traveling back in time to me, Ann."

"Well, the Lord has been preparing me for some time, I can assure you. I had a monumental task in convincing Dad and Mom to let me come. Actually, Mom was much harder to convince than Dad. Oh, Aunt Sarah! When we saw the carving on Stone Mountain next to the pirate's carving after you disappeared, we knew you were safe and that our Lord was using you for what we termed a 'mission trip.' Thank you so much for doing that for us."

Samuel and Sarah exchanged happy glances. "So it worked. You got my message. It was Samuel's idea to make the carving. When did you see it?"

"Just hours after you disappeared. Well, it was a rough few hours not knowing where you were, I can tell you. Mom was stricken, and Dad frantically searched for you. Then Shelby suggested that we look for you at the pirate's carving because you had liked it so much. When we got there, we saw your message. It was such a relief to find it."

Sarah held her hand out to her beloved husband, and he grasped it affectionately. "Thank you, my darling. You are very wise," Sarah said, feeling exceedingly grateful that her family had received her message so quickly.

Ann continued, "Ever since I turned nineteen years old, I've had the strongest feeling that I had to come back in time to help you in some way. When I finally convinced Mom and then Dad, they helped me to get ready." Patting her stuffed knapsack, she continued, "I have a lot of medicines in here for all ages and for all types of illnesses, compliments of Dr. Dad, of course."

Samuel interjected, "This carrying of a knapsack seems to be a family trait, and I thank the Lord it is. You wouldn't happen to have a Hershey bar in there now, would you, Ann?

A mischievous smile lit up her face. "Uncle Samuel, how would you know about Hershey bars? They haven't been invented yet."

"Your sweet Aunt gave her last Hershey bar to me as a wedding present. Of course, I shared it with her. I remember it to be splendid."

Reaching into her knapsack, Ann drew out a six-pack of the dark-brown delicacy, giving three bars to Sarah and one to each of the other family members.

Sarah gave two of hers to her husband and said, "You have waited ten years for another taste. I am going to make sure that it is a big one."

"You are so generous as always, Aunt Sarah. But you also have waited ten years for another taste," protested Ann.

"Yes, dear, but I ate so many Hershey bars in my lifetime that I surely devoured my whole life's quota before I turned twenty-three years old." They all chuckled and felt their stress levels begin to decrease.

"I checked before I left. The year 1894 is when Hershey chocolate gets invented, so just be patient," Ann said triumphantly.

"Well, that will be a day to look forward to, for sure, Ann." Samuel and Sarah exchanged a smile.

They didn't diminish Ann's announcement by stating that Sarah had already told her husband of that very fact. Nor did they reveal their plans to invest in the Hershey Company when the time came. Even though Hershey, Pennsylvania, was in the north, there was now no animosity between the CSA and the USA. Businesses were thriving, and importing and exporting between the two countries had been established with amiability and profit for both nations. The North had even joined the South in abolishing slavery and had instituted the indentured servants' program for all nationalities wanting to come and become citizens of the USA and the CSA.

As everyone ecstatically munched on his or her priceless treat, Ann asked Sarah, "Did you feel any different when you came through time? I didn't feel anything at all. I just walked up to the slave cabin, stepped through the doorway, and saw you. Actually, I thought I was still in 2028 and that I had interrupted a family's private moment."

"It was the same with me; only it took me a little bit longer to realize I had gone back in time. When I went out of the slave cabin to meet up with you all at the restrooms, I bumped into General Stonewall Jackson himself. I thought he was a man in a costume. Then I met Samuel's sister, Rebecca, and then Samuel. Oh, I have so much to tell you."

Gathering the Hershey bar wrappers, Samuel said, "Let's go back to the manor. We will be more comfortable to talk there. Our desired trip to the future has certainly ended up as a great surprise. Our son has his needed medicine, and we have you, Ann. Let's get you settled in, shall we?"

The girls walked on ahead of the adults, still licking their chocolate-covered fingers.

Ann said, "Well, we know God sent me here to bring lifesaving medicine for my little cousin, Henry, but I wonder what else He has in store for me."

They all strolled toward the manor and enjoyed a whisper of a breeze. After being in the intense atmosphere of the slave cabin, the fragrance of fresh air was a breath of hope and sweet life.

"I can tell you from experience, dear Ann, that God will reveal His will to you. Just live each day as His willing servant. Just as you knew you had to come here, you will know what is in your future, one day at a time," Sarah encouraged her niece.

The baby cried out his familiar cry of wanting to nurse. Sarah was so happy, and she began to nurse him right away as they walked. How good to know that he wished to have nourishment once again!

Sarah shared, "I am so glad that God had a better plan than I had imagined and requested in my prayer. I miss my brother and our family, of course, but I have grown to love living here in this time." She smiled up at her sweet husband, who smiled back at her.

"Oh! It is so good to see you, Ann!" They hugged again in joy.

Sarah checked her baby son's face for any signs of improvement. The fever flush and his skin tone looked a little more normal as his body responded quickly to the powerful medicines. Since he wasn't accustomed to antibiotics, they worked very fast.

"Aunt Sarah, we all missed you so much, but we realized you were perfect for this mission trip. Dad remembered vividly your unexplainable interest in the Civil War, ever since you were a child."

"You mean the War of Northern Aggression, and I'm sure you know God used your amazing Aunt Sarah to help the South win. I will be interested to find out how things changed for you after your aunt came here with us," Samuel said.

"Yes, sir, I will let you know as much as I can. It may take us a while. I actually brought a book about the war too." Ann patted her knapsack and smiled as she continued to walk.

"Oh! What is that marvelous fragrance?" Ann tilted her head backward and breathed in a lung full of sweet aroma.

"That is our gardenia bush. See it here? It is now in full bloom. It is quite marvelous, isn't it?" Sarah replied, indicating the five-foot-tall gardenia plant in full bloom. Ann stood next to the white petals and drank in the beautiful, heady bouquet of the delicate flowers. She had never smelled anything as delightful as these gardenias.

Sarah asked, "Since you have come back in time to me, Ann, do you think any other of our family line could be time travelers in our past or in our future?"

Ann replied with a shrug, "Well, Aunt Sarah, who knows? It is quite possible. As we always say, 'God works in mysterious ways!'" They said it in unison and smiled.

"Yes, Ann, we all plan our lives, but God's perfect plans often change our purposes." Sarah smiled at Samuel, who nodded in agreement. She raised her eyebrows for emphasis.

As they strolled toward the manor, Ann suddenly remembered something important and stopped. She said, "Oh, Aunt Sarah, here! I have letters for you." Reaching into the zippered part of her knapsack, she removed the letters their family had written for Sarah. Ann triumphantly handed them to her.

Shaken, Sarah handed their beloved son to Samuel and took the precious letters from her niece. As she read the outside of each envelope, she instantly recognized the familiar handwriting and could identify the author. Sarah traced the lettering with her finger. When she came to the last ones, which were from her parents and Lexi, Sarah broke into a choked sob and put her hand on her heart. She looked up lovingly at her husband with joyful, grateful tears streaming down her happy face.

"Oh Samuel, God let them live! My parents and Lexi live. Oh, happy day! I feel like playing a jig—"Middlin' Thank You" to be exact. Let's go get my fiddle. Tenderly holding her letters written by her family in the future, Sarah bounded ahead with a light step. She turned and said to the others, "I will savor these letters later, over and over. What treasures! Thank you, dear Ann."

"You are so welcome, Aunt Sarah. I knew you would love having them." Ann smiled brightly.

Entering into the manor foyer, Sarah said with sudden realization, "Now I have some small understanding of Jesus's words from John 10:10, when He said, 'I am come that they might have life, and that they might have it more abundantly.' Family, we are so blessed!"

Ann, Samuel, and the girls said a collective "Amen!"

About the Author

Paula Jean Henry holds the conviction of liberty like Patrick Henry. She homeschooled her four children and dedicated them to God. Later, she filled her empty nest by playing violin in two orchestras, teaching violin, and writing her first novel, Changed Purpose. A dedicated Christian, Paula Jean and her beloved husband, Kenley, reside in the Appalachian Mountains where she is inspired daily by God's magnificent creation.

Author's contact: ChangedPurpose18@gmail.com

CPSIA information can be obtained
at www.ICGtesting.com
Printed in the USA
FSHW011340041218